Praise for *The Magic of Ordinary Days*

"Like *Plainsong*, Creel's novel is quietly and eloquently written . . . an ideal book to read while sipping lemonade on the porch swing this summer."   —*Colorado Springs Gazette*

"Ann Howard Creel explores the effects of mistaken and offered love in 1940s rural Colorado, where World War II, though seemingly distant, reaches deeply into the lives of the innocent and the misled. Rich in reminiscence, *The Magic of Ordinary Days* treats imperfect humanity with respect, tenderness, and understanding, qualities that mature in the characters into the finest of loves. A highly satisfying read."

> —Susan Vreeland, author of *The Passion of Artemisia* and *Girl in Hyacinth Blue*

"This is a gentle but powerful novel, combining the story of bittersweet love with a poignant account of the journey toward self-realization and acceptance."   —*BookPage*

"A gentle love story."
> —*Denver Post and Rocky Mountain News*

"Compelling."
> —*Boulder Daily Camera*

"Like catching a glimpse of a butterfly on the first day of spring, Creel's novel, *The Magic of Ordinary Days*, is a gentle and delightful celebration of life. Here's a story of the surprising and satisfying appearance of love."   —Lynne Hinton, author of *Friendship Cake*

"Delicate, perceptive and fine-boned writing . . . Creel gets it all just right."   —*Publishers Weekly*

"A bittersweet tale of love."
> —*The Florida Times-Un*

"Precisely observed . . . blends histori place."   —*Kirkus Reviews*

T0043029

PENGUIN BOOKS

THE MAGIC OF ORDINARY DAYS

Ann Howard Creel is the author of eight works of fiction: four middle grade novels, three young adult, and one adult novel. Her children's books have won numerous awards, and her adult novel, *The Magic of Ordinary Days*, was made into a Hallmark Hall of Fame movie for CBS. She has a home in Denver and divides her time between Colorado and the East Coast.

The
Magic of
Ordinary Days

Ann Howard Creel

Penguin Books

PENGUIN BOOKS

Published by the Penguin Group
Penguin Group (USA) Inc., 375 Hudson Street, New York, New York 10014, U.S.A.
Penguin Group (Canada), 90 Eglinton Avenue East, Suite 700, Toronto,
Ontario, Canada M4P 2Y3 (a division of Pearson Penguin Canada Inc.)
Penguin Books Ltd, 80 Strand, London WC2R 0RL, England
Penguin Ireland, 25 St Stephen's Green, Dublin 2, Ireland (a division of Penguin Books Ltd)
Penguin Group (Australia), 250 Camberwell Road, Camberwell,
Victoria 3124, Australia (a division of Pearson Australia Group Pty Ltd)
Penguin Books India Pvt Ltd, 11 Community Centre, Panchsheel Park, New Delhi – 110 017, India
Penguin Group (NZ), 67 Apollo Drive, Rosedale, Auckland 0632,
New Zealand (a division of Pearson New Zealand Ltd)
Penguin Books (South Africa) (Pty) Ltd, 24 Sturdee Avenue,
Rosebank, Johannesburg 2196, South Africa

Penguin Books Ltd, Registered Offices:
80 Strand, London WC2R 0RL, England

First published in the United States of America by Viking Penguin,
a member of Penguin Putnam, Inc. 2001
Published in Penguin Books 2002
This edition published in Penguin Books 2011

PUBLISHER'S NOTE
This is a work of fiction. Names, characters, places, and incidents are either the product
of the author's imagination or are used fictitiously, and any resemblance to actual persons,
living or dead, business establishments, events, or locales is entirely coincidental.

THE LIBRARY OF CONGRESS HAS CATALOGED THE HARDCOVER EDITION AS FOLLOWS:
Creel, Ann Howard.
The magic of ordinary days / Ann Howard Creel.
p. cm.
ISBN 0-670-91027-9 (hc.)
ISBN 978-0-14-311995-1 (pbk.)
PS3553.R339 M34 2001
813'.54—dc21   00-049643

Printed in the United States of America
Designed by Nancy Resnick

For my parents, who lived the war

Acknowledgments

My thanks go to Lee and Eleanor Hancock of Rocky Ford, who shared accounts of everyday life and farming during the war years, and Don Lowman of the Otero County Museum Association, who aided me with information and resources.

A number of books were helpful, too many to mention, but in particular Frances Bollacker Keck's *Conquistadors to the 21st Century: A History of Otero and Crowley Counties, Colorado* and James L. Colwell's *La Junta Army Air Field in WWII*. I gleaned much information from Mark Jonathan Harris, Franklin Mitchell, and Steven Schechter's book *The Homefront: America During World War II*, from Arnold Krammer's *Nazi Prisoners of War in America*, Larry Dane Brimner's *Voices from the Camps: Internment of Japanese Americans During World War II*, and from Roger Daniels's *Prisoners Without Trial: Japanese Americans in World War II*. Pictorial inspiration came from *V Is for Victory: America's Homefront During World War II* by Stan Cohen.

Thanks to my circle of Colorado friends, especially Nancy, kind reader of the first draft, and Lynn, faithful supporter of every small step. My gratitude will always go to Lisa Erbach Vance of the Aaron Priest Literary Agency, editor Frances Jalet-Miller, also of the Aaron Priest Agency, and my editor at Viking, Carolyn Carlson, for her excellent input.

Finally, thanks to every member of my family, most of all, to my husband, David.

The

Magic *of*

Ordinary Days

Prologue

I don't often think back to that year, the last year of the war—its days, its decisions—not unless I'm out walking the dawn of a quiet winter morning, when new snowfall has stunned into silence the lands around me, when even the ice crystals in the air hold still. On those mornings of frozen perfection, when most living creatures keep to a warm bed or a deep ground hole, I pull on my heaviest old boots and set out to make first tracks through the topcrust and let the early dawn know I'm still alive and appreciating every last minute of her fine lavender light.

Then I remember.

I'll begin this tale on the day of my sister's wedding, almost twenty-four years to the day after I came crying out onto earth's slippery soil.

It was April 1944. The Allied forces were preparing to invade France and put an end to the worst war in history, while back on the home front, some of us managed to go on with what might have been considered normal lives. On a Saturday, a buttery spring day along the Front Range of the Rockies, my baby sister

Beatrice was marrying her high school sweetheart, then a newly commissioned Army officer, and leaving me the only Dunne daughter not yet married. The oldest of three sisters and still unmarried, it was an oddity that would not go unnoticed, especially by my aunts. As we waited in the receiving line, Aunt Eloise commented about the quality of the catches made by my sisters. During the war, officers commanded the highest regard, and Abigail, nearest to me in age, still held top rank in that department, as she had caught herself a high-ranking officer, and a medical doctor to boot.

"If only you hadn't always been compared to those sisters of yours," Aunt Eloise said.

Aunt Pearl added, "You might have been considered quite attractive by yourself."

My aunts were not cruel, you understand. They loved to talk, and at every available opportunity they gave away the neatly wrapped presents of their thoughts, confident that no one would refuse them. And although I sometimes ached to talk back to them, I had been taught well by my parents to respect my elders.

Instead of pursuing marriage, at summer's end and after completion of only two more classes and the approval of my thesis, I would receive my master's in history from the University of Denver. My fascination with history started with the first lesson ever taught to me in grammar school. As my teacher described the sea passages of Christopher Columbus, I could so easily imagine myself a stowaway girl on one of his ships. I could see the promise of full sails billowing out above me and feel the sharp tips of saltwater winds. If I had been there, I would've climbed the ship's mast and looked out to the horizon for new lands myself. Formal study at the university had always seemed more destiny than choice.

Unfortunately the war had forced postponement of my fall plans to travel overseas as part of an academic expedition. Because of a world gone astray, my path was strewn with the debris of war, and my journey with archaeologists, anthropologists, and other historians to study the excavation sites of the land of sealed tombs, Egypt, and the ancient city of Horizon-of-the-Aten, would have to wait.

During Bea's wedding reception, my aunts pointed out to me that now, more than ever, single girls had good odds of husband catching. From MPs training in Golden, to airmen at Lowry Air Base and Buckley Field, to medical personnel at Fitzsimons, available soldiers filled Denver's streets, USOs, and bars. But not just any private would do. Those in our social circle wanted to duplicate Bea's catch by latching on to at least an officer, perhaps even a doctor like Abby's, or a pilot, the loftiest catch in the hierarchy of the uniform.

But I had never run my life in order to meet men or find romance, although I wasn't immune to those things, either. I'd always dreamed that someday love would come into my life in some spectacular fashion. Probably it would happen in another country, on board a ship; most likely it would unfold during one of my future treks to uncover a secret of history. One side of me knew that these were the dreams of an inexperienced girl, and yes, I was inexperienced with love. But it didn't bother me. Every day, it didn't bother me.

Secretly I hoped to always disagree with my aunts. That way I'd know I hadn't succumbed to the limited view of so many of their generation. But my dear mother—I could see how my aunts' comments wounded her. Recently, however, I'd convinced her to stop stepping in on my behalf. Early on, I had learned my place on the family wall and found it not such an uncomfortable place to hang. My sisters and I weren't speechless, motionless tulips or ferns in a pattern of wallpaper. In the years of our girlhood, we could mingle and socialize during family outings. Abby, Bea, and I often stood at the front of my father's church, in the theater lobby, at the country club or museum, and we had become well practiced in the art of pastoral family presentations. And after years spent before others, at the easy perusal of relatives and friends, I knew exactly what I was.

I was the practice rug.

Among the Navajo, traditional weavers learn their art by first weaving a rough rug. It is a chance to hone their skills; the rug may contain loose weft, uneven corners, and other flaws. After this essential practice, however, the weaver may go on to produce masterpieces. And so it was with my family. I thought of myself as the first, rather average attempt at a daughter; then, after my birth, my parents brought into the world two rare beauties. I had the most common color of brown hair, a forehead a bit too broad, and a small, lima-bean-shaped birthmark just above my upper lip. My sisters were masterpieces woven of warm wool, natural blondes with unmarked skin and real smiles, not painted on hard canvas, and they were approachable, so that admirers did not hold themselves back. So unusually blessed, Abigail and Beatrice neither competed with me, nor did they gloat.

Despite the inevitable comparisons, Mother always pointed out the good qualities I did have. She'd say that my fingers were long and tapered, that I always sat tall in a chair, and that my teeth had come in straight and white like a row of dominoes.

"And you're as sharp as a tack, you are," she'd say with a hug. "Someday you're going to go places."

As we grew up, my sisters played with dollhouses and dreamed of futures beside successful husbands, whereas I became gripped by the past. The stories and struggles of olden days worked their way from the crepe paper pages of old books and under the seal of my skin. I was the Shoshone guide Sacajawea leading Lewis and Clark on their expeditions, or I was a pioneer woman leading her clan out west on one of the first wagon trains. As I grew into a young woman, a need to understand and experience began to drive me. My whole body became part of the chase; the desire for a fresh find seeped out of my every pore. It was Mother who understood. She helped me fill in my application for the university and collect references. She plotted out on the map with me all the places I might want to go.

But although many a learned woman wanted to deny its importance, even Mother admitted that in our society, beauty was still prized above knowledge and wisdom in a woman. Despite female accomplishments that for the first time held us up in a place where our feet could walk the earth at the same level as our male counterparts, many men most wanted a pretty image hooked on their arms. And yes, although a woman no longer needed a husband, Mother hoped that maybe someday I'd want one, one who could appreciate me, mind and all.

Mother's honesty was something I had always thought I would have; I relied on it.

Whenever I remember Bea's wedding day, I always remember the flowers. Before Bea left for her honeymoon, she gave me a white rose she had singled out and plucked from the bouquet before the bridal toss, and this I waxed and kept on the polished top of my dresser in the months that followed. And on that day, not only had the church and the country club been filled with lilies, gardenias, and roses, but outside on the city streets and in the parks, the crabapple trees had been blooming, every branch decked with blooms of pink, white, and fuchsia so deep in color it almost came to purple. That spring, the crabapple blossoms fell to the ground over a period of several weeks, coating the sidewalks and streets with cupped petals so thick the concrete beneath them disappeared.

My mother had always loved the crabapple blossoms, and I liked to believe their abundance that spring was gifted to her. During the wedding and reception, she held herself up well, with plenty of smiles and gracious small talk in the face of compliments for the wedding. Once I had heard that every person must complete something of importance before he or she dies, and perhaps witnessing her youngest daughter's marriage had been just that for Mother. She smiled and chatted with friends and members of Father's congregation throughout the long reception, as if it would have been impolite to show any sign of her illness. Father directed the event and would have tolerated little less than perfection.

Then afterward, Mother slipped away over several weeks, like water in slow-moving streams gradually sinks into the soil. My sisters busy with marriage and my father preoccupied with church duties, I was the one who left school to be with her. I was the one who eased her away.

Perhaps it was Mother's untimely death, perhaps because the cancer caused her to suffer so, or perhaps another absence between us caused the course of it all to change. But after her death, even my father lost his typical stern control. In the first weeks, he all but abandoned our two-story house in Denver's Park Hill neighborhood that Mother had always maintained with pride. In our house, fingerprints had rarely lasted long on the furniture, and any chipped dishes had been given away. Father let stacks of mail pile up on the foyer table, and he closed up other rooms to collect dust. He submerged himself in even more work of the church.

And although we kept two radios, one in the kitchen and another in his study, Father would allow no music in the house. After all, a singer's voice might sound like hers. And we couldn't have flowers around again, although at the time of her death, the gladiolas were up, their tall stalks stabbing the sky and their blooms open, silently screaming.

I've often wondered, even to this day, why during painful times some people seem to step away from themselves and make decisions that fall far out of their usual line of character and behavior. Perhaps a natural reluctance to sit still is central, or perhaps, like the lesser animals, instinct forces us to go on even if grief has left us not up to the task. But no one could have guessed that the oldest, the strongest, the most independent daughter would be the one most altered by her death.

In the next few months, I put into motion the strange set of circumstances that would later find me losing my plans, the ones I'd mapped out with my mother. In one fleeting moment, I stripped away the petals of my future, let them catch wind, and fly away.

One

On August 30, 1944, only four months after Bea's wedding, my sisters accompanied me to Union Station to send me off on a journey that would please only my aunts. I thought of Aunt Eloise and Aunt Pearl often on that day. A shame they had missed this farewell into matrimony. Without knowledge of the circumstances, they would have been joyous.

During the war, Denver's Union Station served as a crossroads for some four million American soldiers who passed through its doors. Among the throng of uniformed servicemen and -women who daily boarded and debarked trains and made connections, Abby, Bea, and I walked to the ticket window and purchased a ticket for travel south, to launch the first step of a journey much different from the academic missions I'd once imagined. On that day, I would leave the city for the countryside, to carry out the plans for marriage arranged and urged on by my father.

Into my hand, Abby pressed gifts wrapped in new linen handkerchiefs and tied with ribbon. She held her face still. "I'm sorry Father couldn't make it."

"He tried," Bea said, but her youth betrayed her. Barely twenty years old and although a married woman, she hadn't yet learned to mask untruths on her face. It still flashed every emotion, just as it had when we three sisters shared a bed and huddled under a play tent of quilts in the sting of winter mornings. How little of the world she had experienced.

"Call us," was all else she could say.

On that morning, just after the liberation of Paris, the entire country sat perched on the sill of celebration. Laughter was louder, and in everyone's eyes gleamed a hopeful prospect, a wish we all held on to for easy victory, despite doubting its likelihood. Inside the passenger car I rode, the air grew dense with smoke from unfiltered cigarettes held loosely between fingers, passed about, and shared. In 1944, cigarettes had become scarce, but not so on that day.

Near me, only one other woman traveled alone, a thirtyish woman with hair dyed platinum blond like Jean Harlow's. I thought of asking her to play a hand of rummy, anything to break the monotony of the ride and divert my attention. In the university library, once I'd introduced myself to a girl named Dot who later became one of my best friends. But the blond woman seemed engrossed in reading her newspaper, and perhaps I pondered on it too long. Perhaps people traveling alone wanted to be left alone.

I studied the scenes outside the window. In the last days of summer, wood ducks skimmed over low-water ponds, and razored pines swayed in the hills between Denver and Colorado Springs. Just outside of Pueblo, I saw a huge pile of salvaged rubber tires, precious commodities during the war, chained and watched over by a guard. In Pueblo, a town that held an Army air base and therefore another teeming depot, I debarked from the train, following the blond woman but preceding the throng of servicemen. An hour later, I changed trains and headed east. I tried to buy lunch in the dining car but changed my mind after I found it full of people pressed in against each other.

Across the plain, the land shook free of mountain, hill, and mesa, becoming instead long and close-fit to the earth's contours, as a sheet fits a bed. Wild sunflowers grew in patches just feet away from the tracks. They made me remember something Mother once said to me. I had everyone beat in the eyes. Mine, she had said, like her own mother's, were as big and as deeply brown as sunflower centers. And that memory nudged another one. Hadn't Mother once told us a story about sunflowers? During the years of our girlhood, she had whispered to us so many fairy tales, myths, and even some stories of her own making, that it was difficult to recall them all. In her own girlhood, she had once had aims of becoming a novelist, and in my opinion, she had an imagination fresh enough to have succeeded as a writer. Once I asked her if she'd ever regretted her decision to marry and have children, but she'd only laughed and rubbed my head. "Who better to tell my stories to than you girls?"

The story had been something about the sunflower heads, about how they follow the track of the sun. With my eyes closed, I reached far back onto the shelf of distant memory, but still I could not remember it.

The train made five stops between Pueblo and my destination, including one at Nepesta, where the Missouri Pacific and the Santa Fe Railroads crossed. Outside my window, occasional ranch houses, signs of modest human habitation, dotted land that seemed most suitable for gophers and field mice. Then abruptly, outside of Fowler, the untrodden prairie ended, and miles of rowed crops in the fertile bottomlands of the lower Arkansas River began. For a few moments at a time, I saw stretches of the river—a silver-blue strand of waterway that curled back on itself and braided through stands of cottonwoods and willows. Near Rocky Ford, trucks piled high with ripe honeydew melons waited to cross the tracks, reminding me that summer was still at hand.

The train stopped at La Junta, home to another Army air base, where pilots received training in flying B-25 bombers. I debarked along with still more servicemen. La Junta, Spanish for "the junction," was probably named for its location at the convergence of the old Santa Fe and Navajo Trails, and still served as a transportation hub, only now for trains and planes instead of horses and wagons. The train station was huge compared to the buildings in the surrounding area and contained a roundhouse, docks, restaurants, and hotel rooms.

I expected to see my party as soon as I arrived; however, for a time that seemed much longer than it surely was, I stood on the platform with my large traveling case sitting upright at my side, waiting alone.

My father's old friend from seminary, the Reverend Willard Case, was to meet me and introduce me to the man who would become my husband. I had not seen the reverend in almost twelve years and wondered if I would recognize him. But as the depot finally began to clear of uniformed men and family members bustling about, I saw him striding toward me down the platform. He looked much as I had remembered him—wire-thin with a brisk walk. He removed a felt hat, the kind men found fashionable to wear with their suits during the war years, and I saw that since I'd last seen him, his once dark and unruly hair had turned into ribbons of silver strung away from his face.

As Reverend Case laid eyes upon me, recognition lit his face.

"Ah, Olivia," he said as he approached me with an outstretched hand. "We were late in arriving." He took my hand in both of his. "And how was the journey?"

"Fine, fine," I answered, glancing up not at him but instead at the man who accompanied him. He had a face that wasn't unpleasant. No feature was too big or too small, but the resulting mixture was one that couldn't be called distinctive or handsome, either, and he had thinning red-brown hair that made him appear older than the thirty years I had been told was his age. He was tall and broad and appeared strong, as I would've guessed a farmer to be. Dressed in a brown suit with faded knees and elbows, he held himself a step back, completely still, his hat in one hand.

Revered Case followed my eyes. "Yes, let me make the introductions. Mr. Ray Singleton, this is Miss Olivia Dunne."

"Livvy," I said as we shook hands. "Most everyone calls me Livvy, for short."

I saw the lift of a smile in one cheek, but for only the slightest second, and then it was gone. Mr. Ray Singleton, who would become my husband as of this day, provided neither of us changed our minds, simply nodded in my direction. Then he stood back again, and holding his hat with both hands now, he shuffled it about in a circle.

He allowed Reverend Case to take the lead in conversation. "Any problems getting here?" the reverend asked me.

"Just a crowded train," I answered.

He pointed to my bag. "Is this it?"

Funny how I had fit what was left of me into that one case. "For now, yes," I answered.

Reverend Case directed our next moves. "We have the car parked nearby. Quite a little drive ahead of us," he said with the smile that now I remembered. Although they shared the same profession, Reverend Case's face and expressions lacked the hard edge that marked my father. While in Denver for the yearly conference, he had stayed in our guest room and had tolerated the spying games and antics of three young girls. Twelve years ago, even then I had wondered how this gentle man could have once been a close friend to my father. Or had my father perhaps been softer in his youth?

"Do we need to use the station services?" he asked me.

I nodded. "Please pardon me."

In the ladies' room, I removed my hat and pinned away feathers of hair that had escaped from the French twist hairstyle Bea had assisted me to put up for my special occasion. I checked my suit jacket from neck to waist, straightened my skirt, and smoothed out the lines that had creased my hem from hours of sitting in one place. And I regretted that because of rationing, I hadn't been able to purchase nylons to wear.

This man, Ray Singleton, didn't look anything like my sisters' husbands, but then again, I didn't look like my sisters. My body was lean and firm over the bones, not the sort that had ever lent itself to wolf whistles or men's admiring comments.

I pulled out my compact and powdered my nose. I ran the puff three times over the birthmark above my upper lip, which softened its color. But until I started to pin the hat back in place on my head, until I began dropping hatpins that clinked and bounced on the concrete flooring, until I crouched down to retrieve the pins, I hadn't noticed what I'd done to my shoes. On the train, I'd crossed the heels of my pumps over each other so many times that I'd worn ruts into the leather.

Two

⁂

*U*pon my return, Reverend Case advised Mr. Singleton to carry my suitcase, and then he led us to his aged DeSoto motorcar, a square-looking vehicle with balding tires and torn seats. I sat on the front bench seat beside Reverend Case, and Mr. Singleton sat directly behind me.

Just as a troop train was steaming into the station, we pulled away and headed east on the two-lane dirt and gravel road out of La Junta toward Las Animas, passing through the rural, nearly flat farmlands of the Arkansas River Valley. I'd come here once before, on a field trip to the old Bent's Fort, arguably the most important trading post in U.S. history, but hadn't taken much notice of the surroundings. With the windows down and the wind taking those loose hairs out from underneath my hat again, I gazed out at land that appeared more akin to Kansas than to the state that boasted the highest mountains on the mainland. We passed by straight rows of fields irrigated by canals, herds of cattle in numerous shades of brown and black, and shallow livestock ponds. How different from the clipped campus of the university where I had spent so much of my time before leaving to care for my mother. Reverend Case kept up a running description of every well, farm, and outbuilding we passed along the way.

"Now, Olivia, you should know this. The Singletons," he said, nodding toward the man in the backseat, "have some of the best acreage in all of Otero County. Held it in the same family since the homesteading days. Isn't that right, Ray?"

"Yes, sir."

The reverend smiled and nodded to himself as he continued. "Out here we grow sugar beets, vegetables, and a bit of grains. And what with the war going on, farmers are held in highest regard." He tapped the steering wheel with the heel of one hand and glanced my way. "No gasoline shortages for farmers. They get all they want. Right, Ray?"

"Yes, sir."

"Farming," the reverend said. "Feeding hungry mouths." He wrapped his hand around the steering wheel now and nodded. "It's a good life, Olivia."

Outside my window, locoweed growing along the side of the road made me recall the story of Johann Gottfried Zinn, an explorer who wandered the mountains of Mexico. When he discovered some purple flowers he had never seen before, admiring them, Zinn pulled the flowers and put them in his bag. When thieves later attacked him, they tore open his sack and found the wilted flowers. Assuming he was a simpleton, they let him go, believing it to be bad luck to harm the dim-witted. Perhaps if I bolted from the car and dove out headfirst into the wild grass, maybe they'd deem me unfit for marriage. Maybe they'd let me go, too.

We came to the town of Wilson, which lay along the Fort

Lyon irrigation canal. North of the Arkansas River and surrounded by farms and ranches that ranged from modest to impoverished, the town consisted of a church, cemetery, school, and post office. The reverend parked in front of a wood-framed church building covered with red peeling paint and topped with a narrow steeple complete with belfry. As Reverend Case showed us inside the church building, I again found it difficult to envision the friendship between my father and this man. Reverend Case had once studied alongside my father at one of the finest seminaries in the country. Certainly he could have served in many churches, but it seemed he focused his ministry out here by choice. After ushering us into the kitchen, the reverend said he would leave Mr. Singleton and me to ourselves for a spell, that he would await our decision in his office.

Before the ceremony, it was one final chance to change our minds.

Ray Singleton poured lemonade from the icebox and sat down across from me at a long table where I could easily imagine the church buffets spread out on Sunday after services. He cleared his throat but seemed unable to speak.

"Mr. Singleton," I began.

His cheeks reddened before he spoke. "Ray, please."

"Ray, then."

I hoped he wasn't too bashful to answer the question that had plagued me ever since first mention of this arrangement. Since the beginning of the war, the pressure on women to marry soldiers had been as powerful as the pressure put on men to enlist. It was everywhere: in the newspapers, magazines, songs, and movies. After all, the soldier was often heading to war to risk it all—his health, his body, his youth, even his life. A good girl didn't have sex before marriage, so if a soldier wanted her, the best choice was marriage. In the popular movie *The Clock*, Judy Garland agreed to marry a serviceman within hours of meeting him. Women had been marrying soldiers they barely knew out of some patriotic code, but I wondered why a single man would agree to a union such as this one, sight unseen, and for no apparent benefit of his own. "I was wondering . . ." But I was having trouble asking it. "I was wondering why you have agreed to this marriage."

He shifted his weight in the chair, and one deep line sank into the center of his forehead. "When the pastor come out to see me and told me about your situation, I thought . . ." He paused and swallowed hard. "I thought, maybe it'd be God's will."

God's will. Hadn't I been damning God and His will of recent? And had the reverend imposed some kind of religious pressure on Ray, similar to the patriotic pressure that had been placed on so many girls?

Ray waited long enough to take one deep breath. "And seeing as how my folks are passed on, and my brother got killed over there at Pearl Harbor . . ." He cleared his throat again, raised a loose fist to his mouth, and half coughed into it. "Out there at my place, it's been right lonely lately."

Lonely, he said. Loneliness was a reason to marry I could accept. After all, marriages of convenience had inked the scrolls of history far back into earliest recorded time. Politics, power, greed, and graft, not to speak of family honor, had spurred on many a union between man and woman, but how many marriages had come to pass simply because of a need for human companionship? Out of simple loneliness? And how many more arranged marriages had come to fruition than those of personal choice? I remembered back to my study of Bent's Fort. One of the Bent brothers had married Owl Woman, the daughter of a Cheyenne priest, to keep the peace with Plains Indians, upon whose land the post was located. I found it fitting that I, who had always reveled in learning the history of humankind, would now be participating in one of its longest, time-honored traditions: a marriage of convenience.

But in our modern days, I felt that no one should enter marriage without free will. I said to Ray, "Now that you've had a chance to meet me . . ." I tried to get him to look at me. "To see me in person, Ray, have you any doubts?"

"Oh, no, mah'm," he said, finally looking up at me with soft eyes. "You're so fine, I can't believe no man would ever do this to you."

I had to look away, down to the linoleum flooring. *No man would ever do this to you?*

I fought against it, but the pressure started building in my face. My inappropriate reaction to overwhelming emotion was about to begin. I sneezed once—a painful explosion that came from within my cheekbones instead of my nose—then I sneezed again. From out of his chest pocket, Ray handed over a handkerchief as white as new paper. Within minutes, I had sneezed several more times into it. The pressure in my cheekbones made tears well into my eyes, but I could bat them away. I covered my nose with Ray's handkerchief and waited for it to pass.

Words of kindness had always been more difficult for me to handle than the harsh reprimands handed out by my father. Ever since I had been quite young, I could resist those who went against me, had been able to deny their opinions. I had handled my father's perfectionism, the criticism of my aunts, and the resistance to women's higher education, even by some at the university. And going through those battles I believed had formed me into a body a bit more solid and a mind a bit more fierce than those who grew up easy and mild. My inner strength came from an ability to handle, then separate myself from, adversity. Compassion, however, brought up more raw emotion than judgments could ever stir.

At that moment, I remembered the story of the sunflowers. And as it came to me, I also remembered the circumstances of its telling and felt again the magic only Mother could create. Mother first told us the Greek myth about the origin of sunflowers in the midst of a midwinter night, as we snuggled up together in our long nightgowns, spellbound by her every word and dreaming of summer to come.

"The sunflower is the visage of Clytie, a water nymph who died of a broken heart when her love for the sun god Helius was not returned."

"What happened, Mother?" Abby had asked.

"Why did she die?" asked Bea.

Mother plumped up the covers about our necks. "Clytie pined away for Helius until she died. Then her arms and legs dissolved and took root in the earth. Her body metamorphosed into a stalk, and her face changed into a sunflower that followed the path of the sun, day after day."

I shook off the memory, closed my eyes, and willed away the urge to sneeze, then sniffed myself back under control. This wasn't the first time I'd sneezed in taxing situations and for reasons even I couldn't understand. It had started in grade school. Mother had once assured me that I would outgrow it, but instead, the problem had followed me into adulthood. I had even sneezed at the funeral.

Looking down, I could see that my face powder had soiled Ray's handkerchief with flesh-toned smears. "I'll launder and press this for you tomorrow," I said and crumpled the cloth inside my fist.

"It's no bother."

I found his eyes. "Do you think you'll be able to love the baby?"

"Yes," he said without hesitation. "I do."

"Have you always been kind?"

"Not at all," he answered.

Three

*R*ay's sister Martha and her husband came to the church to act as witnesses to our union. Martha resembled Ray in that she had the same shade of red-brown hair, but hers was thick and unruly and refused to stay back in a knot at the back of her head. Instead, pieces of hair stuck out around her face like the arms of a sunburst. She was ruddy-skinned from years spent outside in the sun and was older than Ray, probably by about ten years. When we met, she introduced herself and her husband, Hank, a lean cow-bone of a man who moved forward to shake my hand, every inch in slow motion.

"We've been blessed with four children, ranging all the way from sixteen down to five," Martha said. She adjusted her fabric belt and straightened her hat. Her hands looked roughened by hard work, but were broad and steady. "We hesitated to bring them today. Thought maybe we'd let you get a chance to settle in first."

Hank walked to the church window. Each of his steps started at the hip and rolled down his leg to the foot, one muscle at a time. He pointed outside and spoke on low speed, too. "My family land sets just east of yours."

"Soon you should come for supper," said Martha.

The ceremony itself was over in minutes. Reverend Case skipped the part about kissing the bride, and I wondered if he had done so at Ray's request or simply as a matter of his own kind consideration. After he pronounced us, Martha came forward to squeeze my hand, and before leaving, she gave me a warm casserole dish wrapped up in cup towels.

"You must be tired from all your traveling," she said as she passed it over.

In the truck, I rode beside Ray and held the dish in my lap. He drove us north out Red Church Road, a dirt one-lane that cut wide-weaving arcs out of prairie and field. Ray informed me that our farm, as he now called it, sat at its end.

By then it was well into afternoon. Darts of sunlight came through the windshield, and Ray had to shade his eyes from the glare. I gazed out the side window and soon found myself lost in the rows of crops that fanned away as long arms, blending into shoulders at the horizon and ever moving as we passed them by.

"I don't have a ring," Ray said out of the silence.

I was reminded of the column in the *Rocky Mountain News* that featured Molly Mayfield doling out advice to lonely servicemen and their sweethearts. In the midst of this war, one girl had written in to complain that her fiancé had yet to come up with a diamond engagement ring. I didn't read the column, but everyone else did, so I always heard about the stories anyway. "I don't need one."

I felt him glance my way one time, then again. "Maybe later."

The Singleton farm did indeed sit at the end of the road. Just over the last bridge that crossed a dry creekbed, I could see the spinning flower-top of a windmill and the peaked roof of a barn. As we drew in closer, I could see other weather-beaten outbuildings, a few cows grazing at pasture, and a distant grove of trees. And in all directions now, fields of crops spread away like green stripes on a uniform of brown dirt.

Across an open area of tread-striped dirt sat the house, its stair steps of roof shingles etched into blue sky. I stepped down from the floorboard before Ray had a chance to come around and assist me. In front of the house, I saw the remnants of a flower garden, one that looked as if at one time or another a woman had cared for it. I could see the female touch in the now tilted over and faded whirligigs and in the polished stones arranged on the soil as ornaments. I could also see neglect in the form of weeds, dried leaves, and randomly growing lilac bushes that had managed on their own to survive.

I asked, "Was the garden your mother's?"

"Yes," he said, then removed his hat. "Don't have time to look after it now."

The house was a white framed one-story with steps that led up to a covered porch. Inside, a combined kitchen, den, and dining area made up the largest room. In the center stood a round oak table with claw feet, and along one wall sat a sagging divan covered with a slipcover.

"A good-size icebox," Ray said as he swung open the door to give me a look.

He showed me a bedroom that had belonged to his parents and a bunkroom where he, Martha, and his brother Daniel had grown up. He saved the best for last—a bathroom he had recently converted with indoor plumbing. Until that moment, I hadn't considered living without such conveniences. But on the drive out, I'd seen many a farmhouse with an outhouse slumped behind it.

The bathroom, a large square-shaped room that probably had once been used for putting clothes through the wringer, scrubbing, and ironing, now held a tall sink, commode, a tub with overhead shower, and a washing machine. Along a bar on the wall hung several towels, all of them bleached white and smelling of laundry soap, and in the sink I could see the chalky remains of scouring powder. Obviously Ray had tried to clean up the place, but had forgotten some of the most telling details. Cobwebs draped the line where wall met ceiling, and all over the house, the wood floors were as scratched and scarred as those in a grammar school classroom.

After Ray brought in my luggage, we sat together at the table and shared Martha's casserole of beef, carrots, potatoes, and dumplings. After taking a few bites, Ray stopped and wiped his face with a napkin. "How was that train ride out of Denver?"

I seemed to remember answering this question several times already. "Fine."

A few minutes later, he said, "Bet that ride was tiring. Do you need to lie down?"

"The seats were comfortable. No, I'm fine, thank you."

We both finished large portions of the casserole, then out of the cupboard Ray brought the remains of a cake. "Mrs. Pratt from church," he explained. "She makes something for me nearly every week."

"How nice," I said. "Let's hope she continues." Then I laughed.

He looked surprised, but he shouldn't have been. Plenty of college coeds knew little of domestics, me among them. When Abby, Bea, and I were still small enough to sit on the kitchen countertops, we would climb up and watch Mother bake. I remembered clouds of flour floating in the air as she worked. By the time we were old enough to learn anything, however, she had become preoccupied with her charity work. She hired on a housekeeper and cook, and because it was only fun to watch Mother work in the kitchen, I never gained skills in managing a kitchen or in coming up with concoctions suitable to eat. "I never learned how to bake a thing," I told Ray.

He blinked, looking surprised again. "Mrs. Pratt would come over and teach you, I bet. Or my sister."

"Don't worry." This man was doubtless unaware that women were now going into professions alongside men, that we didn't solely stick to household cleaning and other chores that didn't require expansion of a bright, young, and impressionable mind. Not only were women filling the college campuses, but labor needs had resulted in jobs for women in industries that had traditionally been male dominated. Women were working as welders, engine mechanics, machinists, truck drivers, and crane operators. In factories they assembled shells, bombs, tanks, and ships. Cowgirls and lumberjills, female writers and radio announcers, even women at the stock exchange, had transformed female roles forever. "I'll manage somehow."

He looked embarrassed. "The truth is, I can cook a fair bit."

"Don't bother," I said, smiling. "I'll teach myself."

At sunset, he explained to me that farmers went early to bed, then he disappeared into the bunkroom. Upon our arrival, he had placed my bag in his parents' bedroom, so I could only assume I was to sleep in there, alone. This didn't surprise me. Women in my condition were considered most delicate. And although Ray and I had just gotten married, we'd also just met.

I cleaned and dried the dishes, watched the waning sunset,

then waited. It was so silent the whir of grasshopper wings in the front garden sounded like shouting. I found myself passing through the screen door and out onto the porch. At the railing, I stopped. A full moon slowly rose over the top fringes of dark distant cottonwood trees rimming the banks of creeks that fed into the Arkansas. Not yet silver, the moon reflected the honey gold of the setting sun, lighting her face from continents away.

Finally, I let myself exhale.

My father's plan to give the baby a name had come to fruition. And in the end, he had saved himself the disgrace of preaching morality to others while at the same time housing his own daughter, a girl in trouble. Would I now be able to sleep? Certainly my body needed rest, and flailing about during the quiet hours after midnight could not be good for mother or baby. Would I grow roots here, as Clytie had? Perhaps, in this silent land at the end of the road, I would find rest.

But if I did rest, I prayed not to sleep so deeply as to dream, and most of all, not to dream of him.

Four

Once I read about the homesteaders who first populated the plains of eastern Colorado, and I learned something not widely written about in history books. The isolation of the homesteaders throughout the West drove many to the brink of insanity. The government required homesteaders to live on their claims, and because of the difficulty of travel in those days, compounded by bad weather and much work to do, many settlers went for long months at a time without social contact. This was particularly tough on the women and, for some reason, on those of Scandinavian descent, who had proportionately the highest numbers of immigrants ending up in insane asylums.

I could understand that descent. I could understand why one settler wrote in his memoirs that during his youth, he read over and over again the copy of a New York newspaper his father had put up to paper the walls. And as to the question of the Scandinavians— they had emigrated to the U.S. after living in small, close-knit villages where folk dances and community celebrations had been common. Surely their lives there had been tough at times, but never lonely.

The first morning after my wedding day, I awakened to the sounds of pans and utensils clanging together in the kitchen. I rolled over and checked my watch. Five-fifteen, and outside, still dark. Amazingly, I had slept well and could've used even more sleep. I thought of getting up and offering to make my husband something for breakfast. That was what farm wives were probably supposed to do. But hadn't the man been living by himself for several years now? I flopped over, hugged the pillow to my chest, and drifted back to sleep. When I awakened after nine, the only sign of Ray was the kitchen mess from a large breakfast he had left behind.

I bathed and dressed, ate something for myself, did the dishes, and cleaned up. Then I went investigating. In the kitchen, the cupboards held basic cooking implements and pottery dishes, a fair amount of canned goods, and a breadbox. A radio sat on the countertop. In the bathroom, I found only a few extra towels and washcloths, one brush, one comb. I also found Ray's shaving set and shaving powder, a tube of Brylcreem, but no men's after-shave. Outside on a narrow back porch, I saw a contraption I found out later was a cream separator. A propane tank sat on the ground below the back porch.

In the room where I'd slept, the closets and dresser drawers were empty except for one pewter-framed photo of a plain-faced couple that could only be Ray's parents. No other family photos and nothing of the brother who had been killed at Pearl Harbor. No jewelry boxes, family memorabilia, or books. Assuming I was going to remain in the same room as last night, I opened my case and unpacked my clothes. I set out my most treasured remembrances, starting with the last photo taken of my family together, intended for the church roster book. On the dresser, I placed the other belongings I'd chosen to bring with me: a small jewelry chest that had been Mother's, the waxed rose from Bea's wedding bouquet, one book on ancient Egypt, and antique hatpins—my last birthday gift from Abby. Finally, I opened the gifts Abby and Bea had sent off with me. Inside the new handkerchiefs were two pairs of heirloom earrings—a pair of pearl drops and a pair of bead clusters on ear screws. These I set on the dresser top, too, although I wondered where now I would ever wear them.

In the bunkroom, I found Ray's bed made and only a clock, a Bible, and a calendar sitting on the nightstand. In the closet, his clothes sagged off wire hangers—only some clean work shirts, two white shirts, some slacks, and an overcoat. Off to one side I found the brown suit he had worn the day before. Shoved into the corner were the shoes. Only one tie and no jewelry. On top of his dresser, the hat and the cufflinks he'd worn to the station sat above a stack of closed bureau drawers. I touched the top drawer. Inside, among his personal belongings, must be clues as to who this man was.

When we were girls, Abby used to keep a diary. She wrote in it every day, then she wrapped the book with rubber bands and hid it among her clothing in her drawers. I remembered how Bea had complained about it. She couldn't understand why Abby would want to keep anything from us. But later, Bea started hiding letters from her pen pal in Canada, just as Abby had hidden her diary.

Perhaps in these drawers, Ray kept old letters or yearbooks from high school. Perhaps photographs from his younger days. I wrapped my fingers around the drawer's round knob and started to pull. It was so silent I thought I could hear something ticking inside, something like a clock, or maybe a bomb.

I pulled my hand back. What was I doing? Now I stared at the dresser and admonished myself. Whatever these drawers held was private. Certainly I couldn't have fallen this far.

I walked away from the bunkroom and then carried one of the kitchen chairs out to the porch, where I placed it for good viewing. To one side of the barn was a fenced pen holding some hogs, on the other side a pasture for the dairy cows and draft horses. Occasionally a loose chicken squawked and fluttered out the barn doors. A tuxedo-clad magpie who landed on the back of a cow looked as out of place as I did sitting on the porch in one of my school dresses with matching belt and shoes. Soon my eyes began to sting. When I started picking up pebbles on the planks beneath me and flinging them out onto the dirt, without first realizing I was doing it, I stopped myself. Like the Scandinavians, surely I might go insane here, too.

Just before noon, Ray returned carrying a pail of milk and handed over some eggs out of a basket. "Morning." He glanced over at the clean kitchen and smiled. "How're you?"

"I should have gotten up with you."

"No need." He removed an old felt hat and set it on the table. "You got to have rest."

I wasn't sure why he had returned. "Shall I make lunch?"

He shook his head. "I don't eat midday. Mostly, I'm far off. Unless I got work nearby, I can't come back during the day." He went to the coffeepot and filled his thermos.

"Are you working nearby today?"

He turned red, even to the ears. I'd never have believed a man could be so bashful. Finally he looked up and nodded.

I took off the apron I'd been wearing. "If you're not too busy, then, would you show me around?"

"You mean the farm?"

"I guess so." I shrugged. "Or anything else of interest."

He moved to the icebox and poured the fresh milk into a wide-lipped glass bottle. Then he drew water from the tap. After he gulped down a full glass, he said, "Okay."

He drove the truck down a narrow road that ran between fields. "We have us a good-size farm." He glanced my way. "A hundred and sixty acres."

Ray looked to me as if he wanted my approval. It was wartime, and farming had become an important, crucial industry to feed the country, our troops, and much of the world. Clearly, Ray was proud of what he did, and war needs had raised the status of the family farmer far beyond what it had been during peaceful times, equal at least to that of other businessmen. I remembered one of the government's wartime slogans: "Food will win the war and write the peace." And a government poster I'd seen at the train station featured a uniformed soldier telling a farmer, "Those overalls are your uniform, bud."

I watched the fields and irrigation furrows go by and I asked him, "What are your crops?"

Ray gestured out the window at the fields. "Those there are sugar beets." When I nodded, he said, "Our best crop. We have over half of our acres planted in them."

"I notice that some of the fields are empty."

"You bet," said Ray. "We've already taken the cash crops—green peas, green beans, sweet corn—in June, to get some money coming in. The cucumbers came out in July, the tomatoes in August. We just finished them up. Pretty soon the big work starts up—onions and dry beans. It's almost time."

"To harvest?"

He nodded. "And after that, we'll take the sugar beets."

It seemed I had come at the busiest time of the year. "May I help?"

His face drained of expression. "I doubt it."

I almost laughed. Our situation seemed so absurd. "You're right. I don't know anything about farming."

After a period of silence, he said, "But you have the house to take care of."

Ray turned up a wider road, where he picked up speed. The wind started blowing in through the truck window and hitting me full in the face, wind that carried the odor of manure. I scooted over to the center of the bench seat, but as soon as I did, Ray sat taller in the seat and gripped the steering wheel with callused knuckles. Too late I realized I had moved too close. For the remainder of the drive, I could feel his unease.

At first it baffled me. The man was thirty years old. But then I thought of some of the young men I'd known in high school. In the sad hierarchy that ranked persons primarily by looks, I remembered several groups of young men who were both unattractive and terribly shy, who never went out on dates and never got invited to parties. Many of them never got accustomed to contact with girls, and judging by his reactions to me, Ray must have been just like them. In comparison, my social life, although nothing to brag about, had at least given me the opportunity to befriend a few men. In high school and even in college, my girlfriends and I weren't the most popular, but we had our occasional dates and didn't grow up uncomfortable with the opposite sex, either. When we went to the cinema or the ice-skating rink, often a few of the studious guys or a brother or two of one of the girls came along.

Those timid young men in high school had long since graduated and gone into the service. Rumor held that in the Army, innocence was quickly lost. However, Ray apparently had worked away into adulthood, stuck out here on this farm. He was as lost as one of those pimple-faced and innocent boys on a first date back in high school, more self-conscious and jittery than I'd imagined a grown man could be.

I wondered if I should move back next to the window, but then, how would he take that? I didn't know what to do, so I ended up staying penciled in the seat next to Ray. But as we drove through some curves, I made certain I didn't accidentally fall over and brush up against him.

He showed me the bean fields, the onions fields, and finally the "head gates" that brought water from the canals onto his land and down feeder ditches to the crops. "We get our water from the Fort Lyon, the longest canal in Colorado. A hundred and thirteen miles long."

"Ah," I said.

We never left Singleton land. We never saw another soul, either. On the way back, Ray started telling me the names of weeds growing along the roadway. Rabbit brush, apparently, had just finished blooming.

Over the next few days, I saw Ray early in the morning before dawn and late in the evening just before sunset, when he arrived back at the house, sweaty and hungry. For dinner, I experimented with baking the beef, pork, and chicken I found in the icebox, fresh meat Ray had swapped with other farmers in the area, and for side dishes I heated cans of vegetables. Eating out of cans was considered most luxurious in those days, but the only fresh vegetables Ray brought in were some of the last tomatoes, so I had little choice. Usually I started my preparations way too early, then I had to let the meal sit and wait on the table until Ray returned.

After he tromped in, he headed for the shower first, then sat and silently prayed for long minutes while the food continued to turn colder.

During the day, I cleaned the house and swept off the porch. I ironed all the clothes in my closet and refolded my lingerie in the drawers. Outside, the animals snorted and brayed to remind me I wasn't totally alone, but Ray stopped coming back and checking on me midday. The only reading material I had was the *La Junta Tribune*, which came a day late, delivered by the rural mail carriers on the star route. We had no telephone, and no one came to call.

In the evenings, Ray and I ate dinner together at the table. After eating, Ray always took an hour or so to work on farm business. He spread out receipts and ledger books on the table, pondered over them, and scratched down notes with a pencil. After he finished, he shoved everything back into one manila folder, marked simply "1944," and crammed it inside a kitchen drawer. Afterward, he usually opened his Bible and read a few pages, then we listened to radio programs or worked on making conversation.

After four long days of this, I told him over dinner, "We could stand to stock up on groceries."

He glanced up between bites of bread. "Sure thing. I'll drive you into town tomorrow."

"I can drive a car."

He rumpled the napkin to his face and said, "Sure enough?" But his eyes told me he was uncertain. "Sometimes the clutch on that truck tends to stick."

"I'll learn how to handle it." I wanted to pat his hand or his back in the same manner one assures a child, but most certainly he would've crumbled into ash if I'd touched him. "If it would make you feel better, I'll drive with you along first, so you can see for yourself."

He still looked as if he had just chewed cactus. "Tomorrow, then," he said.

The next morning, I drove with him in the truck, the "beet box," as Ray called it, west toward La Junta, where I got my first glimpse of Japanese interns toiling in the fields along the way, their dark hair like ripe blackberries among the greenery.

Ray gestured that way and said, "They're from Camp Amache."

"But isn't that a long way east of here?"

"The government brings them in, puts them up, so they can work where needed."

"Will they come to your farm?"

"You mean our farm?"

A second later, I nodded.

"Sure enough."

We passed through La Junta and drove the paved road southwest all the way to Trinidad. Ray said it had a feed store with the best prices, and therefore justified the farther traveling. But as I was driving, I realized he had chosen the route purposefully. Maybe he wanted to drive all that distance so I could see some variety in terrain, or maybe he wanted me to get a long drive under my belt, or maybe he wanted to observe my driving skills on less-traveled roads. I didn't know or ask why. At any rate, I enjoyed taking the same route that had once been part of the Santa Fe Trail, the path that had brought pioneers, trappers, and traders into the former hunting grounds of roaming bands of Arapaho and Cheyenne. Now the road passed quickly through farmlands that changed to range lands, then through virgin prairie land still not tilled or grazed.

By the time we reached Trinidad, I was used to the stiff clutch and loose steering of Ray's truck. I even backed it into a spot between two others along the former trail, now Main Street.

The town of Trinidad struck me as a conundrum of differences: adobe buildings next to brick Victorians, coal miners among sheep and cattle ranchers, citizens of Mexican descent among Anglos. Cobblestones covered the hilly streets of old downtown not far from the smoothly paved blacktop highway. Without a military base nearby, the town was distinctive for extremes of ages, too. Children ran in and out of the shadows cast by storefronts, whereas a prevalence of older men and women seemed to thrive inside the shadows, becoming a denser part of the darkness themselves.

"I've read about Trinidad," I told Ray and handed him back the keys to the ignition. "This is one of the oldest towns in the state."

Ray headed for the feed store while I headed for the library. I hadn't opened my book on Egypt yet; somehow I couldn't do it here. But I was desperate for something to read.

As I walked the downtown area, I noticed the lack of attention I received. People passing me on the street looked beyond me, as if one sideways glimpse had already told them I didn't belong. During the war, we were taught that anyone could be a spy, even a nice-appearing or pleasant person. Posters everywhere featured Uncle Sam holding a finger to his lips. "Shhh." Don't give away secrets. "Loose lips sink ships." The message was on the radio, in the newspapers, and in movies. But as I walked on, I doubted that distrust was the reason I was being ignored in this place. In the city, passersby on the street didn't notice each other, either, but it had to do more with preoccupation and hurriedness. Here, I got the impression that newcomers or visitors simply didn't matter.

I sped up. By the time I reached the library, I was salivating like Pavlov's dog. Inside the door, I paused for a minute, breathing it in. I loved everything about the library, even the smell of dust on the bookshelves. I loved fingering through tight card catalogs, perusing the rows of endless subject matter, lifting books so word-heavy they felt as though they might break my arm. In the local history section, I read up on Trinidad. First a favorite camping spot for nomadic tribes and later mountain men, the town became a stopping point for Conestoga wagons heading south over Raton Pass on the trail to Santa Fe.

When I ran out of reading time, I signed up for a library card and checked out the most detailed local history book I could find, a basic cookbook, and *The Sun Also Rises*. I had read some of Hemingway's later books, but had always intended to read this early one that had made him famous. Now would be my chance.

On the way back, Ray drove. I tried enjoying the silence. Before me, the domed sky was even larger than the sage lands below it. As we passed under the shade of high clouds, I turned to face Ray across the seat. "Do you know much about the history of this land we're driving through?"

He shrugged and kept his eyes focused on the empty road ahead. "Can't say that I do."

"I found it in this book." I spread my fingers over the wrinkled leather cover. "It was once part of a huge land grant belonging to Mexican citizens."

He shook his head. "Didn't know that."

"The grant covered four million acres, but U.S. courts threw out Mexican claims for lack of written proof, and the lands were opened up for homesteading, for example, to your family." I only wanted to share a conversation, but as the words came out of my mouth, I realized they sounded like a school report.

"That so?" Ray said. He glanced over his shoulder at the things he'd piled in the truck bed. Clearly he wasn't interested in what I was saying.

"What about your family, Ray? How did they come here and why?"

He crunched himself deeper into the driver's seat. "Well. They came out here and started farming."

"In what year? Where did they live?"

Again, he focused straight ahead. "Don't rightly know the details. Better ask Martha," he said. "Our grandma used to tell us all about that stuff, but I'm sorry to say I've gone and forgot it."

Now I looked straight ahead, too. Shimmering distances on the horizon never came closer. After we passed a train going in the opposite direction, I waited until the high whine of the steam whistle left the still air, then I pointed to the tracks. "In some places the ruts are so deep you can still see the old Santa Fe Trail. Right there, between the tracks and this road."

"Sure enough?" he said, but that was all.

Afterward, I tried reading my book but had to stop because it was making me motion sick. And the only other thing Ray told me was the name of the high point along the road, Jack's Point, a grazing spot for mules. When we stopped for groceries in La Junta, I couldn't think of anything to talk to him about as we walked the few aisles picking out canned goods and produce together.

Before we left town I bought a copy of the other La Junta newspaper, the *Democrat,* and looked over copies of both the *Rocky Mountain News* and the *Denver Post,* all of which I found out were available for mail delivery. I decided to subscribe to the *Denver Post.* Reading about events a day late was better than not reading about them at all.

The following morning, I got up out of a sound sleep to make Ray breakfast. He shoveled it down and headed out the door, then I returned to my room and napped until a more reasonable time for awakening. The next two days, however, Ray started staying around later in the mornings. I heard him up before dawn, just as before, but then he'd be shuffling around the house instead of leaving it. When I got up, there he was, waiting around in the kitchen for breakfast and drinking down coffee.

One morning I told him, "You don't have to stay in because of me."

He had continued sipping out of his mug and didn't look up. "I just been more tired, is all."

I opened my mouth, just about to do it, to correct his English. Most of the time Ray spoke correctly, but every so often he slipped up. He reminded me of fellow students I'd known who had grown up without proper English having been spoken in their households. They knew the correct ways from schooling, but sometimes what they heard at home accidentally sneaked out of them, and how those errors embarrassed them, especially around students such as me, who rarely even slumped to slang. So I closed my mouth before I could say a word to Ray.

The next morning, after I'd made pancakes and fried eggs for breakfast, Ray drank coffee and lingered until the sun was well up into the eastern sky. I asked him about the harvest, and he answered by naming machinery and listing a nondescript course of events I had difficulty following. He told me about various fields, reminding me that he had shown them to me during our drive. But I couldn't remember one field from another, although I pretended I could.

After he went out to the truck and drove away, I sat until my coffee turned cold. I finished cleaning the kitchen and watched the breeze coming in through the window screen, how it lifted the curtain into an arc, dropped it, then lifted it again.

How could something as big as this farm feel so confining? I'd only been here a week, but it felt more like a month. And I'd never spent so much time alone before. Already I'd discovered the weird things I was capable of doing, the thoughts I was capable of entertaining, during too much free time. I'd already examined my hair up close in the mirror and categorized all the different strands of color I found there. I'd studied my toes, counted clouds in the sky, and tried to discern the different facial expressions that could be made by a cow. I'd wondered how many people would die overseas in the time it took me to make up my bed.

Soon I folded up my apron, changed from loafers to sneakers, and headed for the outbuildings I'd been staring down ever since my arrival. I found the barn guarded at the open doors by a milk cow that was so big up close I hate to admit it scared me. From behind the cow, a long-eared hound plodded out the barn doors. I had seen him from afar several times before, but he'd kept his distance from the house. Now as I stood outside the barn, he chugged up to me like a streetcar going uphill. He padded circles about me, sniffing my scent that had fallen down into the dust. I reached down and rubbed the bony top of his head and stroked down his backbone—a string of marbles set out under a rug.

"Hey, boy," I whispered to him.

Now he sniffed around my neck and huffed out dog breath that made me smile and remember. When I was a child, we'd never been allowed a pet. But Abby, Bea, and I had often visited a neighbor who kept a yard full of schnauzers and miniature poodles, so we grew up with some knowledge of pets and no fear of dogs. When one of the poodles gave birth to a litter, we each chose a favorite before those pups had a chance to open their eyes. Although we couldn't take them home, Abby and Bea chose fat white ones, and I picked a wriggling black that reminded me of a caterpillar. I still remember the name I gave him: Shadow.

That old hound padded along with me as I moved on. We passed by rows of crops lined out to the horizon. This was a place of leaves, stalks, and stems in every shade of green, ordered and watered by man but grown by the blue, dry sky. The land was breathing deeply. Human exchange of air seemed meager compared to all the synthesis going on at ground level, and the houses and buildings seemed simply like small boxes of right angles and deadwood planks surrounded by all these big, buzzing fields.

A clay-colored tumbleweed wedged between rows of green leaves caught my eye. Thorny, trapped, and out of place, it let me know the insignificance of any one, distinctive thing caught in a place so mapped with sameness. Aunt Eloise and Aunt Pearl had once accused me of hiding out in school. Instead Father had sent me into hiding here, where the openness of land and sky made hiding out about as unlikely as finding clover among the sage.

I went past a windmill that pumped water out of the well, a wind charger that Ray had told me provided our electricity, and a gasoline storage tank. Behind the barn and next to the livestock pond, I found the last of the outbuildings. Stacked with crates and old tools, the inside of the shed smelled like the attic where my mother had once kept boxes of our old dolls and dresses. On a shelf, I found the hand tools Ray's mother must have used for flower gardening. I picked up a small trowel, brushed off the dirt, and passed it slowly from one hand to the other. It was already too late to start summer annuals, but in the fall, I could still plant bulbs.

I searched over and under the other shelves in the shed and

found things I hadn't expected to find. In the house, there seemed to be room for only the most practical of items. But here, I found pieces of the past—an old wooden butter churn, a small pie safe, buttonhooks, and a flat pan with a long handle that was once used to heat bedding. Pioneers would heat the pan over the fire, then run it in between the sheets to warm them before slipping in for the night.

The butter churn and the pie safe needed to be sanded and refinished, but the buttonhooks and pan simply needed polishing. Everything I found could be worked on and restored. I could even learn to do the restoration myself. Soon I found an empty burlap bag, shook it open, and began stacking it inside with the things I wanted.

That evening, Ray came in early. I was just about to tell him about the shed when he asked, "What do you say we go and visit my sister tonight?" Then he headed for the bathroom.

Maybe he sensed I needed a change, or maybe he needed one himself. "For dinner?" I called after him.

"You bet," he said as he closed the door.

I looked about for the telephone before remembering we didn't have one. "Don't we need to let her know we're coming?" I called back.

"No need," he answered from behind the door.

While he showered, I chose my khaki-colored dress with collar and shoulder pads that I had bought while shopping with my friend Dot shortly after Mother's death. Never before had I bought anything so military-inspired, as was the latest fashion, but after I had tried it on at May Company and with Dot's reassurances, I had decided it was a good fit and quite flattering. I donned the dress, polished my shoes, and then combed out my hair and put it up in pincurls so that just before we left, I could take it down and style it in a bob to graze my shoulders.

Ray came out dressed in his better slacks and a clean plaid shirt. He had washed his hair and combed it over the thinning area on top, but obviously hadn't checked the back of his head. Open to the air, his biggest bald spot shined like an Easter egg in the grasses.

Finally ready, Ray and I slid into the truck. As he started the engine, Ray looked my way. "Onions are ready. This'll be the last chance to get out for a long time coming."

The trip took us nearly twenty minutes of travel down rutted dirt roads, over wooden bridges without railings, and past windmills that creaked around in silent currents of air. As we passed by some spare green plants I hadn't seen before, I asked Ray, "Are those tomatoes?"

"No. Those are potatoes."

"Oh."

"They get grown mostly down in the San Luis Valley." He glanced over at me once, then continued. "But some farmers around here grow a few fields, then send the harvest straight off to the potato chip makers."

"I see."

We kept the windows down for needed cooling, letting the air whip in. I could feel the output of plants landing heavily on my skin. And as we arrived, I could tell my efforts to stay neat had done little good. Dust covered the sleeves and bodice of my dress, and I could feel tangles twisted in my hair.

Martha and Hank greeted us with smiles and handshakes, as if dropping by unexpected weren't unexpected at all. Their farm could have been a replica of ours. Inside the house, which had had a second story added for more bedrooms, they introduced me to their children. Sixteen-year-old Ruth wore a big shirt over denims, and her hair swung behind her in a long, rusty-colored ponytail. Her eyes grew large as she looked me over. "Is that dress ready-made?" she asked.

It hadn't occurred to me until then, but of course store-bought clothes might still be considered quite extraordinary out here. During the Depression, farm wives and children were still wearing chicken-feed-sack dresses and flour-sack underwear. I nodded to Ruth and said, "It's my favorite," but then I wondered if perhaps I should have worn something simpler.

"Oh, I can see why," she replied, still looking me up and down.

Ruth's thirteen-year-old sister Wanda rose from reading a book to be introduced to me. She had copper-colored hair the same shade as her freckles and thick, straight hawk brows that must have spent a lot of time in thought. The two boys, Hank Jr. and Chester, looked more like twins than brothers. "They're only a year apart," Martha explained. As I shook their hands, I noticed they had the same shade of brown eyes that ran in the blood of this family—lighter than mine—the color of brown eggshells.

After a polite exchange of how-do-you-do's, the boys headed back upstairs to finish a game of cards until dinner was served. Wanda took herself back between pages, but Ruth never left my side. Over dinner and dessert, she stared at me. She asked about the fabric of my dress, and later she asked to try on the opal ring I wore on my right hand, a gift from my mother.

In the kitchen, Martha started pulling out pots and pans, ladles and spoons, jars of spices. Ruth and I offered to help her, but she assigned us nothing but the table to set, and working together, we finished it in minutes. As we sat to fold the napkins, Martha kept moving about her kitchen with a certain ease of movement and steady purpose that let everyone around her know she had every-thing under control. Ray and Hank discussed farming business endlessly, and I overheard words and terms I'd never heard before, letting me know for certain just how out of my own element I was.

Beet pullers and feedlots. Fresnos and slips.

At last, Martha took a rest. She sat with me at the kitchen table while dinner baked in the oven. Ruth stayed with us, too, her chair scooted up flush with mine. When I told Martha I was not a cook, she offered to loan me recipe cards she kept in an old oak box, and she told me she knew a secret for perfect piecrust, if ever I wanted to know it. And she offered to pass on her "starter" for baking bread. I thanked her but didn't say I had no wish to spend my one evening out wasting it in talk of nothing but the kitchen.

"How did your ancestors arrive here?" I asked her instead.

"Oh, well, that's a story," she said as she knotted her hands to-gether on the tabletop. "Our grandfather came out here in 1870, one of the first to homestead in these parts. He was only nineteen at the time."

Already she had me hooked. "Where did he come from? Why did he do it?"

Martha looked puzzled. "I guess I don't truthfully know for certain why he did it. Most likely it was the lure of free land. For poor folks, owning land was the only way to get respectable," she said with a smile. "Anyway, he came out from New York City's Lower East Side, traveling by rail and by steamship and then by rail again all the way to Granada. From there he loaded a wagon and followed the Arkansas."

"And he was alone?"

"At the beginning of the journey, yes." She smiled and gazed as though remembering something pleasant. "I heard the story many times as a young girl. He met our grandmother, a pretty little thing of only seventeen, on the steamship and convinced her father that he would be a good husband. He was quite the smooth talker, I heard. They were married by the ship's captain, and she finished the journey along with him."

Martha went on to tell me that through tough times and often disappointing farming, her grandparents had built crude homes, then other homes, and stayed on. Martha had a gift for storytelling, like that of my mother. If only her brother shared the same gift.

"In the earliest days," she told me, "farming wasn't very successful without irrigation. They had to try to raise crops just on rainwater, which isn't much. Then, beginning in the 1870s, the irrigation companies put in canals off the river, but the farmer still had to dig out his own ditches." She sat back in her chair and pulled at a loose thread on the tablecloth. "I doubt any of us could work that hard nowadays."

She studied my face now, but without a hint of hardness. "I keep a box of old photographs and papers in the attic. If you ever want to take a look, you're most welcome."

I nodded. "I have to say I find the history of the farm more interesting than present-day operations."

Martha smiled; then, after a period of silence, she glanced over toward the divan at her brother. "When Daniel joined up, Ray decided to stay behind and run the farm." She looked down at her hands. "It's funny. They never fought over anything. And they never spoke of dividing up the land between them, either. Most brothers would have done that, you know." She caught my eye for a moment, then looked back at her hands. "They always planned on running the farm together. When Daniel returned."

Ruth was still right beside me, but now she looked away.

I said the useless words, "I'm sorry," to Martha, although after my mother's death, while I was still walking pure grief, those words had done nothing for me. I had wanted people to do something bold, take action, shout and rage, anything to express the magnitude of my loss. But I said the words, "I'm sorry," to Martha because I was incapable of creating anything else.

Martha took a long breath. "Now that he's gone . . ." But by then, her air was gone, too.

I finished saying it for her. "Of the Singletons, now only the two of you remain."

She looked up at me. "No longer."

I puzzled, and then she smiled. "Now we have you."

Later the two boys joined us at the table. They wanted to know everything about living in Denver. Did I go often to the cinema, was the capitol building really made of gold, what card games were played at the USO, and had I ever met the governor? When Martha excused herself, the oldest boy, Hank Jr., moved to my side. After he checked to make sure his father wasn't listening, he whispered, "I want to tell you something, but it's a secret."

I crossed my heart. "Promise not to tell."

"When I grow up, I don't want to be a farmer. I want to live in the city like you did, and I want to work in one of those factories that make ships for the Navy."

I touched his shoulder. This youngest generation had known nothing of a world without war. "Let's hope the Navy doesn't need warships by then."

After dinner, Martha took me outside and showed me the new porch swing they had recently hung. "Let's sit, Livvy," she said.

But Ruth slipped down on the seat beside me before Martha had a chance. The boys stood across from me and thought up more questions for me to answer. As I continued to chat about the city life, Ruth inched her way closer to me. I could feel her studying the movements of my face, and I could feel her breath land on my shoulder, soft, like warm air without wind.

In the middle of our conversation, Ruth blurted out to her mother, "I want to cut off my hair." Then she touched one of the curls resting on my shoulder. "I want a bob, just like Livvy's."

And after that, I couldn't make myself meet Martha's eyes.

Five

⁂

$\mathcal{I}$ filled the next two days by cooking and cleaning. I waxed the wood flooring over and over all throughout the house until I got it as shiny as a new desktop. During the sunny afternoons, I washed clothes and linens and hung the wet pieces out to dry on the clothesline. One morning I asked Ray to show me how to be of more use around the farm, and he took me out to the barn, where he let me gather the fresh eggs from the chicken coops. He also offered to show me how to milk the cows, but I declined, too embarrassed to tell him I was fearful of those big, noisily chewing animals. The next morning, he showed me how to operate the cream separator. Along with the extra eggs, he took the cream stored in five-gallon cans into La Junta to sell. He gave the remaining skimmed milk to the hogs.

While the laundry dried outside, I wrote letters to Abby and Bea and then drove the truck to town to post them right away. I kept up with news of the war by way of La Junta's station KOKO on Ray's battery-run Philco radio and by reading the newspaper that came in the mail.

As the Allies slowly reclaimed Europe, more reports of Nazi

atrocities against the Jews were beginning to come to light. Soviet soldiers had overrun the Polish death camp Majdanek in late July. They hadn't found many prisoners but had found eight hundred thousand pairs of shoes. Throughout the war, occasionally I'd read articles, usually ones buried in the depths of the newspaper, relaying unbelievable reports of mass murder. Now the news came in of more discovered killing centers, and as I allowed myself to accept that some of the earlier reports might have been true after all, I felt the pages of this new history curl and recoil. I remember the moment I let myself at least partially believe. I remember the smell of bacon lingering in the kitchen after breakfast, the way the light came in softly through the curtains from the window, how it fell on the yellow cotton of my shirtdress. Everything around me stilled and quieted. The apple butter jar sitting open, breadcrumbs scattered about, and Ray's hat off to one side on the table. As I loitered with little to do, perhaps some of the most dreadful events of human history were daily coming to light, each new report more gruesome than the ones before it.

The Allies and the Red Army slowly progressed. Unthinkable tales of mass graves and gas chambers and other evils still too horrendous to fathom for those of us living comfortably in our own country were slowly emerging. The press coverage was brief, however, and given the exaggeration of atrocities during World War I, an air of disbelief still prevailed. One evening I read a small article I'd found in the back of the news section of the Denver paper. It said that ten thousand Polish Jews had been killed daily; a million Hungarian Jews had been massacred. I remembered a vision that had stuck with me, the eight hundred thousand pairs of shoes.

I had to let the paper drop to my lap.

Ray looked up at me quizzically, so I relayed to him what I'd just read. And I told him about the shoes at Majdanek. "What do you suppose happened to the people who had been wearing all those pairs of shoes?" The numbers were staggering. "Could they all have been killed?"

But Ray looked unfazed. He only shrugged and went back to studying his folder of papers, obviously too concerned with pressing matters here on this farm to let the outside world bother him. Or was the thought of so much death simply too painful for him, especially because of Daniel's death? Maybe he couldn't let it sink in just yet.

I continued reading alone. I found out that thousands of Axis soldiers were being taken prisoner, many of them starved and sick, and some of them ending up in American POW camps, one of them in nearby Trinidad. The news reports were full of ruin in Europe, including hunger that most of us couldn't imagine. In another article, I learned that the Dutch had been forced to eat their tulip bulbs just to survive. But with no servicemen around Wilson and surrounded by lush pastures and full fields, the only signs of warfare were the news reports on the radio, what I read in the newspapers, and occasional low-flying practice runs made by pilots from the base at La Junta. It often felt like the war wasn't real, the way we had felt during the first months of the war, when the entire city of Denver seemed to deny the whole thing.

Back in December 1941, everyone in our posh neighborhood had still lit their houses with Christmas lights. But within a year, we were attending war bond rallies, learning what to do during air raids, sewing blackout curtains, even rationing gasoline and holding on to old tires. We saved our toothpaste tubes, tin cans, and fat. We were told that one pound of fat could be turned into a pound of black powder, and that the iron in one old tool could be converted into four hand grenades. Father had to turn over his spare tires and drive around on bald ones. He supported the war, but secretly he sometimes purchased black market gasoline so he could travel around the city as he wished. He wasn't about to ride the streetcar, although many of the rest of us had begun to do so.

By the time the onion and bean harvest began on the farm two days later, I was aching for the city life again, even with its wartime restrictions. The first day of harvest, Ray tried to inform me about what to expect from the busiest season of the year. "Onions and beans got to be pulled by hand. The high school kids are back in school, and all the older boys are in the service," he said. "We need help, and the government needs our food so bad, now they send in the workers."

He sat longer and shuffled his hat about on the table. He kept glancing up at me as if waiting for a response or praise or something else, I didn't know. He reminded me of those men classified as 4-F, those disappointed boys who couldn't enlist because of bad vision or holes in their eardrums or some other problem. Treated a bit like freaks, they often went into civilian defense to play their part, anything to gain acceptance. Many of the male students left in college had told me they were asked regularly why they weren't in the service. Ray was so like them, the way he boasted about the importance of farmers.

I groped for something to say. "The harvest must go on."

Ray reached for his hat and started to rise from the table. "Things are sure going to get busy around here."

Thank goodness, I thought.

During the day, the farm was different. The fields filled with Japanese workers from Camp Amache in nearby Granada. In the morning Ray took the sides down on the beet box so he could pick them up. They debarked from the truck in front of the house and made their way to the fields, where they worked until sundown.

I tried not to stare, but they were such a study in contrasts. As they arrived in the mornings or as they left at sundown, I found it difficult not to follow them from my kitchen window. Ranging in age from teenage to elderly, some of the younger ones dressed just as the students at the university had been dressing, with rolled-up denims the latest in fashion, and their hair styled in the most recent 'dos. Many of the older women, however, dressed in long skirts and long-sleeved robes tied with a wide cloth belt, and they pinned their hair in a simple bun at the nape of the neck.

I tried to remember the Japanese Americans I'd seen in person before. Colorado was home to a small contingent of farmers of Japanese descent and even some city dwellers northeast of downtown. I remembered their dark coloring and short, compact statures, but my most vivid memory came from a photo I'd once seen, a photo of picture brides. Among the Issei, immigrant men in the U.S., it had been a common practice to send back to Japan for their wives. Young women who didn't speak a word of English would arrive from the old country, and their future husbands would pick them out from the crowd using the photographs sent by members of their family. As I watched the older women, I wondered how many had come to the U.S. for an arranged marriage. And wasn't I a bit like them? But Ray had decided to marry me knowing I was pregnant and without ever seeing a picture.

What surprised me most were not the interns' differences in dress and appearance. What surprised me was their impeccable demeanor. Despite their imprisonment, despite the fact that we were at war with the country of their ancestors, every one of the workers demonstrated the finest of manners. Every day they pulled the dry bean pods and shelled the beans. They pulled up fat onions out of the ground by hand and cropped the tops with sheep shears, grueling work to say the least. But as they boarded the trucks in the evening, even the oldest and most stooped workers still wore smiles on their faces, smiles that to my amazement seemed true.

After the first few days of harvest, I told Ray over breakfast, "Today I'd like to come and watch."

He looked confused.

"To watch what you're doing, to see what it is to harvest."

Ray stopped eating. "I don't understand. Everything's going just fine."

Now I stopped eating, too. "I won't interfere. I just want to learn."

He looked into his plate. "But it's not needed."

Obviously I had hurt him instead of flattered him by my interest. In the past, I had found most people more than willing to show off their skills and knowledge. I thought others enjoyed demonstrating what they knew, but not Ray. He didn't want me to learn anything about farming firsthand, only through his infrequent and bland descriptions.

"Never mind," I said and picked up my fork again. "I'm sorry I mentioned it."

That night, after all the workers had left and Ray came in exhausted and dirty, he took me out beside the barn and showed me the collapsible wooden crates packed with fresh onions. He offered to drive me over to the place where the crates were stored for months at a time in adobe storage buildings. But I could tell he was only doing so to placate me, so I declined. And after that, although I'd been on the farm for only two weeks, I'd already decided to keep my distance from the business of farming.

The next day, I began work on the flower garden. I pulled up the old faded whirligigs, set them aside for repainting, and gathered up the colored stones that Ray's mother had collected. As Ray drove the first truckload of onion crates away toward the storage buildings, I chopped up the deep-rooted weeds in the old flower garden and prepared the soil for bulbs. These things my mother had taught me. Always, she had liked the feel of dirt between her fingers, and of course the results of her efforts— blooming flowers. Even after she had hired on household help, she cared for the flower gardens herself, often taking us girls outside with her. Mother taught us how to break up the frost-hardened topsoil after winter, how to turn and mix the dirt beds in spring, how to plant seeds and bulbs, how to shape and prune the emerging new plants. It was one of the few times we were allowed to get dirty.

In the kitchen, I expanded my efforts beyond basic dishes. Once I cooked two Mexico-style omelets from a recipe I found in the library cookbook. While he ate, Ray glanced up at me after every bite or two. He also made overly kind remarks about the quality of my cooking, but when he thought I wasn't looking, I could see him picking out the chopped onions I had folded into the eggs.

In the afternoons, I walked about the house, outbuildings, and stock pond. Sometimes I could see the dark spots of the workers' bodies far off in the distant fields. I worked in the flower garden and then made my way to the back shed. There I found other artifacts—a wire rug beater, a box of fabric scraps that had probably been collected for quilting, an aluminum teakettle, and a parlor carpet broom. The hound, whose name I found out was Franklin, dubbed in honor of our President, kept me company and often smacked his loose lips or rolled on his back as I was expanding my collection. But I wondered what to do with it all. Certainly the artifacts should be kept for future generations to study and enjoy, perhaps even in a museum. But whom could I trust to do that? Each day I was adding to the burlap bag until it rose to the brim with the pieces I thought were most worth salvaging. But what then? Perhaps, on my next trip to town, I would inquire of any collectors in the area.

Over dinner, I said to Ray, "Martha told me your grandparents once built a tarpaper shack near here. Do you know where the remains are?"

Ray finished chewing. "I know where they used to be."

"Used to be?"

He shrugged. "I tore it down and plowed under the ground about two springs ago."

I had to laugh. "You have to be joking."

Now he looked confused. "It was just a bunch of weathered old boards. That's all that was left." His lips came together, barely moving as he spoke. "It wasn't anything to look at, I tell you."

"In the ground," I told him. "There's no telling what pieces of history might have been in the ground, under those boards."

He cleared his throat. "I needed that land for crops. People overseas are starving."

Of course, I knew this already. "In just one look inside one of your sheds, I found valuable antiques. There's no telling what I might have found around that shack."

He bumped the edge of the table with his fist. "Never thought of it."

"Well, it's done." I found myself shaking my head, then made myself stop. "Ray, I've noticed that you have no family photos, no personal items that belonged to your parents in this house." I deliberately didn't mention Daniel. "Where do you keep those things?"

He cleared his throat again. "Don't rightly know. Better ask Martha."

I couldn't hide my frustration. "You have nothing?"

He shrugged, then rose from the table. He took long strides across the room and clumped through the door of the bunkroom. He let the door close heavily behind him.

The next evening, with Franklin sniffing along at my heels, I walked one of the narrow roadways, down rutted tracks between fields. In the distance, I could see the workers. Bent over the ground, their bodies hooked like boomerangs, they were working later than usual that day. As I drew close to a recently dug onion field, I could hear the hum of their conversations marked with occasional spurts of laughter. Two young women stood apart from the rest of the workers, directly in my path. Engrossed in pursuit and moving ever so cautiously, they were either studying the ground or something near to it. One of the girls held a notebook in her hand. They didn't see me move near.

I took another step closer, and they jumped together. "Excuse us," one of them said. Then they turned away and began to walk off.

"No please," I said. "What are you studying?"

They turned back, and one girl answered with a smile, "Butterflies."

Standing and facing me together now, I saw that they were nearly identical in stature, with the same shade of glossy, blue-black hair fixed in bubble-cut style. They wore checkered cotton work shirts and slacks over sneakers. The older of the two had a fuller face with a few pockmarks on her cheeks. The younger of the two had a face perfectly oval in shape and not a mark on it. A practice rug and a masterpiece, I thought. And certainly they were sisters.

"Do you collect?"

They laughed together, at the same pitch and stopping at the same moment. But there the similarities ended. Lorelei, the younger of the two Umahara sisters, introduced herself, flipped a curl around her ear, and said, "Rose could never kill anything." She held my eyes with a firm, bold-eyed gaze and spoke with a siren of a voice that told me she didn't bow to anyone.

Rose's voice had half the strength of her sister's, and she talked with crossed arms and lowered lids, as if uncertainty were her frequent companion. "We log our observations in this notebook."

"I'm Livvy." Turning back toward the house, I said, "I live in the farmhouse."

When both girls looked back down to the ground, back to the place where earlier they had been studying, I asked, "And what did I cause you to miss?"

Again they laughed. "We thought it was the Purple Hairstreak, a butterfly only found in Colorado or nearby," Rose answered. "But upon closer look, we found that it wasn't."

"We look for butterflies," Lorelei said. "It's our hobby."

I knew little of insects and honestly had never found them of much interest, but I didn't want them to leave yet. "Are there many species?" I asked.

"Oh, yes. Thousands of varieties," answered Lorelei. "And the names are as wonderful as the creatures themselves."

"Silver-Spotted Skippers," said Rose.

"Eyed Hawkmoths," said Lorelei.

"And Speckled Woods."

My mother had once felt the same way about flower names. I remembered how the words had rolled off her tongue like silk off the bolt. Lady Slippers, Monkeyflowers, Snapdragons, and Johnny Jump-ups. At the university, the professors who genuinely loved their subjects were always the most interesting teachers. Enthusiasm for a topic made it enticing to others. And these two girls were clearly crazy for butterflies.

"Lovely," I said.

After a moment of silence, Franklin weaseled up between the girls and me, sniffing over the ground and effectively scaring off any butterflies that might still have been near. Lorelei folded the notebook and stuck it under her arm. Rose glanced back over her shoulder, toward the other workers. Clearly they were reluctant to talk longer, but before they left, I invited them to come visit me at the house. "I have cold bottles of Coca-Cola in the icebox that I'd love to share," I told them.

They smiled, nodded, and said they would come, but I didn't know whether to plan on it or not. They turned back to the field, and I headed back to the house. Before I left their sight completely, however, I looked back over my shoulder. As they walked away, both girls, their silhouettes dark against the deepening sunshine, stepped about on tiptoes, around the dandelions, looking for what I could only presume were more butterflies. The sight of them together, backed by the sunlight, made me turn and walk away even faster.

Abby and Bea. Only a few hours' travel away in Denver, they might as well have been oceans away.

Six

*T*he U.S. forces infiltrated Germany for the first time in mid-September, and we in the U.S. heard details of the offensive over the next few days by radio and newspapers. The progress made an Allied victory in Europe seem inevitable, but in the Pacific, over nine thousand men died in eleven days of fighting to capture just one small island named Peleliu. Even as the end of the war drew nearer, the news kept getting bleaker.

The following Sunday, Ray convinced me to attend church, something that, for reasons not yet clear to me, I had been avoiding. But I longed for a change of company, so I donned what had always been my favorite Sunday suit and joined Ray, who wore his brown suit again for the first time since our wedding day.

Outside the church building, I saw many parked cars and trucks, all of them covered in the layer of brown dust that had already grown familiar to me, grime that disguised the true colors of most everything. Groups of people worked their way into the building, letting me know that despite the outward appearance of emptiness down the web of roads, indeed many people lived there.

Before the service began, I met some of the congregation members and noticed that here, wartime fashion had yet to be introduced. In the face of plain prints and faded hats, I became conscious of the quality of my suit. Ray introduced me as his wife, and judging by the surprised looks we received, I didn't think he had told anyone I was coming. At Ray's side, however, I received a much different response from the one I'd received in Trinidad, alone. With him, people didn't hesitate to smile and greet me.

"So pleased to meet you," one woman said. "Goodness me." Then she congratulated Ray.

Another woman said, "We had no idea."

Her husband pumped Ray's hand up and down, then patted him on the back before we entered the sanctuary.

Reverend Case began his service with the usual prayers, hymns, and Bible readings. But then he moved from behind the pulpit and spoke directly to the congregation without the burden of that barrier between us. In the sermon, his message was one of forgiveness and sympathy for our enemies.

"I hope we can be so great a nation that we choose charity in the face of victory." He paused for reflection. "Sympathy over condemnation."

It felt as if he were engaged in intimate conversation alone and with each one of us. "I hope that we may find love for the countrymen of our enemy." Then he stood perfectly still. "The common man among our enemies may be more victim than we know."

Graciousness against our enemies? In Denver, I had been more accustomed to dirty "Heine" jokes and "Jinx the Japs" rallies than to the substance of this talk. At one point in the early years of the war, a game atmosphere had even prevailed. Everyone had believed that the U.S. forces were obviously superior, that victory would be easy. Bent on revenge for Pearl Harbor, we caricatured our enemy, attended parties and rallies, and held parades. It was definitely a good-versus-evil thing, and we in the U.S. were the good guys. But after years of it, I had grown weary of celebrations and children wearing cast-off uniforms and shooting toy guns. And now, in this unlikely place, I was listening to words that mirrored my sentiments. The difference between Reverend Case and the stern men of the pulpit I had known before was remarkable. After the first years of the war, I never thought of celebrating victories in the same way that once I'd done it before. With so much loss taken along the way, victories didn't feel very triumphant anyway.

"Let us pray for the relief of all suffering, for comfort and prosperity for all, for the end to every skirmish, battle, and war in this world."

"Amen," we said together.

After the service ended, Reverend Case held me back in the sanctuary for a moment. With one of his gracious smiles, he said, "I'm so happy to see you again. How are you liking it here?"

I didn't want to lie. "It's peaceful." But still, he looked concerned. "I enjoyed your sermon."

He put one hand on my back and gave a soft pat. "You're among friends here, Olivia." Then he led me into the kitchen area, where we chatted with Martha, Hank, and the children.

Ray then introduced me to the infamous Mrs. Pratt, who indeed handed over a cake. She grinned and touched my sleeve. "What a wonderful thing that Ray has finally married." Cake in hand, Ray headed for the door. Mrs. Pratt moved closer. "And how did you and Ray meet?"

In one instant, I knew why I hadn't wanted to attend church.

My father planned to tell everyone in Denver that I had eloped.

During the war years, two people taking off together and marrying on the sly was a perfectly acceptable thing to do. Rushed weddings happened every day, sometimes just hours before a soldier was shipping out. Not until the baby came would people realize that I had to get married.

I said, "I eloped."

Mrs. Pratt looked baffled. Then Ray was back at my side. "We met in Denver several months ago."

"How romantic." She was genuinely pleased. "I never knew you traveled to Denver," she said to Ray, then winked.

Although a potluck was planned for noontime, we declined to stay, as Ray said he had another place he wished to take me. On the way home, he explained, "There's a fishing hole nearby. Thought you might like to see it."

Truthfully, I'd never liked fishing. Once my uncle had taken Abby, Bea, and me out to a pier on a lake, but after a few minutes of no bites, my sisters and I had abandoned our poles and gone off exploring in the woods on our own. But anything would be an improvement over spending the rest of the day at the house. So when Ray drove us home, we changed into denims and shirts, then headed out again. At the edge of Holbrook Lake, Ray led me to an overturned rowboat. He righted it and slipped the bow into the water, keeping the stern on shore so I could hop in without getting wet. A minute or so later, he pushed us off. Ray dipped the oar on one side and then the other. Soon we were in the center of the lake surrounded by dragonflies courting over the surface of the water.

"Middle of the day's not the best time for fishing," Ray said. "But maybe we'll get lucky."

Rimming the bank were stands of cottonwoods and fingery willows. Pheasants prattled about in the branches near the ground, and in the top of the tallest tree, a bleached bone of spindly arms, I saw a tangled nest that could only have been home to something quite large, perhaps a hawk or an eagle. Ray cast out a line and waited. I leaned back on the wooden slat that served as my seat and closed my eyes into the sunlight. I had to admit it was restful here, on this pond.

"It's nice," I said to Ray without opening my eyes. "Thank you for bringing me." And thank you for lying to Mrs. Pratt.

I could barely hear his voice over the sound of whirring dragonflies and tender licks of water against the sides of the boat. "Hoped you'd like it."

I kicked off my sneakers in the bottom of the boat and fanned out my toes. Later, I felt Ray shift his weight, then I heard him reeling in his line. In the bright light outside my lids, I saw that he had caught something. "Cutthroat," Ray said as the fish flipped in the water at our side. Ray lifted it into the air, where the creature began its struggle for life.

But I had to look away.

"Trout are good eating. And this one's fair size." I could hear him working on getting the hook out of its mouth.

"I don't think I could eat anything I've seen breathing."

"Well," he said, still working. "Fish don't really breathe."

"I know. Gills instead of lungs."

"Look," Ray said.

I saw that he had removed the hook, that he was slowly sinking the trout back in the water. He held that fish so gently in his large drum of a hand that it surprised me. For a few seconds, he held on, letting the fish move within his hand. He explained, "Got to let it get used to the feel of water on its gills again." After a few more seconds he let it go. "See, it's okay. It's swimming off now."

I watched the silver shadow disappear into deeper water. "You didn't have to do that."

Ray took off his hat, wiped his brow with the back of his hand, then replaced the hat. Looking off into the willows, he said, "Being out here is the point. Fishing is just . . ." He searched for the right word. "An excuse, I suspect."

"Thanks for letting it go."

"You bet."

"I can't fillet a fish anyway."

"I can," he said, nodding. "But it's a heap of trouble."

The surface of the lake became flat and still and solid as marble. I stretched out in the boat like a cat on a windowsill. To my surprise, I enjoyed this day. Ray was enjoying it, too, and that worried me more than being miserable.

Seven

The next day, in late afternoon, Rose and Lorelei showed up on my porch, smiling and looking as if they'd just come from the beauty shop, not from the fields. Their hair looked freshly curled and styled, their cotton shirts still held creases along the tops of the sleeves, and their denims showed no sign of dirt, no tears or faded patches, either. Only their dusty, scraped shoes gave away that these girls had just come from working in the dirt. How did they do it? Obviously they wore gloves to protect their hands, but how were they able to keep their clothing so untouched?

"We skipped off from our overseer," Rose explained.

"She's Issei, very strict," said Lorelei.

I welcomed them in as I recalled the meaning of the name, Issei. First-generation Japanese emigrated to the U.S. were called by this name; they retained much of their traditional values and mores. These two sisters were clearly Nisei or Sansei, second- or third-generation American citizens by birth. As we later sat on the steps sipping Cokes out of green bottles through paper straws, they told me they had both been enrolled at UCLA before the evacuation notices went up.

Rose said, "When I was only seven, I won first place in the spelling bee at my school. And ever since, I've wanted to teach English." She finished her Coke and set the bottle down on the porch step without making a sound. "The language and the words," she said, "must be perfect."

"And perfectly spelled," Lorelei said, elbowing her sister.

Rose spoke back, but her quiet voice could barely manage to criticize. "At least I've set my plans."

Lorelei played with her hair, flipping it just under her ear. She explained to me, "Back at school, I hadn't settled on a major yet. Too many things interested me, so I was taking all the required courses first."

Rose snickered. "She studied the senior boys."

Lorelei laughed aloud, covered her mouth, and then blushed. "Only the clever ones. Or the dashing ones," she said. She hung her hands over her feet and sat so that their shadow covered her work shoes.

Later I told them about the history studies I, too, had abandoned. That once I had planned to go on expedition to Egypt, to help decipher the hieroglyphs, to aid in recording the excavation of tomb chambers buried in the sands.

"Ah, King Tut," Rose said.

At last, a conversation about another part of the world, off this farm. The discovery of King Tut-ankh-amen's tomb in 1922 had awakened much of the general population to the wonders of ancient Egypt, but I doubted that its reach had extended to many others in the onion fields. "And so many other tombs, so many other kings and princesses, as well," I said. "I was particularly interested in studying the pharaoh who ruled before King Tut, named Akh-en-aten."

They looked as if they wanted me to continue.

"Historians think he had a misshapen head and hips because portraits reveal this about him. And he believed in only one god, Aten, and he built a great holy city, Horizon-of-the-Aten, in his honor."

Rose looked at her hands, then she turned and asked me, "Do you miss it?"

I hadn't expected such a direct question. "Yes," I answered her. Then I hugged my knees to my chest. "But in many ways, just listening to the radio news is a study in history. Especially now."

Rose looked out over the open fields. "I miss all the lively conversations, the sharing of ideas. A classroom of students may read the same piece of poetry or the same passage in a novel, and each person will interpret it differently."

I turned to face her. "It's the same," I said. "Exactly the same way with history, too."

"Is it?"

"Think about it," I told her. "Even the facts of history are tainted by personal views. Depending on beliefs, every side in every conflict has been seen as both right and wrong."

Rose answered softly, "Of course."

Then it dawned on me. These girls would understand differences in views better than most. After all, they had been moved and confined by a country at war with the country of their ancestors. They were living among people who assumed our white brains superior to theirs. The surprise attack on Pearl Harbor and the hardships of the war in the Pacific had come as a shock to those Americans who thought Japan incapable of executing anything intelligent or difficult. Yet Rose and Lorelei were as American as I was. What internal struggles must torment them?

"In years to come, all of this present history may be viewed differently," I said.

"Just as books and poems are continually being reread and reevaluated," said Rose.

"Literature has had a profound effect on history."

"For example, *Uncle Tom's Cabin*."

"Exactly."

Later we walked about the farm, visited the pond, and tossed sticks for Franklin to lazily retrieve. I invited them to come over again, and when I explained I had a truck available to me, one with plentiful gasoline, their faces lit up like tinfoil left out in the sun.

"We could look for butterflies in the thickets," said Lorelei.

"Or on the open prairie," added Rose.

I could hardly wait. "Come again and we'll go driving."

That night, I found myself moving without effort. I remembered running on younger legs, the wind whipping between campus buildings, and the feel of new book pages beneath my fingers. I remembered the classroom discussions that had taken my thoughts down new paths, records played on the radio, and whispered thoughts only girlfriends have the courage to share.

As I was cooking dinner, Ray came up behind me. He looked over my shoulder at the tuna fish casserole I was stirring up in a bowl. Something surely did seem to please him, and I thought it was the food. "Does it look good?" I asked him.

"Sure enough," he said. "But that's not why I'm standing here. I wanted to listen better."

I stopped stirring. Then he told me, "You were singing to yourself."

Eight

Ray and I began to attend church every Sunday. Despite a few sets of questioning eyes, I didn't object because it was my only chance to escape the farm, and I enjoyed the peaceful messages of Reverend Case's sermons. And, too, I enjoyed seeking out Martha and trying to piece together an early picture of life on the land where now I lived.

"Ray tore down the old shack," I told her on a Sunday in early October.

"Oh, dear," she said with a smile. "Hank would have done the same, I'm afraid. But you ought to be able to find the dugout."

I almost choked on my coffee. "They started with a dugout?"

Martha nodded. "It's along the creekbed just south of the bridge, but you shouldn't try to find it on your own."

"A dugout?" I still couldn't believe my luck. "How long did they live in it?"

"At least the first few years." Martha looked concerned. "You won't go down there by yourself, will you?"

I squeezed her arm. "Don't worry, and thank you."

"Promise me you won't go down there on your own."

But how could I wait? I planned to find it the next day, but before I had time to go outside, Lorelei and Rose showed up again on my doorstep. With almost all the onions and beans harvested out of Singleton soil, they had some break time, and they wanted to spend it with me.

They asked to travel south, so we slid in together on the truck seat and headed through La Junta in the direction of Trinidad. Along the way, we searched streambeds, patches of brush, and open sage prairie. Whenever we saw wildflowers that might attract butterflies, we pulled over. In one meadow, we'd searched for only a few minutes before the girls spotted a swallowtail among the thistle flowers. The black and yellow butterfly opened and closed its wings and turned about in the sunlight as if showing off for us. Rose said it was definitely swallowtail, probably a Western Tiger Swallowtail, but she wouldn't be certain of its exact identity until she researched it later in one of their books. As Rose moved in closer, Lorelei held back and outlined a sketch in the notebook, shading the wing patterns with colored pencils.

I studied them at work, and I studied the swallowtail. On the butterfly's hind wings, I saw two large circles of red and blue. "The large spots on the wings are quite beautiful, aren't they?" I said.

"False eyes," Lorelei said as she worked on her drawing.

At last, the swallowtail fled. I noticed that it didn't flutter away; instead, with just one flap, it caught a current of air and soared.

Rose brushed off her hands. "The false eyes confuse the butterfly's enemies."

Lorelei had to explain, "They scare birds and lizards away. Those large spots appear like eyes of a much larger animal."

"So predators think the butterfly must be something else."

Lorelei added, "It's a protection for the butterfly, evolved over time."

"Many moths have them, too," said Rose.

I had learned something new, something I'd never noticed before—false eyes on butterflies. But more importantly, I had uncovered the pattern of the sisters' speech. Perhaps they weren't aware of it themselves, that they finished thoughts and sentences for each other. Layer upon layer, they added on to each other's phrases until a more complete picture emerged, one more vivid than if it had come from a single voice.

"Amazing," I told them.

We stopped at a service station outside La Junta, where I treated us to bottles of Dad's root beer out of the drink machine. We leaned up against the side of the truck and sipped while we talked.

Rose flipped through the butterfly notebook that Lorelei usually took in her charge. "Since we've been in Colorado, we've seen over twenty new varieties," Rose said. She stopped turning pages. "Now what's this?" she asked Lorelei.

I glanced over. In the midst of all the butterfly sketches was a full-page drawing of an American soldier complete with uniform and butch haircut.

"Give it to me," Lorelei yelped as she reached for the notebook.

Rose jerked it away. "This was supposed to be for our records."

Lorelei covered her mouth and giggled. Then she looped a strand of hair around her finger. "I couldn't help myself. He was so handsome."

Rose looked defeated. "Now our book is ruined."

"No, it's not. Here, let me have it." She grabbed the book away from Rose, ripped out the paper drawing of the soldier, folded it, and stuffed it into her pocket. "You're no fun. Rules, rules, rules. Always Rose has to follow the rules."

"Things need to stay in their right places."

"Oh, yes," Lorelei said, nodding exaggeratedly. "Like we need to stay in the camp."

The camp. It was the first time either one of them had mentioned their confinement. I studied the bubbles in my root beer bottle and listened.

Rose shot back, "I never said that."

"But you go along all too well."

They stared at each other, then turned away. Obviously, this was a subject they hadn't meant to discuss, at least not in front of me. I watched the road and saw a cottontail scurry across it. I looked away until the moment had passed, and soon Rose and Lorelei were talking about men and swigging down their drinks again.

We traveled farther south. Along the Purgatoire River, we found tiny Silvery Blues, Painted Ladies, and Viceroys—orange and black butterflies I had always thought were Monarchs. We watched the Viceroys gather along the riverbank. Hundreds of them came together and overlapped their wings into one wave of color, a bright scarf flowing in the breeze.

"That's called mud puddling," pointed out Lorelei.

"They gather together to drink the shallow water out of the soil, water rich in mineral salts," added Rose.

After a few moments of silence, Lorelei turned to me. "How much farther to New Mexico?"

"The border is only a short drive away. Why do you ask?"

She shrugged. "We've never seen that state."

I checked my watch. "Maybe next time we can get an earlier start."

When I slid back in behind the steering wheel, I caught Rose studying my belt.

"What?" I asked her.

She shook her head and looked out through the windshield. Then, apparently changing her mind, she turned back to me and asked, "Are you expecting?"

My keys fell to the floorboard.

I couldn't believe it. I was unable to speak, unable to answer her question. Already it was noticeable, and so soon. I had seen a doctor for verification back in Denver but hadn't suffered one morning of sickness, hadn't felt weak or faint, and hadn't even realized my abdomen was growing. Checking off the time, I realized it had been over three months, that certainly it made sense I should now be showing. As I searched the floorboard for the keys, I felt the powerlessness once again rush in and consume me. I remembered the first day I had allowed myself to acknowledge the possibility, and by then I was over a month late. It was too unbelievable that I couldn't control the processes transpiring inside the confines of my own flesh, so unbelievable that I had ignored the clear signs. Although I had feared the truth, I told no one for another two weeks in hopes that it was just some cruel trick of nature. But after weeks of walking around with a bomb buried inside me, I finally went to Abby, and she went to Father.

Abby had meant me no harm. She had assumed that Father, as the head of our family, needed to know, that he would come up with a sensible plan. Father didn't speak to me for two more weeks; he wouldn't even meet my eyes. Then he summoned Abby and Bea over to the house, where he ushered the three of us into his study. He sat us down and announced that he had been in touch with his old friend Reverend Case, and that I would marry a bean farmer out on the plains. I remembered sitting there in his cool leather chair and staring at the perfect part in his hair. It was so straight. Had he sectioned it off with an ice pick?

Bea had begun to cry.

"Oh, Father, please," Abby was saying. "There must be other options."

Bea spoke up between sobs. "She could go to a home for unwed mothers, then give up the baby for adoption."

Abby said, "I knew a girl who went away to visit a maiden aunt for about six months. That was the story. We could say the same—"

"No," Father interrupted her. He stared at me through the spotless lenses of his glasses. "We must all bear the consequences of our actions."

"This is too big," Abby said in a whisper. "This is too big a consequence."

As Abby and Bea continued to plead for me, Father took off his already immaculate eyeglasses and scrubbed the lenses again until every imaginary speck and smudge had vanished. If I had done something we could hide, if no one could have ever found out, I might have been forgiven. For us, family dignity was one of our chief concerns. But this thing—I couldn't even say the word— the P word. It made my transgression so bountifully obvious.

Father placed both hands flat on the desk and began to rise, signaling that our discussion had ended. "My decision is made. The arrangements are all in order." Before he put his glasses back on, for just a second, I thought I glimpsed just a touch of something not totally clear, a fine mist coating his eyes. But he said, "Livvy, you leave on the train next week."

Near the gas pedal, I finally found the keys. I looked up at Rose and Lorelei and almost laughed. Only two nights before, Ray had asked me, "Don't you need to see a doctor?" I had thought he was referring to an accident I'd recently had. While working in the garden, I had cut my foot on an old piece of glass hidden in the dirt. Now it occurred to me—his true concern was the reason I had come here in the first place.

Of course, others would assume this a happy event. I said to Rose and Lorelei, "Yes, I am expecting." Then I managed a smile.

Lorelei squealed and clasped her hands together. "Do you have any clothes?" she asked.

Perhaps I wasn't yet listening to her. She meant maternity clothes, of course. "No, no, I don't."

Rose sat up straight in the seat and smiled. "We can sew. We have our own Singer. Back in California, that was our family business—tailoring. Our father made the finest suits in all of Los Angeles, often for moviemakers. What could we make for you?"

"It isn't necessary," I said, but soon realized that it was necessary, for them. In this way, they could return the favor of my driving. "I'll take that back. I would like a dress for church. In Wilson, a minister preaches on Sundays. A man I most admire."

"What are your favorite colors?"

I didn't care, but I remembered the false eyes. "Blue and red, like the eyes of the swallowtail."

Lorelei asked, "Are you hoping for a boy or girl?"

Again I was momentarily unable to answer, for it was another question I had never considered. "I suppose the Singleton family would prefer a boy."

"But what about you? Would you prefer a daughter or son?" asked Lorelei.

I remembered a young man I'd known at the university, a quiet, soft-spoken, serious student who had always dressed as if he were going to church. He'd avoided the draft all through college, then, at his father's urging, had joined the Marines upon graduation and became a Corps pilot. He was shot down and killed during his first combat mission in the Battle for the Eastern Solomons, never once having the chance to teach blind children, as had been his ambition.

"If I were able to choose, I'd take a daughter." I met Rose's eyes. "At least girls don't get drafted, don't get pressured to go off and fight in wars."

"Do you ever wonder," began Rose slowly, "why there must be so much war?"

What a question it was, and one I'd often asked my professors. "All the time I wonder. Throughout all of my history studies, I was constantly amazed and distraught by the near constancy of it, all across time."

Lorelei chewed a nail. "Do you think that human beings are naturally warlike?"

I shook my head. "I can't believe that. I can't let myself believe that."

"I don't believe it, either," said Rose. "Most of us would find some other way to settle our disputes."

I agreed. "Most of us are naturally peaceful."

"It's only when the wrong leaders come into power that the peace disintegrates," Lorelei concluded.

"If only the leaders of all countries could be women," I said, and we laughed together at the notion, the impossible nature of it.

Then we were silent, each of us lost in our own gnawing thoughts.

Rose put a hand on my arm. "It must be a difficult time to be carrying a baby."

I hadn't thought of it until then. This baby would most likely be born while this deadly war, the worst and most brutal in history, still raged. And Rose's sympathy for me in the face of what was happening to her, in the face of her lost home, lost education, and imprisonment, touched me profoundly. I swallowed back tears. "I'm sure it'll end up okay."

"Yes," said Rose. "We must all believe that, mustn't we?"

Lorelei studied me over the next few moments of silence. Her eyes saw more than I thought I was showing. "Is Ray Singleton your husband?"

I realized then, that in all the time I'd spent with them, I'd never introduced Ray or even mentioned him in our conversations.

"Yes," I answered. And legally, he was.

Nine

Back in La Junta, we found a Woolworth's with a section for sewing, including a row of fabric bolts lined up along the back wall. First, we searched through a pattern book until we found a maternity dress we all approved of and decided would suit me. Then we looked at fabric.

As she ran her hand along the bolts, Rose said, "All of the jackets my father made were lined with the finest silks."

Lorelei said, "We did all the finish work by hand, with tiny stitches our grandmother taught us to make. You couldn't see them from the finished side."

I selected jersey fabric of navy blue with tiny white polka dots, a package of pearly buttons, and needed notions. Then we took turns trying on wide-brimmed straw hats. Already my face was checkered with big freckles darker than my birthmark. Rose, Lorelei, and I chose for each other the most flattering hats to save our faces from the endless prairie sun. Then we flipped through dime novels and picked one to buy, pass between us and read, and then later discuss.

All during the time we spent in the store, I had the same feeling of disbelief that had sheltered me during the months since Mother's funeral. I moved and spoke just as before, in a manner that looked so normal. No one would know that the center of me had been hollowed out with a shovel. But on our way back to the truck, we passed by a soldier in uniform, and my own feelings of reproach welled so powerfully within me that I lost my step. Lorelei fell a step behind, too, but for an entirely different reason. She turned around and swooned over the soldier as he walked behind her and down the street.

"What did I tell you?" whispered Rose. "She's boy-crazy."

As we drove back, we followed truckloads of other Japanese interns traveling back from the fields. Farther north, we came upon a truckload of German POWs sitting on the flatbed of a truck similar to Ray's. The truck was pulling onto the highway and coming our way. I knew they had to be POWs because, although they wore regular clothes and looked average enough, they were accompanied by three armed MPs.

I sat up in the seat. I had known the Axis POWs were near, but had never seen any of them before. Ray had told me that while they were working the area, they stayed in barracks set up at the Rocky Ford fairgrounds. He'd even had some help from them earlier in the summer when he was harvesting the cash crops.

Germans, possibly Nazis, right here in our country, as faces on human beings. Amazingly, I had heard nothing but good reports about the German and Italian POWs. Some of those from Camp Trinidad were so likable and trustworthy they had earned the friendship of the people in the bordering community. Teachers and other civilians were even volunteering to go into the camps to teach classes in English, one of many educational opportunities offered to the prisoners and the subject most requested by them. On the radio, once I heard that one group of women who baked and cooked for the POWs found themselves so carried away in adoration, the sheriff of the county had cautioned them to stop, reminding them we were still at war.

I eased off the accelerator. I wondered how the Germans would appear in person, without the flattening effect of the newspaper pictures and impersonal newsreels. The truck went by me so fast, however, that I saw only a blur of many faces turned toward the road and not enough to form an impression.

Rose, who sat closest to me, must have been reading my thoughts. "Some of them are nice enough."

"Have you met?" I asked her

"Often we work the same farms."

Remembering the reports I'd recently read, I asked, "Are the POWs still Nazis?"

Rose lifted her shoulders and sighed. "I suppose some of them are. But most of them are just beginning to learn English, so we can't talk in much depth. And when we do talk, we don't usually discuss politics."

As I accelerated again, I asked, "Have you read anything about the death camps?"

"Yes," Rose answered.

"Do you believe the numbers of murders that are being reported?"

Rose frowned. "I'm beginning to. Yes."

I had to make myself concentrate on driving. But I couldn't stop thinking about it, either. Those eight hundred thousand pairs of shoes. At Majdanek alone. "Do you think the average German soldier knew?"

"If they did, they probably wouldn't admit it. And regardless, they would probably disavow any connection to it. Just as we want to claim no part of the war conducted by Japan."

Lorelei peered around her sister. "Do you want to know what song is their favorite?" She waited for my nod, then said, " 'Don't Fence Me In.' Isn't that funny?"

But I found it all too awful to be funny.

In Wilson, I pulled over and gathered out all the coins I could find in my change purse. Inside the booth, first I dialed Abby, who didn't answer. When I tried Bea, however, she answered on the first ring.

She sounded so young. "Livvy, I can't believe it's really you. We've missed you so badly. How are you?"

"Fine."

"Oh, my dear, it's been so gruesome here without you. Are you well? When can you come to visit?"

When I didn't answer, she went on. "Father has had the influenza, but he's fine, really fine now. And you don't know the news about Abby and Kent. He's being shipped off, away from Fitzsimons, assigned to go overseas." Bea paused. "But Abby is acting so brave, wouldn't you know it? Always the strong supporter. Saying they need him on the front lines more than she does, especially now more than ever, with the end so near."

Finally I found my voice. "If only it would end before he has to go. Tell Abby I'll pray for Kent every night."

"Of course I will." Bea waited, then her voice deepened. "Oh, how is it really, Livvy? Is he good to you? Because if he isn't, remember what Abby advised. You always have options."

Options? I could remember once having options. "I can't think about that now."

"Of course you can't. Just take a rest out there, and after the baby comes, things will look clearer. Now. Do you think you'll be able to come home for the holidays?" When I couldn't keep up with her, Bea filled the dead space. "It's going to be so terribly sad without Mother for the first time. We can't possibly manage without you, too. You'll just have to come. We simply won't take no for an answer."

Bea went on in this manner for quite some time, almost carrying on a conversation with herself. But her voice sounded so good to me that I let her go on and on. I added more coins as the operator asked for them, until I had completely run out of change, and Bea and I were forced to say a rushed goodbye.

As I hung up the receiver and looked outside the telephone booth, I realized that for just the briefest moment, I had escaped. Bea's voice had picked me up and plunked me back in the home where I had once belonged. Although Rose and Lorelei waited for me in the truck, it took me a while before I was able to move toward them.

Options, Bea had said. Back in Denver and before I left, we had discussed those options. With no place to go and no personal means, I couldn't disappear on my own, but staying in Denver was impossible, too. Having a baby without a husband ruined a girl's life forever. Abby's suggestion had been to marry as Father insisted, give the child a name, then divorce and return with the baby to Denver. Our mother had always taught us that divorce was a distasteful thing reserved for the lower classes and for movie stars, but our generation was more enlightened. We were fighting the worst war in history, and if humanity survived it, we wouldn't sacrifice everything in our lives, ever again. Already the divorce rate was soaring, probably due to the large number of hasty wartime marriages. Of course, Mother had also taught her daughters to stay virgins until after marriage, something Abby and Bea had managed to do.

I slipped back into the driver's seat and turned over the ignition. Earlier that morning, I had met Rose and Lorelei at the pay telephone in town, as they had assured me they could walk that far. But now they directed me to a large horse barn outside of Wilson where many of the farmworkers lucky enough to participate in the Agricultural Leave Program spent their nights. Draped by lanterns, the open doors revealed beds of hay inside, personal belongings and clothing stacked on hay bales and on overturned crates, workers milling about as if in preparation for the night to come.

I tried to remember the first time I had heard of Congress's plans for Japanese American internment. I recalled that my first impression had been one of approval, that certainly we couldn't chance domestic disloyalty in the face of this terrible world war. But now, as I sat beside Rose and Lorelei and gazed out at this barn—this farm camp, as they called it—I wavered. Certainly these two girls posed no threat to our country. In fact, all the farmworkers seemed to be the most peaceful of people. They had volunteered to help with the harvest, tough physical labor at best, to leave the camp and stay here in conditions little better than those provided for our livestock, all to earn a measly nineteen dollars a month.

This was temporary, I kept telling myself. At war's end, they could return to the homes, businesses, and places in society where they had lived before. I found myself wishing I'd never seen this camp.

Perhaps someday, we could all make it back to the places where we started.

I didn't believe it, but I tried to.

Ten

$\mathcal{B}$y the time I reached home, it was after sunset. On moonless nights, black sky and prairie horizon blended into one dark veil. But with no blackout curtains required here in the middle of the countryside, I could see stark white light coming from the kitchen window, letting me know that Ray was inside. I climbed the steps and found him sitting at the table eating heated-up leftover chicken.

"Sorry about that," I said.

He set down his fork. "I got by on my own for years before."

I slid down onto the chair next to him and checked the pot. Perhaps I'd try some myself.

Ray said, "We're thinking on trying winter wheat this year." He picked up his fork and started to eat again. "We plant it in the fall and let it grow for a couple of weeks until the cold makes it go dormant. If winter's not too bad, then in spring, the wheat'll come alive again."

But I'd long lost my initial curiosity about farming. Now I had to pretend to be interested. "How will you know?"

"If we get a lot of snow, it protects the plants like a blanket.

But if winter's cold and dry," he said, shaking his head, "they're lost."

I grabbed a plate and picked out a chicken breast. "Is it worth the risk?"

He looked surprised. "Of course it is. That wheat could feed a lot of folks."

I found myself staring at the oily indentation across his forehead caused by wearing that old hat of his all day long.

He finished eating, then leaned back in the chair. "Where were you today?"

It wasn't a demand. I took one bite. "Sightseeing," I answered.

He rocked forward. "The truck's not for sightseeing. We get gasoline to move workers and do our business."

Of course, he was right. Because of gasoline shortages and war needs, most everyone frowned on pleasure driving, and at one time, the government had banned it altogether. In January of 1943, the government had tried making pleasure driving a punishable offense, but with enforcement nearly impossible, they lifted the ban later that same year, in September.

I said, "Then that's what I did."

Ray started on his dessert, stale cake from Mrs. Pratt. "It's not just the gasoline, but the tires, too. I'm using a tractor with steel wheels 'cause you can't get tires nowadays. And every fall after harvest, I have to take the tires off that old wagon hitched behind the barn and put them on the truck. Otherwise, the truck tires would be worn out, and all I could buy is reclaimed ones that don't last a hundred miles."

"That's illegal, isn't it?"

Ray gulped.

"Switching out tires? Keeping more than one set?"

"I do it 'cause I need to."

"Well, I needed to transport farmworkers."

"Who'd that be?"

"Rose and Lorelei."

He looked baffled, and then a flash of recognition crossed his face. "The Japanese girls."

"They're American."

He chewed with effort. I think the man hadn't a clue what I meant. "Okay. The American girls who look Japanese."

That chicken wasn't such a good idea after all. I shoved my plate away. "Do you dislike them because of Pearl Harbor? Because of Daniel?"

He gave me a hard look. "I'm not as stupid as you think. I know they're not the same people who bombed Pearl Harbor. And they're great people, good workers. They've kept our harvest going over the past few years."

I slumped back. "I never said you were stupid."

Now Ray looked at his dessert instead of eating it. "And I never said I disliked them. I just said they were Japanese, is all."

"And you keep your distance."

"I have a lot to do around here." Ray wiped his face with a napkin. "I got to keep this farm going pretty much on my own. I don't go into the fields to socialize."

Eating with him now was out of the question. I got up from the table and went outside to the porch without slamming the screen door. I sat in my chair and listened to the sounds made by crickets in the night while I tried to slow my breathing. He left me alone for close to an hour, then before he went to bed, he stepped outside.

The breeze that night came in from the direction of the creekbed, and although it ran dry, the ditch always held a pocket of cold air that chilled me each time I walked the bridge that crossed it. Ray's looming, boxy shape blocked the moonlight but not the cold air coming up from the creekbed. A chill ran up my bare forearms, and I wished I had brought out a sweater.

"You should eat something," he said.

But I couldn't even look his way.

Eleven

⬥⬥⬥

he work of the harvest continued, the fields full of workers, the roads run up and down with piled-high trucks. One day as I was driving to La Junta to buy groceries, I saw some of the German POWs at work on one of the farms near us. The enlisted men were watched over by guards, Army MPs stationed at each end of the field and one in the middle. But other POWs weren't guarded at all. Ray told me later it was because they were officers and could be trusted pretty much on their own.

During long days around the house, however, all was quiet. I had no visitors except for the bulk gasoline agent who drove out one day with a tanker truck to fill Ray's storage tank. When I saw him, I wandered outside, yearning for conversation. But as he filled the tank, all we talked about was the war and both of his sons who were off fighting in Europe.

Everyone on all the surrounding farms and in the communities was busy; however, I still had few chores to make myself feel productive. Often I wondered how my itching feet had landed on such a stationary plot. I had already planted the bulbs in the front flower garden, cleaned the house numerous times, and thumbed through cookbooks so many times I thought I might memorize the recipes. I gathered eggs in the morning and separated the cream from the raw milk, and every couple of days I started taking eggs and cream into La Junta to sell for Ray. I read Susan Shelby Magoffin's diary, *Down the Santa Fe Trail and into Mexico,* over the course of one long day.

One morning, I decided to go in search of the dugout. Even though Martha had warned me not to go alone, I couldn't wait any longer. And if I took Franklin along with me, technically, I said to myself, I wouldn't be going alone.

Outside it was warm, and the sun was a butterscotch disk on a blue paper sky. After making myself a sandwich, I headed out the front door toward the bridge, calling after Franklin to join me. He came shuffling up with tongue hanging out to one side. Following Martha's directions, I went to the creek and carefully scrambled down one side of the bank until I found myself on the ditch bottom. The bed was sandy, flat, and easy to walk, the only impediments occasional smooth stones. Franklin was sniffing up behind me.

We walked south. I saw one carved-out, semi-cave a few feet up on the bank about a hundred yards south. But it was too small. I continued walking down the creekbed until I arrived at a bend filled with tangled branches and debris that blocked my way. The creekbed dropped away at that point and began a rocky descent. I stood and thought. The indention I had seen earlier must have been the right place after all. Soon I had made my way back to it.

Looking up, I saw that the dugout was only about five feet deep and no more than ten feet across. None of the willows and reeds that had most likely been used to extend the roof and walls remained. Probably on one of the occasions when water ran high through this bed, it had all been swept away, or else the winds had taken it. I climbed up to the front of the cavelike opening, and leaning over, I went inside with Franklin on my heels. When I looked up and saw the earthen and stone roof at the back of the dugout still stained black with the smoke from fires, I knew I had discovered the right place. And for just a second, I thought I smelled something cooking.

Franklin went off to explore on his own while I sat on the cool dirt floor of a place that had once been a home. I pulled out my sandwich and bit in as I took in the same view that Ray's ancestors must have studied, day after day of their lives. Opposite from me, the far bank cut a swath of blond color across the sky. A stunted tree along the rim became a woman dancing in a long, flowing skirt. Dark stones strewn about on the pale sand of the creekbed stood out like buttons on a white dress.

I closed my eyes. After a couple of B-25 trainers passed overhead, near silence returned. From far away came the call of a hawk, hunting. I could hear the scuff of critters in the underbrush below me and a sigh of wind sailing through nearby juniper trees. When I opened my eyes and took another bite, I wondered about those early pioneers' lives. What had they thought about? What of their hopes and dreams? And how did they handle the solitude and not lose their minds?

After I finished eating, I searched the ground around me. Any fabric or paper would've long since deteriorated, but pieces of broken china or tools might have survived. I found droppings indicating coyotes had at one time or another used the dugout as a den, but nothing else until I arrived in the far corner. There, I pulled something long and stiff out of the dirt. It was a tarnished black fork with two missing tines, a piece of civilization that had probably been brought out as a prized possession by the first Mrs. Singleton. Not long after her arrival, she had most likely discovered how little use she had for such niceties as silverware, and when the tines broke off, she had probably just tossed this treasure away.

Back at the house, I found silver polish underneath the kitchen sink cupboard, and then I went to work on that fork. By the time Ray returned home, I had it shining mirror-silver again.

"Look what I found," I told Ray when he came in.

He took a look, then said, "It's broken."

"That's not the point," I said. "It came from what's left of the dugout, where your grandparents first lived on this land. I found it in the corner. Isn't that amazing?"

With a smile, he said, "You bet."

But once he had finished eating, he went to work again. After raking the sweaty hair off his forehead, he pulled out some ledgers and started scratching figures on the pages with a stubbed pencil. Every so often, he'd stop and rub his eyes with both fists, then resume working. Finally, he went to bed without ever touching the treasure.

For long days at a time, I managed on my own. Once Ray disappeared out into the harvesting fields, he never returned, all day. He arrived home in late evening, only after the sunlight no longer lit his workplace. But Rose and Lorelei were able to get away. Often they came by for lemonade or Cokes and a rest on the porch steps. One day I glimpsed them through the screen door before they knocked, and then I saw how they managed to stay looking so neat. They were taking turns brushing each other off, taking great pains to remove every fleck of grass and dirt that had landed on their clothes.

After I answered the door, they handed over a sack containing the maternity dress made of polka-dot jersey that already they had managed to sew.

"It's wonderful," I told them and held it up to get a better look. The tailoring was excellent; all the seams were perfectly smooth and flat, and the handwork, just as they had claimed, was imperceptible. The finished product looked more professional than the picture on the front of the pattern. "I'll wear it soon."

Both girls barely smiled. Rose said a shy, "Thank you."

"You did an outstanding job."

Rose looked away, and Lorelei toyed with her hair. "It's nothing."

"Really," said Rose.

Perhaps I had praised too much, embarrassing them. I refolded the dress and stared at the truck sitting on the dirt drive. Ray had told me over breakfast that he would be spending the afternoon cleaning up and collecting garbage that had accumulated from the harvest. And he would be working with the tractor that day, not the truck. A few minutes later, I suggested to Rose and Lorelei that we go for a drive.

As we headed out, Rose said, "Father worries that his customers won't dress so well anymore, now that he's gone."

Lorelei said, "They're certain to miss his attention to detail."

I paused for a moment, then curiosity overcame me. "What became of the business?"

At first they didn't answer, and I feared I had pried too much, gone too far again. But then Rose replied, "We were forced to close it before evacuating. But it was just as well. Even my father's most loyal customers no longer came in."

"What of your home?"

"We had to sell it, too. Our bank accounts had been frozen, and we didn't want to come out here without any of our own money."

Lorelei blurted out, "We cleaned it for them."

"You what?"

"We had to sell our house for half its worth, yet my parents insisted we clean it for the new owners. We even waxed the floors."

Rose sighed at her sister. "I still don't understand why the cleaning angers you so. We had to leave it clean. For our own sakes."

Lorelei snickered. "I would've invited everyone I knew over for a dance and left it filthy."

"Lorelei!" Rose snapped, then turned away.

Lately I'd been reading everything I could put my hands on about Japanese American internment. Our former governor, Ralph Carr, was one of the only politicians who had been bold enough to welcome and defend Americans of Japanese descent. It hadn't been a popular stance, and some people even thought it had cost him the last election. The *Denver Post* expressed bigotry toward anyone of Japanese descent. One of their editors constructed a large effigy of a Japanese man complete with monkey face, whereas the *Rocky Mountain News* had been more open-minded, even pointing out to readers that Americans of German descent hadn't been singled out. In truth, I think the common man and woman in Denver had given little thought to the struggle of Japanese Americans. As long as large numbers of Japanese hadn't moved into their own neighborhoods, as long as nothing suspicious occurred, the average citizen went on with his or her life unaffected.

I drove on, swerving past trucks that rumbled up and down the roads, past fields swarmed with workers. With the harvest in full swing, most everyone was engaged in the effort to provide food for others. I remembered what Ray had said to me about pleasure driving, and a bit of guilt pinched me. Of course it was wrong of me. Perhaps if I could conduct some business along the way? I couldn't give up this time with Rose and Lorelei. I wanted to learn as much as I could about them, and without driving, how would I continue to get to know them?

I told the girls I needed to stop at the grocery store, but in the end, I bought only a loaf of bread. Most farmers' wives considered it lazy to buy bread in the store, but the opposite logic appealed to me. Why bake something that could so easily be bought? My preferences in shopping leaned toward ease of preparation, and already my blue point coupons for buying canned and processed foods were running low.

We drove on to Rocky Ford, a farming community that looked huge compared to Wilson. Named for the safe crossing point on the Arkansas River it had provided pioneers, it had become well-known for cantaloupes, watermelons, and honeydews. We managed to buy some of the last of the fall crop at a roadside stand. Later, we stopped for gasoline and sodas in the town of Swink, and as the girls and I relaxed around the truck in the sunshine, a conversation nearby caught my attention.

I saw a man talking to the attendant while a woman waited for him inside their car. I thought I recognized the couple from church, but wasn't altogether certain. The man glanced up at me once, but he seemed unsure if he recognized me, too. A minute later, he showed his R coupon card to the attendant and paid him, then he began to walk in my direction. He kept moving my way until his expression changed. He stopped walking.

At first I thought he was reacting to the slacks that all three of us wore. Not long ago, even some men in Denver wouldn't give women wearing slacks a seat on the streetcar. But then I saw the true reason for his displeasure. As he looked over Rose and Lorelei, something not kind crossed his face, the same look I had often seen when Negroes entered a nice restaurant in downtown Denver. The man apparently changed his mind about coming over to speak to me. Instead, he turned on a stiff heel and walked the other way.

Rose and Lorelei kept on sipping their sodas as if nothing had happened. Surely they had noticed. But I didn't know—were they able to dismiss it? Or perhaps had they become so accustomed to prejudices that it no longer found a way to pierce their reserve?

I tried to converse and keep on smiling, but I found myself unable to fathom the source of that man's displeasure. Daily, Japanese evacuees worked diligently and pleasantly in the farmlands around us. I had heard Ray and Hank both comment on the quality of the Japanese interns' work and how much they wished to please. On their occasional days off, those at Camp Amache were allowed to venture away from the camp, and all of them returned voluntarily.

I had often wondered why Rose and Lorelei were staying in the camp and putting up with all of this. The release of some college students from camps had begun as early as 1942. The Nisei were allowed to leave camps and resettle in any of forty-four states if they so chose, the only requirements being sworn loyalty to the U.S. and gainful employment. But the questionnaire required of them contained some tricky wording, and even with war jobs plentiful, most remained in the camps. Now the very thing I had just witnessed gave me my answer. Perhaps the intolerance and prejudice I had just seen kept them in confinement together, in the somewhat sheltered isolation of the camp.

As we leaned against the side of the truck, I found myself

studying my friends' faces. So much alike and yet so different, just like my own sisters and me. Lorelei became more beautiful every time I saw her, but Rose's face had become beautiful to me, too. The sunlight danced off their hair like shine on black patent leather shoes. Always their posture was perfect, their exotic faces reflected composure, poise, and grace.

Rose looked back at me in a different way. She set down her Coke bottle and started talking in a changed tone. "I was on my way to take a final in English lit," she said. "It was in 1941, before Pearl Harbor. A woman stopped me to ask me my views about Emperor Hirohito. And when I told her my views would be no more valuable than those of any other student, that I had never lived under his rule in Japan, she thanked me for my time, and we each went on our own way."

Lorelei stopped drinking as Rose continued. "It was a pleasant conversation. But for me, it was a preview of things to come, like a prologue to a book I was someday going to have to read, although I'd not have chosen it for myself. She saw me as Japanese, nothing else. Certainly not American."

"We left school even before the evacuation notices went up," said Lorelei.

"When they did, I was almost relieved."

"Well, I wasn't," countered Lorelei.

Now I could see it. Despite the poise, I could see the suffering in their eyes. I tried to think of something to say, but what? The leaders of our country had determined that Japanese American presence in the coastal states posed a threat to national security. Loyalty had been questioned, and with so many lives and secrets at stake, perhaps most people felt that Congress had made a prudent decision. But I had begun to think they had reacted hastily and irresponsibly toward good citizens. After all, except for the American Indians, we were all immigrants or descendants of immigrants.

I longed for the right words to explain that for which there was no explanation. "It isn't you they dislike. For some people . . ." I thought for a minute. "For a lot of people, it's difficult to separate those of you living and working over here from the enemy overseas. Those people probably aren't naturally hateful, just ill-informed. They tend to group all persons of a certain creed or nationality together in one category. It isn't right, but still they do it."

"We are the enemy," said Lorelei.

I sighed. "Of course you're not."

"We are Japanese."

"You were born in this country."

Lorelei shrugged. "No matter. We look Japanese, the same face as the enemy that bombed Pearl Harbor."

"Look," I said, "many others believe as I do. That a person's individual accomplishments and personality are what matter. I believe we're beginning to see a shift in this country, starting with our generation. In the future, these problems will get better."

Lorelei and Rose finished the last of their sodas, whereas mine turned warm in the bottle. As I stood there, new thoughts showered me with sharp pebbles. In Denver, there had been just as many divisions. I had grown up attending an all-white and affluent church, my father's. But in the city, there had also been Negro churches and Mexican churches, and never once did we join together for activities or socials. Soldiers were routinely segregated in the services, and there was even a separate USO for Negro soldiers located in the Five Points area of Denver. Even on the university campus, my friends and I had been a pasty collection who stood for equality for all, but did we really embrace it?

I asked, "Have you ever considered leaving the camp? Have you considered moving to Denver, going back to college, or getting a factory job?"

"We could never leave our parents and grandparents," said Rose.

"They're Issei," said Lorelei. "They aren't free to go."

Lorelei leaned around her sister to look at my face. "Would it be any better in Denver? Would others find us acceptable there any more than they do here?"

"In the city, there are more people of various views."

Lorelei asked in a louder voice, "But would it truly be any different?"

My shoulders fell. "Probably not."

Twelve

*L*ater, I drove us away into wisps of dust that never got a chance to settle back to the ground during harvest days. Dirt and grime layered the air and coated the buildings, equipment, and vehicles. Even the trains became smoky phantoms emerging out of the earth, instead of riding the ground above it. The sky-blue engines called the Blue Gooses were as grimy brown as the solid black steam engines of other trains.

That evening, I carried the maternity dress into my room, folded it, and smoothed it out flat inside one of my drawers. Eventually, I realized, I'd be wearing it. After all, my old coverings weren't going to suffice forever.

The next day, Ray and I drove to church in the evening for a "social," as he put it. I wore the plainest dress I'd brought with me and kept my hair down. Inside the church kitchen, I found women sitting at the table, pooling and trading ration coupons. I realized too late I should've brought my coupons along. Ray raised enough chicken and pork to feed us, so I could have traded our meat coupons for more canned goods, or even for nylons.

Another group of women was trading off vegetables. I started to pull up a chair to listen and watch, but then I heard some of the conversation going on. One woman sitting next to Mrs. Pratt was complaining about women leaving their children at home, working in factories, and simply by their presence wooing married men, and of course wearing slacks. I ended up joining the women who were ripping up worn sheets and rolling them into bandages for the injured. We also filled paper bags with shaving goods, packs of cigarettes, and chocolate bars for men in hospitals. Here the conversation was more bearable. A woman was telling us all about her son, a bombardier with the Fifth Air Force, who was back from combat attending B-29 school. She told us that his uniforms were custom-made in Australia and they were cream-colored, the loveliest she'd ever seen. And apparently the Electrolux man was in town. He had come out to one woman's house and had done all her floors while she was out doing her shopping, just to thank her for buying one.

They discussed making butter and cheese, canning preserves, and making sausage, conversations I couldn't even comment on. Soon I went to the window and looked outside to see what the men were doing. Hood up, some farmer's old car was the center of attention. Leaning in, the men passed tools around and worked together.

Mrs. Pratt came up to stand behind me. "They're fixing the fluid drive on our old Chrysler, but we won't tell the factory." She pointed outside. "They have to take the drum apart, put in new seals, and get us driving again."

I watched Ray in the midst of the group leaning over the engine. "Is it dangerous?"

"I doubt it. The factory says you're not supposed to do it, but we have to figure out our own ways, nowadays." She smiled at me. "Don't worry. He's going to be all right."

I looked back outside. Children were running around the church building and the broken-down car, engaged in fantasy and games, and I wished I could join them.

That night, long after the interns had boarded the trucks and returned to their camp, I went walking on the farm. I left the narrow roadway and walked out into an open cleared field for the first time. Out in the middle, I looked over the remains of tangled bean vines, overturned stones, clods of dirt, and occasional pieces of trash and leaves blown in by the wind. And stamped down into the soil, I saw hundreds of small shoe prints, many of them as small as children's, footprints that could only belong to the Japanese interns.

Once we had talked of shoes. Arriving from the mild climate of Long Beach, Rose and Lorelei had brought with them only sneakers and sandals. Many of the Issei had come to camp with just their Japanese slippers. Rose found it a good excuse to buy boots she'd always wanted, but Lorelei complained about the cold winters. Never before had she felt such cold toes. I recalled an article that had once been published in *Reader's Digest* entitled "One Small Unwilling Captain." A Japanese man, in a letter to an American friend, had written, "I am a small man. I am an unwilling man. I am a captain in the Japanese Imperial Army, and I do not want to do this."

Regardless of the view taken and despite the thousands of conflicts I'd once studied in classes, war's effect on the innocent had never come to me so strongly as it did at that moment. It came in the remembrance of that letter and in those footprints pressed down into Singleton soil. As I walked back to the cluster of house and outbuildings, I couldn't shake the vision of those prints. The wind blew in grit that coated my lips and peppered my eyes. Up ahead, I could see that Ray was home but still out working, piling up trash behind the barn. I stopped and watched from a distance.

As I stood there, a chill swept over me. In one instant, I knew what he had done.

I began to run. A pitiful sound came out of me—wail or cry, growl or moan—I didn't know what it was. I didn't even know I was capable of making such a beastly sound, but it came out of me without my will as I tore down the embankment to the barn. At the brink of the pile, I stopped and raked my hair with claw fingers. The trash heap now appeared as nothing but a mass of splintered wood pieces mixed with animal offal and bits of soggy newspaper. Pressure was building in my face.

"What is it?" Ray yelled as he jumped down from the tractor.

"My things. All the things I was collecting. The old tools, the antiques. I was collecting them in that burlap bag." Now I glared at him. "Did you take it?"

I turned and walked back to the house without waiting for an answer, because I knew it already. Except for Rose and Lorelei, the only things I cared about in this dreadful place were now gone. My few sources of pleasure, and he had gone and destroyed them.

In the house, I cooked dinner, but I kept having a hard time focusing on the pages of my cookbook. Instead, the words kept blurring on the page, and I kept banging pans together as I moved them around. Even my arms were angry. The veins stood up on top of the skin in tightly pulled ropes.

Nightfall came and still no sign of Ray.

At last, later than he'd ever returned before, he clumped up the steps to the house. He came in and stood before me with muddy water dripping down his face and pieces of smelly debris clinging to his clothes. His arms hung at both sides, and in one fist he held the burlap bag, which he set down on the floor.

"It was in the pile but near the bottom. It's still okay." At that moment, I saw more expression on his face than I'd seen in all the previous weeks we had spent together. What was his expression? Pain? Exasperation? Defeat? Disbelief?

He was struggling for speech. Then his words came out in a desperate plea. "You should have told me you loved them."

That night we ate in silence. I had tried to bake pork chops but had cooked them too long, making them tough. Cutting into those chops was like cutting into cardboard, and chewing the meat made my teeth hurt.

Ray ate it anyway, then he sat back. "This here's a working farm, Livvy. Everything we keep around here ought to have some use. I was just cleaning things out a bit, and when I saw an old sack, I thought it'd be trash."

I wouldn't look up. "It's not trash. Besides, that stuff looked as if it had been in the same shed for years. Why did you need to clean it out now?"

"I have some used equipment coming in and no place to put it up for winter."

Now I tried eating again. "Well, it was an accident."

He was still just sitting. "How much of that old stuff do you want to keep?"

I stared blankly ahead. I honestly didn't know.

For a long stretch of minutes, we continued to sit without moving. The air in between us grew as thick as the low fog that rises out of a night plain. I could feel it pressing in on my skin, wrapping me up. When it started to push down on my chest, too, finally I made myself look over at him. I saw his eyes barely well up, the tears men seldom cry just held back in check.

He said, "I'd do anything to make you happy."

I breathed out then. "I know."

Thirteen

The next Sunday, we left church shortly after the service ended. Ray drove us away in silence, not once glancing over at me as he usually did. After passing through the town, he pulled to a stop in front of a graveyard run over with grama grass, then he got out and walked inside the rusty iron gate without me. I didn't know if I was supposed to follow him or leave him alone, so for a few minutes I lingered in the car until I couldn't sit still any longer.

I found him standing over a grave, hat off and held in both hands, staring at the headstone of his brother, Daniel Singleton, born 1919, died 1941. Ray stood in the same way without moving for what was at least a half hour, and all I could guess was that in this way, he grieved. Only once did his eyes mist over, only once did he barely pass beyond the emotional boundaries of men, so self-imposed.

He grieved for his brother and I for my mother. We both suffered from the loss of someone we loved. Wasn't this a common thread so strong it should pull us together? I should've tried to comfort him, to console him for the pain of losing one so young as Daniel, his only brother. I should do something, I kept saying to myself. As I stood there, I tried to summon up affectionate feelings for him, but the only good memories I could recall were of the afternoon out on the fishing pond. And on the same day, he had rescued me from Mrs. Pratt, had even told a lie for me, something I imagined he rarely did. He had done it to protect me, and I would protect him from this awful sorrow if only I could. But unfortunately, I knew the truth from my own experience. Nothing could pull a person out from under this load.

I stood beside him until the sun started to singe the tiny hairs that grew almost invisibly on my forearms. Finally Ray turned and walked back to the truck. He slumped into the seat and gripped the steering wheel, still staring straight ahead at nothing but empty air.

We drove back to the farm in silence. I spent the rest of the day reading, while Ray disappeared inside the barn. In the evening, he came indoors to hear Walter Winchell on the radio, but we didn't talk over any of the news or the day's events. And for once, I retired to bed earlier than he did.

As the onion and bean harvest was finishing up, the interns spent long days on the Singleton farm. With Rose and Lorelei nearby, we met every day for their midday break and for other snatches of time when they could escape away from their overseer.

One day, on the front porch steps, Rose kept looking me over. "Are you well?" she asked me.

"I'm fine, just fine," I told her. I touched the strands of hair that lay out over my shoulders. I hadn't bothered cutting or curling my hair lately. Maybe I needed a trip to the beauty shop for a trim.

They glanced at each other. Then Lorelei peered into my face. "Are you certain?"

"Yes, of course." I was having trouble meeting her gaze. I

looked down at my sneakers and saw that I had forgotten to tie the laces. "Why wouldn't I be?"

"You don't look well," said Lorelei.

"In what way?"

They didn't answer. Instead, Rose said to me, "There's a very old woman in the camp, an Issei who used to help women in your condition back in the old country. She can tell you what to do."

I shook my head. Maybe it was the extra weight. "Nothing's wrong."

Lorelei said, "She can make you feel better. And she can predict boy or girl."

Again, I shook my head. "Not yet."

That evening, Ray took me out into the elm grove. Those vase-shaped trees had lately changed to their autumn color, making a mesh of floating gold above us. Under our feet, leaves already fallen cushioned the ground as we walked into the shade.

"It's going to be a good harvest." Ray reached down and picked up a stem fingered out with yellow leaves. He handed it to me. "When the war's over, the price regulations will be lifted. All the farmers I know are thinking that, come soon, we'll be able to get good money for our crops."

I rolled the stem around in my hand, then passed it back to him. As I caught his eye, he had to look away. Whenever I looked into the heart of his eyes now, he did this. He couldn't hold my gaze. And in the brief second I got a glimpse of his eyes, I saw what lay there—that same look of reservation, of hesitation, of sadness and vulnerability he didn't want to reveal, but which I saw almost every day now.

"This harvest is still one of the best we've ever had in these parts."

"You're a good farmer, Ray."

"This is good land. Never let us down. Not once, since I was a boy."

I looked out to the horizon that always sat at eye level. "Lucky for the world."

"Lucky for us, too." He readjusted the hat on his head. "This year'll pull in more money than ever before. We could add onto the house if you like."

Now I looked back in that direction. "The house is fine."

"I could add on a room for all those antiques of yours." He shifted his weight from one foot and then to the other. "Or I could put in a nursery."

"Please, no. Everything is fine the way it is. Your house," I said, turning in that direction.

"Our house."

"It's perfectly fine. And it's probably full of memories of your family just as it sits now." Already I could feel the weight of the burden I carried. "We don't need to change a thing."

The following Sunday, when I tried to button the same dress I'd worn just a week earlier to church, I noticed that it was tighter around the waist and through the hips. I tested it by sitting on the edge of the bed and saw that when I sat down, the dress spread open between buttons, revealing my pale and stretching skin. Quickly I tore it off and pulled out the dress that Rose and Lorelei had made for me. I had kept it folded in the drawer, not yet wanting to realize the inevitable. This morning, however, the time had come. I slipped the smocklike, loose dress over my neck and studied myself in the mirror.

People always say that pregnant women are beautiful, and as I've reached into old age, I find that I mostly agree. But back in those days, I could see no beauty in my newfound weight about the middle or in the watery pockets about the eyes. And again, as

I looked at myself in the shapeless dress of a mother-to-be, it all came sweeping in over me. I had not anticipated any of it, that nature would surpass my will, that I would find myself in such a state of circumstances, that I would be feeling the war in such a new way through Rose and Lorelei, and least of all that Ray would fall in love.

When I walked out into the main room with my purse in hand, Ray stood up. He looked me over briefly, but said nothing about my new look, only, "Ready now?"

Before the church service began, I posted a notice on the bulletin board. I had finally come to my senses and realized the illogic in keeping valuable artifacts out on a farm where no one could see them. I would give much of it away, if only I could find someone who could appreciate the pieces, restore them to their former utilitarian beauty, and add them to a collection. I would keep only a few precious pieces for myself: the buttonhooks and my fork from the dugout.

In church, Reverend Case spoke of current topics and events instead of the usual rehashing of moral lessons. He discussed leadership and the ability to inspire, comparing General Dwight D. Eisenhower's leadership power to the spiritual power of Jesus Christ. Then he spoke of gratitude, the good fortune we had experienced living in a safe and prosperous country during such times. I had to agree, and occasionally, even I felt lucky. Ray could have been anyone, a cruel man or one who judged me. Instead, he had turned out to be a decent and kind person, one I couldn't imagine being mean ever at all.

We stayed on for the potluck lunch. I had prepared ambrosia salad, one dish so easy even I couldn't ruin it. Throughout lunch and fellowship time, several older women and a few of the men came up to ask me about the artifacts. Exactly what did I have, could I date the pieces, how was their condition? I invited all of them out to the farm for a look. Giving away the collection would have an added benefit I only just then realized. I could count on some visitors for a change.

After the last inquisitor left me alone to eat my lunch, Martha came to sit beside me. She ate off a plate held high in the air and balanced perfectly with one hand. With her other hand she pulled out a yellowed and curling photograph from her handbag and passed it over to me. "This was our grandfather, Horace Single-ton, and his wife, Irma. The baby in Irma's arms was our father."

I looked at the gaunt faces. It struck me as odd that people in old photographs never smiled. Standing gravely and dressed in suit and full-length dress, the baby in Irma's arms completely cov-ered, they looked tired, as if even the small effort required by pos-ing for a picture had been a chore. "Irma wasn't our grandmother. Our grandmother died after giving birth to our father, and Irma is the woman Horace remarried."

I tried to imagine bringing a baby into this world without medical help, without adequate shelter. Had the baby been born in the dugout?

Martha resumed eating while I studied the photo. "What year was this taken?"

"Turn it over and read the back," Martha said in between bites. "Someone, I think it was my grandfather, labeled it. What does it say?"

I turned the photo over: "Old homestead, 1879."

Martha scanned the crowd. A moment later, she shifted in her seat. Then she arose, and after setting her plate down in the chair, she said, "I'll be right back. There's someone I'd like to introduce to you."

She returned with a white-haired older gentleman on her arm.

"This is the finest doctor in all of two counties. Dr. McCutcheon, this is my sister-in-law, Olivia."

"Livvy, please," I told him.

"So I see you might be in need of a checkup," the doctor said with a smile well engraved into his cheeks.

Martha swooped up her plate and gave the old doctor her seat. "Dr. McCutcheon delivered all four of mine. He traveled out from La Junta for the two girls, but by the time I had the boys, I knew the signs. For those two, I traveled to him and enjoyed the luxury of a hospital bed."

I handed over the photograph. And this was a bit of a conspiracy. If the doctor's office was located in La Junta, why was he attending church services way out here? Obviously he had come on invitation. For a moment, I felt myself an infant with too many parents hovering about the bassinet. But then I relaxed and told myself that surely they only meant well, that it was true—I did need to see a doctor.

"No," Martha said, refusing the photograph from me. "Seeing as you enjoy history so much, I thought you might like to have it for yourself."

"I'll frame it and keep it on my dresser. Thank you," I said before she left me alone with the doctor. Their plan worked well. Before Dr. McCutcheon rose to go off and fix another plate from the selections at the buffet table, I had scheduled an appointment.

Mrs. Pratt soon came to take his place in the seat beside me. Again, she had used her kitchen skills for Ray's benefit. Beet farmers didn't have to ration sugar; therefore she had plenty of it with which to spoil Ray. In the icebox, she had left us a mixed-fruit pie with cream topping. "You'll need to leave it in there until just before you leave church today. Then place it back in your icebox as soon as you've arrived home."

After I thanked her, we sat in silence. Just when I was starting to eat and enjoy the hum of others' conversations all around me, Mrs. Pratt asked, "And when is the happy arrival to occur?"

I stopped chewing. "We're not certain."

Of course, it wasn't true. The doctor in Denver had predicted an early March delivery, only five months away and falling short of seven months after my marriage to Ray. I wondered how long it would take Mrs. Pratt and probably many others to start counting backward. How long would it take the party lines to spread the shocking news?

She picked at her food. "So fortunate to be blessed so soon."

I sat tall and sucked in.

She looked down at my lap. "Do twins run in your family?"

And this question, I couldn't answer.

Fourteen

‹❦›

$\mathcal{A}$round the first of October, the weather turned cooler as a front came in, bringing rain. Then, after a few days of cloudiness, Indian summer returned. I took advantage of the remaining warm days to go walking through the elm grove. Martha once explained to me how the elm trees had come to be planted. "A homesteader could add to his original claim by planting ten acres of trees. Forestation was supposed to increase rain and snowfall here, but of course it didn't work. My grandparents tried some trees, but at first they planted the wrong types, and before irrigation, it was a dismal failure. All of those trees died in less than a year. Then they found out that Chinese elms could survive just about anything."

She also told me that the first tree farm, as she called it, was now the elm grove at the Rocky Ford fairgrounds, the same place where over two hundred German POWs from Camp Trinidad were being housed.

I stepped over twigs and dead branches that had fallen from the trees. With the onions and beans pulled, while we still had warm afternoons for growth, Ray was seeding the winter wheat. And in a few days, the sugar beet harvest would begin, keeping Rose and Lorelei busy for long days at a time. But what would I do?

If we lived closer to Trinidad, I could offer to teach English at the POW camp. It would be interesting to get to know something about the German soldiers firsthand. But what would Ray think about it?

On the first day of beet harvest, Ray explained the process to me. He used the tractor to pull a contraption appropriately called a beet puller behind it. It had two prongs that went into the ground under the beets and forced them up. Then the harvest crew came in with beet knives—short swordlike knives with a straight, narrow hooking device that came off at a right angle from the end of the larger blade. The interns went through the field, leaning down and hooking the beets off the ground, then hacking off their tops with the knives. Later the beets had to be loaded in the truck for transport to one of the nearby factories that could extract the sugar. The beets came out of the ground bulky and dirty. It was the filthiest and most physically demanding work of the entire season, and although it came near the end of an arduous autumn harvest, when all the interns were most likely exhausted, none of our workers ever lodged a complaint. I kept my distance from the fieldwork, as that seemed to be what Ray wanted, but occasionally I'd take a ride with him to the sugar beet factory to drop off a load.

In the midst of the sugar beet harvest, Lorelei and Rose were able to take a day off for another drive. We met in Wilson, then drove all the way south, past Trinidad, over Raton Pass, and into New Mexico. "Will your absence be a problem?" I asked them. I didn't want to cause them any more trouble.

"We have a pass," answered Lorelei.

"Our activities out of camp are not very restricted anymore. It's much more relaxed than when we first arrived."

We crossed the border while still in the mountains, then wound down to rolling land. Farther south, the land became drier and flatter still, more of a pink desert than a green plain, with lavender-blue mountains and mesas scalloping the horizon.

I didn't know what Lorelei and Rose had expected, but surely they looked disappointed, or something else was bothering them, I didn't know what. Along the way, we stopped at various good observation spots for butterflies, but by now, with fall's night chills quickly beginning to scare insects away, we found none of them. It wasn't until we arrived in a spare woodland sheltered by canyon walls that things began to change. The dancing leaves and bright colors of fall had always made the world feel fanciful to me, as if dressed for a party. Orange and crimson, hanging on to the branches for life, the leaves flitted and twirled about whenever a breeze came through. Leaves already fallen to the ground crunched beneath our feet as we walked along the canyon floor. I searched the walls for any petroglyphs left behind by ancient Indians. Deeper into the canyon, rock walls cracked by tree roots sheltered us from the wind.

The mood began to change when Rose stumbled on a Fritillary sunbathing, wings open, on a bare branch exposed to sunlight. The Fritillary was another butterfly of orange and black color, but unlike the Monarch and the Viceroy, its pattern was spotted. While Lorelei was still sketching in the notebook, Rose found another butterfly. This time it was the Purple Hairstreak, the same butterfly they had been seeking on the day we first met. On an orange oak leaf, the butterfly opened and closed its wings, letting us see the gray-brown undersides of its wings contrasted to the purple topsides.

Lorelei only whispered, "The Hairstreak," for me to know this sighting was of great importance to them. She completed her drawing quickly, and then we stood still and watched. Surely the butterfly would take notice of us and be on its way. The Purple Hairstreak remained on the same leaf, however, for longer than I would have liked to stay in one place, particularly if I had owned wings.

Rose was reading my mind again. She asked, "Did we ever tell you about their wings?"

When I shook my head, she continued, "The wings of a butterfly are made up of millions of tiny scales, not one solid part. All the scales come together to form the wing and give the butterfly its color. And every time one flies, some of the scales fall off as dust. By the time the butterfly is old, much of its scales and color are lost."

Lorelei touched the ground with a pointed toe. "All around us is butterfly dust." She looked up and smiled. "We just can't see it."

That butterfly sighting changed everything. Soon Rose and Lorelei were humming favorite tunes and talking in layers again. I shrugged off their earlier solemn disposition. We sat down on some dry buffalo grass that snapped beneath my new heaviness.

"You'll need more clothes soon," said Rose. "We've already begun to make you a suit."

"You can come out for a fitting and meet our parents," Lorelei said.

I had accepted the dress, but a suit was too much. "You shouldn't go to so much trouble on account of me."

Both of their faces fell. Refusing their offer meant something to them, something I didn't understand but could sense anyway. "Well, if you really want to. . . ."

"Oh, we do," Lorelei said as her face brightened.

"Come out as soon as you can. We want you to meet our parents and grandparents anyway, and we'll also be able to mark the fabric for a perfect fit."

I remembered shopping for clothes with Abby and Bea, spending half a day in and out of dressing rooms, then dining out for lunch.

Rose asked, "Where are your parents, Livvy?"

The words came out of my mouth, but no longer from out of me. I was somewhere else, free of it. "My mother died this year. My father and sisters are in Denver."

"Do you see them often?"

"Not since I married. But I'm hoping to visit for the holidays."

Rose folded her hands before her. She had a look in her eyes of years much older than her age. Her voice became even softer. "Livvy, is something wrong?"

For a moment, I considered telling them, telling them all of it. That I had made a mistake, the kind I was supposed to have been too well raised, too smart, too full of good common sense to make. That I had fallen prey to the most feminine of failings.

But in the end, I said, "Of course not."

And on the long ride back, the girls and I had switched places. They were now giggling and jousting with each other, whereas I couldn't get memories of growing up with all my hopes still intact to stop prodding me down deep into the bones.

That night in bed, shafts of dusty worry lit up by the moon came streaming into the window. I threw back the covers and looked at my changing body. I touched it for the first time, the hard mound expanding between navel and groin. Then I lay back and closed my eyes.

I remembered seeing newborn babies at church. Tucked into their mothers' elbows, swathed in blankets, sometimes even their faces covered, they had been difficult for me to study. During christening ceremonies, my father had described healthy infants as incredible gifts from God. Always I had had the impression that babies were precious, fragile, and easily infected. Even as the minister's daughters, we weren't allowed to get close.

How, then, could something so valuable be entrusted to a mother who didn't want it?

Fifteen

On the day of my scheduled obstetric appointment, Ray drove me to La Junta to see Dr. McCutcheon. In the morning, the skies had been cloudy, threatening rain, so we left early and ended up arriving in town almost an hour before my appointment time. Instead of waiting in the office, we went into the Fred Harvey House at the train depot and managed to snag a table by the window in the dining room. We ordered coffee and slices of pie.

Ray sat across from me. He fingered his keys on the tablecloth and stole looks out the window. As the waitress came to deliver our plates, I noticed that he gazed up at her with an expression I could only guess to be pride. I saw it again when he looked up as I was returning to the table from the ladies' room. Then it occurred to me. A married man sitting with his pregnant wife, and all in public to witness his accomplishment. Under normal circumstances, his pride would be understandable. But what of our situation? Wouldn't some people inevitably question the paternity of this child? But I wasn't sure if that kind of tawdry thought ever occurred to Ray.

"What is it?" I asked him as I sat back down at the table.

"Nothing," he answered.

"You looked happy."

Now he smiled. "Something wrong with that?"

I looked around at the other customers. Couples, mostly couples, sitting together, smiling, eating, and chatting away. Probably they had done things the right way. Most likely they had met, dated, fallen in love, then gotten married. If they had both wanted a baby, they had probably sat down and planned it.

Ray's voice was low as he began to speak. "After the baby comes ..." But then the waitress returned with our bill. Ray looked over the check, up at me, then out the window. People stood outside waiting for tables, and by then, it was time to be on our way. Therefore Ray paid the bill and never did finish his sentence.

My checkup began with an examination that detected no problems or abnormalities. Then the nurse ushered me into Dr. McCutcheon's office for an opportunity to ask questions. After the door closed behind me, I sat on the edge of the chair and stated the truth. "I'm nearly four months."

Behind the desk, Dr. McCutcheon rocked back in his chair. "That's about what I would have guessed. Were you told a date?"

"Early March. And not a bit premature."

"March looks about right." The old doctor smiled. "And we never want premature babies."

"No, I suppose not."

"You know, Mrs. Singleton ..." He looked me over as he toyed with a pen on the desktop. "I doctor both young and old. And I've had countless wonderful experiences during all these years of caring for families." He paused. "But the best of all things is getting to bring babies into this world." He glanced over at a wall of newborn infant photos. "A healthy baby is always a blessing."

I shook my head. "This was a mistake."

He looked at me with resolve. "Once the baby gets here, you won't see him or her as a mistake anymore."

I'd heard this before. I remembered one of Mother's friends, at least her age or older, who had become pregnant just about the time her two sons went off to college. Mother had whispered to me that the baby was unplanned, obviously. But once that little girl had arrived, she had stolen everyone's heart with her flashing dark eyes, auburn hair, and smile. Mother's friend never missed an opportunity to show her daughter off in public, always dressing her in the finest clothing from shops in downtown Denver. I took a short breath. "I'd like to believe you."

"Then do so, Mrs. Singleton." He picked up his pen and tapped it once on the desktop. "I've cared for others in your situation, and many times the babies turn out to be some of the most loved of them all."

For a few minutes, we sat in silence. Then he asked, "Any questions?"

When I shook my head, he slipped the pen into his chest pocket. "Then we'll give you a booklet to read, and we'll see you in a month." He rose from his chair. "See you out?"

As Ray and I later walked down the sidewalk, he asked, "Everything go okay?"

I looked at all the people bustling by on the sidewalk. Groups of soldiers, married couples, children. "Everything's right on schedule."

"Did he tell you when the baby's coming?"

"March," I replied, then looked his way. "I could have told you that before."

Ray led me to the truck. He opened my door and helped me in. Then he walked around, slid in himself, and sat focusing out the windshield. "I guess I couldn't ask you before. I could see it hurts you." He glanced my way. "Salt in a wound, you know."

I'd been thinking lately of the pyramids, not the ones in Egypt, but the ones closer by in Mexico. The ancient civilizations of Mexico had been much more advanced than what early explorers ever realized. The Mayans and their culture were some of the most mysterious and misunderstood. And the ruins of their cities often perched on rises overlooking blue-green seas and surrounded by big-leaf jungles holding parrots in the trees.

I said, "It can't be changed."

Ray seemed reluctant to start driving, as if he had more to say or to hear. After almost two months together, he was finally breaking out of his shyness around me. And I decided that he might as well hear thoughts from the darkest corners of me, this woman he thought he loved. "Early on, I kept praying to lose the baby."

He didn't move in the seat. Even his hands were motionless on the steering wheel. "But then, you wouldn't have come here."

Of course, I wouldn't have. Because of Mother's illness, I had missed my summer classes, but by the end of the fall term, I would've caught up again. I would've finished my master's degree and started planning field studies. "People will notice, Ray. People will notice that the baby is early. What will they think then?"

"I don't care what people think."

"That's impossible," I said. Why did people pretend to be immune? "Everyone cares. The child was conceived before we were married. Soon that will be apparent to everyone. People judge, people gossip." I stopped. "Even here."

"They won't say anything."

I turned away. "How do you know?"

"I lived here my whole life. Trust me. No one will say anything to you."

I wanted to understand. "Out of respect to your family?"

"Something like that." I heard him take a big breath and felt him look my way. "Livvy," he said, "when Reverend Case got that call from your father, he could've picked any number of ole bachelors living out here on their own. But he picked me." Now he whispered the words, "This is the best thing to ever happen to me."

I fought back the sting of fresh tears. At first this whole scheme of Father's seemed as if it would hurt only me. I hadn't planned to hurt anyone else. When Father said I would marry a bean farmer, I was in such a state of worry for my own self, I couldn't imagine any of the consequences. I'd never even pictured a real person, a real family, not until I arrived here. My own pain was acceptable, but the pain I was causing Ray was too awful to face.

Closing my eyes, I said, "Ray, I don't know what *this* is."

I could barely hear him say, "It's a beginning."

Then I started sneezing and couldn't stop until my head felt as if it would blow right off of my shoulders. After that, Ray drove us away, and we didn't talk about it anymore. But by that night, any reserve I had left started to crumble away. My own selfishness at accepting Father's plan, such an easy way out and at others' expense, ate at me like termites in the marrow. After midnight, I was still listening to the clock ticking on my nightstand, and from miles away I heard a train whistle calling out like a lure, telling all of us lost souls to jump on board and run away.

Perhaps the sterile conditions of the physician's office had sent the visions flying back to me. As I lay there, I remembered back to the days in May when I had to put Mother to bed for the last time, and how Father had found so much church work of dire importance to do that he left Mother to suffer out her last days on her own, alone except for me. I was the one who learned to inject the morphine that would relieve her pain. I was the one who got up with her in the night. I cleaned and cared for her while he went about his business caring for others and not his own.

Mother appreciated every last thing I did for her. But she never ceased longing for Father's company. Sometimes she would startle herself awake, having heard some noise, real or imaginary, that came from within the house. Then she would whisper to me, "Is your father here?" And I would have to tell her that no, he wasn't. Abby and Bea made time to come and spend hours during the day with her, holding her hand or trying to feed her soup or pudding, but Father, for all good purposes, vanished before our very eyes.

On one of her last days, she asked me to take her outside in the garden where she could feel wind and sunshine on her skin. I carried her brittle cage of a body and set her on a cushioned chair among the flowers. Mother was dying in May, when the irises were blooming. Irises, which took their name from the Greek goddess of the rainbow, whose duty it was to lead the souls of dead women to paradise.

A moan came out of my throat, startling me awake. I hadn't realized I was dreaming, hadn't even realized I'd fallen asleep. In my dream, Mother was in the arms of the goddess of the rainbow, flying off to heaven, but something had gone wrong, and then she was falling, falling down to earth with no one there to catch her. I could still see the speck of her, so insignificant against a huge yellow sky. A snivel of pain escaped out of me.

Ray was in the room. I could see his shadow in the moonlight that shafted in from the window. "Are you okay?" he whispered.

"Yes," I answered.

Then I closed my eyes, took a deep breath, and pretended to go back to sleep. Instead, within the dark closet of my closed lids, I listened to him breathing. I expected him to turn around and leave, but for reasons I couldn't imagine, he stayed in the doorway and watched over me for a long time.

Sixteen

In mid-October, while General MacArthur was in the midst of battle for the Philippines, several visitors dropped by to look at the antiques. Some of them held private collections, and others gathered for the historical society or for local museums. I let my visitors select and take anything they found useful. I also offered refreshments, and we chatted on the porch if weather allowed, sharing thoughts about the history of the area. Most of my visitors were friendly enough, but I noticed fairly soon that conversation beyond niceties was out of the question. I also found it interesting that few people mentioned my obvious pregnancy. Every day now, I wore maternity clothes, and there could be no doubt as to my condition, but most people chose to ignore it. Speaking of pregnancy acknowledged that women were sexual beings, after all. I was reminded of the Spanish word for pregnant, *embarazada*, meaning embarrassed.

I received only a few shy congratulations, and one woman offered to host a baby shower for me as the date drew nearer. Lingering on the porch sipping lemonade, she had said, "We could hold it at the church or at my home, whatever you prefer."

It was a gracious offer, but to my surprise, I found no relief from my loneliness. Perhaps I even felt worse, even more disconnected. I said, "Perhaps the church would be more convenient."

She looked relieved. "Yes, probably."

I was experiencing the strangest mix of feelings. Treated with instant respect because I had married into one of the old-generation farming families, I found myself wanting to scream at her, to shout out the truth. I'd become a woman who dreamed of yelling at people who didn't even know how infuriating I found them.

One day during the sugar beet harvest, Ray came back in the middle of the day, which startled me. I knew something had to be wrong. He had with him a middle-aged male Japanese intern who had a piece of cloth wrapped around his left hand. Through the cloth, I could see blood. Ray quickly explained to me that the man had cut himself while chopping off the top of a sugar beet and that we needed to drive him to Santa Fe Hospital in La Junta to see a doctor. "He's going to need stitches," Ray said to me.

The man smiled at me and bowed. He had leathery, tanned skin that furrowed away from his eyes as he smiled, and he wore suspenders over a work shirt, scuffed pants, and scarred shoes.

I untied my apron strings and grabbed my handbag off the counter. "I can drive him over."

Ray looked relieved. "That'd be great. Then I can get back to the fields and make sure nothing else happens."

I led the man to the truck, got him settled inside, and drove us off. On the way I found out that the gentleman spoke only broken English. But he spoke the language better than he understood it. We managed to carry on a conversation anyway, and I learned that he had been a farmer in Sonoma County, California, that he had arrived here with his wife and three sons via the Merced Assembly Center, that his sons were in junior high and high school, that he hoped to return to his farm at war's end.

I checked him in at the emergency room and filled out the needed papers, naming Ray and me as the responsible parties. I waited while he had his hand stitched up and wondered how much instruction he had been given in how to handle the beet knife. He had been so pleasant with me, not bitter in the least. At the end of the day, when I returned him to the horse barn, he thanked me and said haltingly, "Be back soon."

"Oh, no," I told him. "You must return to Camp Amache. No more work until that hand is healed."

He bowed and smiled out to both ears.

"Promise?"

I'm not sure he understood what I was saying, but he pretended he could. He backed away and I returned home in hopes that I wouldn't see him again on the farm.

At the same time as the sugar beet harvest progressed, overseas, in the battle for the Leyte Gulf in the Philippines, the U.S. Navy claimed victory in the greatest sea battle in history. On the last day of sea fighting off Leyte, however, a new and terrifying warfare tactic was introduced by the Japanese, the kamikaze. From the Japanese word for "divine wind," the kamikazes, a special group of suicide pilots, purposefully crashed their planes into American carriers and battleships.

The news came in, announced on the evening radio news just after sundown. At the kitchen table, I was reading *A Tree Grows in Brooklyn,* and Ray was working on receipts for farm supplies. As the announcement came, we looked up from our work and listened.

I had never heard of such a thing in all my previous years of studying history. Unfortunately, humankind has almost constantly been at war, and always there have been those who stood at the front line. In the awful pecking order of battle, the soldiers first to charge surely must have known their chances of survival were not good. But never had I heard of such calculated suicide missions as that of the kamikaze. Never had I heard of such deliberate sacrifice of a life, and now armed with the machines of modern days, one person bent on suicide was capable of causing the large-scale death of others as never before. Ray and I listened to the long report. The kamikaze had flown into the flight deck of one of our carriers, the *St.-Lo,* causing it to blow up and then sink.

I had made a custard pudding for dessert, but after the news, neither of us felt like trying it. Instead, as the station switched to playing some music, I told Ray, "I need to walk."

"Don't go far," he said.

I bundled up in my overcoat, but at the door, I turned back. "Would you like to come?"

He sat up; then, pushing the receipts aside, he said, "Sure."

Outside, the night air was cold as we walked swiftly in the direction of the bridge. In the creekbed, a tiny trickle of clear water flowed, evidence of recent rain, and ice formed along the bank edges. Low clouds obscured the moon and stars, making the night sky as dark as India ink. Only when lightning lit up distant portions of the sky could we see the rolling undersides of the storm clouds, like smoke from a blue-black fire.

On the bridge, I said, "What a night sky," to Ray as I looked up.

He said, "It'd be even colder without those clouds."

I turned to him. "It's hard to believe we're standing under the same sky as our soldiers are." I shook my head. "All over the world, people are looking at the same stars, the same moon, the same sun, every day." Somehow, I didn't feel so isolated when I thought of it that way.

"I suppose."

I tilted my head to better see those seething clouds and remembered what I had come outside to forget. The kamikaze. I whispered to Ray, "How could something so awful be going on underneath this same sky?"

Ray was following my gaze. "But in the Philippines, it's daytime."

Now I turned to stare at him. "Don't you ever wonder what else is out there?"

He stood still. "I wouldn't expect to find anything I couldn't find here."

"You don't care to see other parts of the world?"

He stuck his hands in his pockets and studied me now. "I always did like a day drive. But I like coming back to my own place. There's something about sleeping on your own soil."

"Your own soil?" I said. "It seems that almost every war in human history has had something to do with 'owning the soil.' I like the Indian's view—that we're just temporary guardians of the land on which we live."

"It's not temporary for me."

"Your family has owned this land for less than a hundred years. In the span of history, that's nothing."

That familiar line sank back in the center of his forehead, letting me know that Ray was thinking. "But in the span of a life, that's near everything."

At that moment, something moved inside me.

I put a hand on the spot where I felt it, low on my abdomen and just to one side of center. It happened again, and this time, the smooth skin bulged under my fingers. At once, I realized that the flutters I had been feeling weren't some unusual cramping, but instead were the movements of another life. Once my mother had told me of this moment. She had said that the earliest stages of pregnancy seemed an illusion to her, a dream, a promise of something unbelievable. But once she felt life, she had told me, everything changed. From that moment onward, the baby became a being separate from her, distinct, and very real. At that moment, I felt it, too, although I didn't know that kind of strength simmered within me. "The baby," I said, looking up at Ray. "It's moving."

Seventeen

Over the next days, the national news reports broadcast on KOKO told us of more kamikaze pilots driving their planes into U.S. Navy ships, sinking them. I listened off and on all day, then drove to the mailbox to retrieve my paper so I could read up on more details. The decisive sea battle for Leyte took only three days and ended in American victory, but the land campaign dragged on. In Europe, although Hitler was backed into his homeland, he still had ten million troops under his command and had recently created a new militia, requiring all men aged sixteen to sixty to serve.

On the Singleton farm, the weather finally turned colder. The last of the sugar beets came out of the soil before any chance of frozen ground. Before the hard freezes came, while we still had sunny and warm afternoons, Ray had plans to dig a new pond.

I was confused because we already had a stock pond down the slope beside the barn, so I asked Ray why we needed another one.

"That other pond's not good enough for swimming, seeing that it sits below the barn, catches all the animal waste. I aim to dig one that I can line with willows and stock with trout and bass.

Build it deep so the water stays clear and in the summertime, you and the children can go swimming."

The children? My mouth opened in a surprised little circle, but I said nothing.

Two days later, the weather turned warm again, especially pleasant for a day in the middle of fall on the High Plains. Ray and Hank borrowed a cranelike machine they called a dragline to begin working on the pond, and because apparently this was a pretty exciting thing to watch, Martha and the kids came along, too. Ray had chosen a site on the same overgrown watershed slope where the livestock pond was located but farther away from the barn. Still within eyesight of the house, the site, he explained, was perfect for collecting rainwater runoff—a "sky pond," it was called.

Martha and I stood on the porch and shielded our eyes from the glare as Wanda read a book nearby on the railing, barely paying any attention to the goings-on at all. As Ray and Hank started out to work with the dragline, I could see the machine backed up against a sky so endlessly blue it nearly hurt my eyes.

"Maynor Tate was the only man in this county who knew how to operate that thing," Martha said to me. "But now he's gone off in the Army."

Ray and Hank were standing around the dragline, then Ray climbed up into the cab, sat down, and started looking over the controls. On the ground nearby, Hank was scratching his head. A minute later the engine roared up, and Martha started down the porch steps. Both Chester and Hank Jr. were standing around the machine, which was now rumbling like the tail of a rattler.

"I don't think I want them so close by," Martha was saying as she started off toward the contraption and the men who were trying to figure out how to operate it.

I was right behind her. "Isn't there an instruction manual or something?"

Martha glanced back in my direction and smirked. "Do you think they'd read it?"

Martha gathered the boys around her like a hen pulls in her chicks. Ray had figured out how to lower the bucket on the dragline and now had it pawing the dirt. It reminded me of a lame animal trying to dig up something to eat.

"Dig it in there, Ray," Hank said.

"I'm figuring out the controls," Ray said as he pushed and pulled on a cable control in the cab of the dragline. He lifted the bucket back into the air, then brought it down with a loud thump on soil that was thickly covered with patches of straw-colored stubble. A low scraping cry came out of the ground as the scoop dug through her top-skin.

"There you go, now," said Hank.

The bucket dragged back through the soil, like an iron hand with claws on its fingers. Ray then took his time figuring out how to lift the scoop, turn the machine around to one side, and then dump the soil away from the hole he was digging. The amount of soil in that first load, however, was disappointing.

"Got to pull in more than that, Ray," Hank was shouting over the sound of the engine.

"Right you are," Ray replied.

The next time he scooped, he dug in deeper and brought out a nearly full load of dirt, gravel, and rocks. Again he deposited the soil on a downside pile that would later serve as a dam.

"Now you're getting the hang of it," Hank told him.

Martha and I stood with the boys as Ray continued to dig the hole deeper and wider. "How deep do they have to go?" I asked Martha after we had been watching for close to a half hour.

"At least ten feet," she said. "Even better if it's deeper than that. Or else the water'll evaporate too fast and only be worthwhile to the mosquitoes."

I wished they'd stop. The deeper they went, the more rickety that old dragline became. The hole was soon a crater of brown earth big enough to hold two cars sitting side by side. But Ray kept going in deeper. The machine balanced on the lip of the crater as its cable ran out fully to scoop up more soil.

Martha and I were just heading back to the house when Ray continued scooping into the hole long and deep again. Over the sound of the engine I heard a creaking sound, metal moaning against itself, and I turned to see the rear of the drag line begin to lift off the ground. As the tracks rose upward, I could hear Hank yelling, "She's too heavy. Drop her! Drop the load!" It was the first time I'd ever heard him say anything so fast.

The rear of the dragline kept coming upward as Martha and I stood by doing nothing except holding our breath, paralyzed by our own helplessness. Up she came, and all I could see ahead was the whole thing tipping over into the hole, Ray stuck inside the cab.

Crows continued flying past us as if nothing were happening.

Down in the hole, Ray must have managed to drop the load he was attempting to lift, but then the dragline stayed frozen in a list, exactly as she was, for long minutes. I hadn't a clue which way she was going to go. Finally she changed her course and slumped back down to the ground with a groaning thud and a wind of dust. Only then did time start ticking forward again.

I had been clutching my throat without even realizing it. Martha looked at me and blinked watery eyes as if saying, *This is what we women must go through.*

"Can't they hire someone else to do this, maybe someone who has a bit more experience with the machine?"

Martha shook her head. "Sometimes it's better not to watch." She grabbed the boys again and headed toward the house. I couldn't seem to move yet. Martha said, "Come on. I don't know how, but they always manage to come out alive."

Ray's face was not moving. Except for the flush on his face, I wouldn't have known he'd nearly crashed into the hole, the dragline on top of him. He and Hank were proceeding as if nothing out of the ordinary had happened. I turned and followed Martha without saying a word to either one of them. Back at the house, I felt like lying down for a while. I found Ruth in my room perched on the edge of the bed looking at the things laid out on the dresser top.

"I hope you don't mind," she said as I came in.

"Of course not." I slipped down on the bed and stretched out on the covers. "Your father and uncle are outside trying to kill themselves." Then it occurred to me that maybe I shouldn't be so outspoken with a girl of only sixteen.

But even at her age, Ruth understood. "Oh, bother." She picked up the photo of my family and held it in her lap. "Your sisters are beautiful."

"Yes," I said and sank down into the pillow. But my eyes stayed open. I kept wondering how the men were managing outside, if they'd managed to tip that machine on its head yet.

"Your mother, too," whispered Ruth.

"She died last May."

"I heard that. I'm sorry."

Those useless words again. But coming from Ruth, they no longer angered me. Lately I'd been remembering things about

Mother that made me smile—the safety of her hand when she had held mine as a little girl, the way she had managed to steer all three of us girls together around her as we crossed a street. While I rested on the bed, Ruth put on my earrings and then picked out a couple of my dresses to model. A pale green one I used to favor for church looked so good on her I insisted that she take it home.

"Only until you can wear it again," she said as she touched the collar and admired herself in the mirror.

"I want you to keep it."

"I couldn't."

"Sure you can. I'll tell your mother it was my idea."

By the end of the day, Ray and Hank had managed to dig a hole deep enough for the beginnings of a pond, then they started shaping the bottom and the banks out with a blade pulled behind the tractor. Finally they were operating a machine they knew. At the end of the day, when Martha finally rounded up her brood and piled them in the car to leave us, her face looked softened with relief. Another day had passed, and no one had died or been seriously wounded.

The next day Hank returned, and by sunset he and Ray had finished digging out the pond, shaping a dam, and building a spillway for overflow.

"When the snow starts to melt next spring, the pond'll begin to fill up," Ray told me that night. "Maybe someday we can go fishing right here on our own land."

"That's great, Ray. But going over to that other pond was nice, too."

He shrugged. "Staying around here can be nice."

I smiled at him and began to eat.

After dinner, a front started blowing in. The winds came out of the Rockies—sharp, dry, and angry. I heard Franklin, who almost never approached the house, out on the porch whimpering and pawing on the planks. Without thinking, I arose from the table and went to the door to let him inside.

Immediately Ray stood up from the table where he had been working and pointed one finger right back at the door. "We don't have animals in this house." You'd have thought I had committed an act of carnage.

I gathered some old newspapers to clean Franklin's paws. "Just for the night," I told him.

He took two long strides and grasped Franklin by the neck. Firmly but not roughly, he led Franklin back to the door and pushed him outside. Then he turned to me. "I grew up here. It means something to me." Pointing, he said, "I ate at that table." He took a deep breath. "For all of my growing up." Then he pointed to the bedroom where for two months I had been sleeping. "My parents both died in that bedroom." He began to get a grip on himself. "I don't let just anyone in this house, and I'm not letting in a dog."

Obviously, I had misjudged. "I understand."

What Ray didn't know was that I had planned to let Franklin curl up with me on the bed during cold winter nights. A few days later I was able to laugh a bit—to myself, of course—when I thought of the reaction I might have received to that idea.

One day, soon after the beet harvest had been completed, I drove out to Camp Amache to have a fitting for my suit. As I drove east, the land became drier, the grasses shorter, and the plant life more spare and stunted. The land looked more suitable for grazing than for growing, and soon, all about me spread away pasture land and bare prairie, small herds of cattle, and large bunches of spongy gray sheep.

As I approached the camp, I saw that Amache was huge. Home

to more than seven thousand evacuees, it rose out of the dirt, a city picked up by tornado winds and plunked down and away from the rest of civilization. Fenced in with barbed wire and watched over by two tall security towers that didn't seem to be manned at the time, the camp contained rowed-out, one-story buildings all uniform and similar in appearance to military barracks. I had hoped these quarters would be superior to what I'd seen at the farm outpost; however, the same feeling of shock and sorrow came over me here, exactly as before. I watched men, women, and children milling about the buildings, smiling and bowing to each other.

The "Yellow Peril," they had been called. "Nips and Japs."

I met a uniformed guard just inside the gate and told him I was to meet Rose and Lorelei Umahara. He asked me where I came from, but he seemed to be making conversation rather than inquiring out of security concerns. He moved slowly and easily, as someone does who feels little stress in his or her work. It was clear there wasn't much concern about escape or danger at Camp Amache. I found out later that only two officers and seventeen men were stationed here to guard the residents. Most of the camp management the evacuees handled for themselves.

A few minutes later, Rose and Lorelei came walking up. They smiled and spoke to the guard, then took me inside, down rows of barracks, and finally to the quarters assigned to their family. Outside I saw a carefully laid out rock garden with stones arranged together by color, size, and even by shapes. They had transplanted some native cholla cacti, sage plants, pincushion cacti, and prickly pears in among the rocks and smooth stones, making it into something neat and attractive. They had turned useless stones and ordinary plants, waste to most of us, into a garden of spare beauty.

Rose gestured out to the desert. "Our father borrowed a wheelbarrow, and we hauled these rocks in from all around."

"I thought he would kill us in the process," Lorelei whispered and then laughed.

"It's lovely. It was worth your effort." But it couldn't have compared to the green gardens they had left behind in California.

Once inside the door to their home, even Lorelei became quiet. The first thing that struck me was how small it was—the space assigned for four adults to live in, their "apartment," as they called it, couldn't have been more than twenty by twenty-four feet. But just as they had done with the outside garden, they had transformed it. The interior was a cheerful, tidy home. It looked as if they had put up walls, then painted and papered them. They had also carved out some niches in the corners and added shelves lined with family photos and built Japanese-style screens to cover the windows. From my readings, I had learned that each internee had been allowed to bring only two bags of belongings to camp and no furniture, but despite that, the Umaharas had managed to furnish this home with pieces made out of crates and scrap wood, the end result as neat and comfortable as humanly possible. In one corner was a table covered with a yellow-and-red-flowered tablecloth and tucked under with chairs. Along the wall sat a dresser and a double-decker bed. The room was lit with two shaded lamps. One corner held a folding screen framed with carved wood and decorated with a Japanese scene.

The furniture, the lampshades, even the floors were spotless, as if just recently polished, dusted, and swept out with a broom. This camp and the land around it was a place of endless sand and dust, much drier even than the farm where I lived, yet they kept it more than habitable. I could see no running water in the room and only a coal stove for heat, yet the room felt warm.

Rose and Lorelei spoke in hushed tones as they introduced me to their father, Masaji, and their mother, Itsu, who were both well dressed in American garb, both smooth-skinned, short of stature, but strong in appearance.

They nodded to me as we met. "What an honor that you have come to our home," said Masaji. His shirt was purest white and pressed.

Itsu offered me hot tea, which I accepted, then she began pulling out pinstriped, gray wool fabric already pieced together using broad hand stitches. As she held the garment up to me, I saw the only sign of her age—tiny vertical lines on her upper lip. The rest of her skin was unmarked, and her hair was as black as her daughters', long, pulled back, and coiled at the back of her head. As she worked, I noticed three majorette uniforms decorated with gold braid and brass buttons hanging on the wall. Lorelei told me later that her parents were making the uniforms for the camp's high school band. Itsu ushered me behind the screen, then all four of them left the "apartment" so I could try on the garment in privacy. As I was slipping myself into the pieced suit, as they waited for me beyond the door, I wondered about their sense of privacy. All four of them, after all, slept inside the same room.

After I was dressed, Rose, Lorelei, and their parents returned to work on the fitting. Itsu and Rose were the only ones to touch me in any personal way—they took the measurements along the hem, across my breasts, and my enlarging waist, whereas Masaji held back and gave them quiet directions, sometimes in English and sometimes in Japanese. Rose and Lorelei had told me before that their parents came to this country as children after having already learned the Japanese language and customs. Their parents' parents had been friendly for years, had come across the ocean at approximately the same time, and the two children had always been friends, had always seemed destined to marry.

It was their mother and father who had suffered most from the disparity between cultures, Rose and Lorelei once told me. As Itsu pinned the fabric for a perfect fit, I remembered. Because they weren't born in this country, they couldn't become citizens, although they had lived most of their lives in the U.S. When Rose and Lorelei were born on this soil, they purposefully chose for them first names common in America, taught them English at home, and sent them to public schools, where they were expected to excel. Obviously Masaji and Itsu had hoped to provide better opportunities for their daughters than had been afforded to them.

As they continued to work on the fitting, I studied the family photos on the shelves across from me. Beside them was another photo of Masaji standing and smiling with a celebrity whose face I recognized but couldn't name. I remembered Rose and Lorelei once telling me that their father had made suits for famous people in Los Angeles.

Later, from the compartment next to theirs, Rose and Lorelei's maternal grandparents came over to meet me. They spoke little English, but instead bowed to me and smiled; then we sat and shared a cup of hot tea. Their grandmother was one of the tiniest women I'd ever seen, with small flitting eyes like those of a bird. She wore a long, silky kimono and cork-soled slippers that slapped silently on her soles as she walked.

Afterward, Rose and Lorelei led me away for a walk about the camp.

"Your suit should be ready for the holidays," Rose said.

"I can't tell you how much I appreciate it." If only I had a place to wear it.

We looked inside the mess hall where Lorelei said they ate their meals. At an empty table, an older woman was teaching a group of younger women an art form called *bon-kei*. Rose told me the woman had learned it in Japan. Sand was a vital ingredient and because sand was in no short supply at Amache, word had spread throughout the camp, and the old woman had ended up with many new students of the art. We stopped to watch for a few minutes as the students worked on creating miniature landscapes inside a tray—some of them of mountain, desert, or beach, and many of them of imaginary scenes in Japan. Each one was different. In another area of the mess hall, high school students were working on their yearbook pages.

We walked back out into the sunlight. "It mustn't seem like much of a problem, but I don't have enough to do on the farm," I said to Rose as we left. "Would the *bon-kei* teacher allow someone from outside the camp in her class?"

"She would," Rose replied. "She would see it as an honor."

"Perhaps I'll join a class, then."

Lorelei said, "Our mother can teach you *ikebana*, Japanese flower arranging."

"It would honor her, too," Rose added.

They looked at me in a new way, expectantly. They had asked so little of me before and given so much. "Then that's what I'll do. I'll learn flower arranging instead."

Rose's face glowed. "We'll tell our mother."

Even Lorelei looked pleased.

A moment later, we walked onward and Lorelei said, "I understand what you mean, Livvy. We're bored here, too. The high school kids call it 'waste time,' and we've too much of it."

Rose spoke up. "Not all of us are bored. I'm taking advantage of the free time and learning the tea ceremony from our grandmother."

Lorelei shot me a sideways glance. "Even though she doesn't really want to."

Rose turned to me. "It's different for us. We can't refuse the wishes of our elders."

"We must please, that's true," Lorelei said. "But I'm never quite pleasing enough." She looked away, out to the softly blowing desert.

As they guided me onward, I began to notice the same thing I'd noticed in Trinidad—the lack of young men. I saw some high school seniors holding a war bond drive, and plenty of young boys running around playing cowboys and Indians. Young girls played with dolls, older men engaged in hobbies or worked, and older women joined groups of quiet conversation over knitting. But the young men had vanished from this place. Rose told me that since 1943, Nisei men had been able to enlist in the all-Nisei 442nd Regiment, now engaged in the fighting in Italy and France. Camp Amache had the highest percentage of eligible males inducted into the armed services, their cousin among them. Plenty of Japanese American young men were anxious and ready to prove their loyalty to the U.S., even with their lives. Already highly decorated, since October 15, the 442nd had led the rescue of the famous "lost battalion" and were then on their way to Germany.

Now I could clearly see the reason for Lorelei's longing for male company. She and Rose were surrounded by older parents and grandparents and by much younger people still in school, but by few others their own age.

Rose showed me to the latrine after I told her I needed to find a bathroom. I entered a community building where toilets sat rowed out next to each other and pieces of plywood had been put up by shy women to afford some bit of privacy. I sat at the last toilet and covered my nose against the odor.

Years later, I would remember that smell. It is odd the things we remember in our older days. From that day onward, I would also remember other things about my first visit to Amache. The endless arc of a sky bigger than earth, the taste of dust on my teeth, rocks arranged in rows, hushed conversations, and the gentle laughter of shy women. Not all of it bad or unpleasant, but all of it was tamped with a sense of isolation and restriction.

How dreadfully their lives had changed.

Moments later, as I readjusted my clothing and prepared to exit the latrine, a sickness, disbelief turned into nausea, came over me. I'd left myself somewhere else and wasn't really in this camp anymore. That way, Rose and Lorelei and their sweet family couldn't be here, either.

Eighteen

In 1944, the winter came quietly. Instead of raging storms, we had heavy, silent snowfalls that covered the dry grasses and the overturned fields with miles of powder.

One of the reasons untouched snow is so breathtaking is that it's, by nature, so fleeting. Even the act of making those first tracks mars it; then on the warmer days in between storms, it gets icy, later slushy, then eventually melts away. But on those mornings when it spreads away, velvety white and sparkling, nothing's finer.

During my childhood, often my family would drive up into the Rockies after the first storm, and there we found ourselves quite alone, as most of the tourists were long gone by that time. We explored the quiet roads back in the days before the bans were placed on pleasure driving. We listened to empty echoes, trudged down roads and out into meadows, seeking out the deer and elk herds that would have to survive the winter season most likely with little food. On Berthoud Pass, we strapped on oak skis to glide down the slopes. And for once, I excelled in something other than studies, and my sisters did not. My father, who skied better than us all, would take off, fast-gliding down the slopes, and only I could come close to keeping up with him. I remember how he would look back over his shoulder at me as I tried to gain on him, and he'd shout out, "Bravo, girl!"

On the morning after about a foot of new snow had fallen, I bundled into my coat and stepped out on the porch. Winter on the plains came as a surprise to me. Our previously bare fields now spread out like a linen cloth on a table sprinkled with sugar. The sun had already burned the clouds away, but the air had yet to begin to warm. Each of my breaths did a smoky dance show before me. All was so silent I could hear the soft whisk of a sparrow hawk as it circled overhead.

Ray came outside to join me. He slurped loudly on his coffee and disturbed the silence. Looking out at the snow, I asked him, "Are you finished with your work now?"

He took another loud sip. "I got plenty of other things that need tending to besides the fields." He gestured beyond the porch. "This snow'll melt off. Usually before Christmastime comes, we'll get some warm days and even some rain."

I still hadn't adjusted to all the talk of weather. Even women and children often discussed the changing conditions of the high prairie at long length. After church, in the town, over supper, and in the stores, it was the favorite topic of conversation of everyone around me.

Ray pointed down the roadway that ran between fields, the same one where I had first met Rose and Lorelei. "I got to grade the ruts out of that road before the ground freezes. Then I need to work on the fences."

I looked back at the snow. So he wouldn't be spending any

more time at home after all. I had thought that after harvest and seeding the winter wheat, he would be around more often.

"Last winter, I worked the midnight shift at the sugar beet factory." He took another sip. "But I won't do that this year."

I said, "Thank you." It would be a bit spooky, out so far and by myself at night.

The silence between Ray's slurps was deafening. Finally, he said, "I want to thank you for being so friendly with Martha."

Ray never ceased to surprise me. "Why wouldn't I be friendly to Martha? She's a wonderful lady, Ray."

He smiled into his coffee mug. "It wasn't easy for her growing up the only girl in the family, with two brothers for bad company." Now he laughed to himself. "When she was a teenager, Daniel and I were 'long about six and ten years old and up to no good at all times. We'd put grasshoppers in her bed and pry open her hairpins, just for sport."

Our quiet house full of childhood romp and antics? I couldn't imagine it. "Tell me more."

"The first time she went out on a date, that ole boyfriend of hers drove all the way out here to pick her up. I tell you, he was dressed in his best, and so was Martha. Daniel and I hid right here, under this porch." He pointed down to the planks beneath our feet. "And while that boy was inside getting drilled by my dad about his intentions, we poured maple syrup on the porch steps. They came out and stepped down in it. For the whole of that date, they were having to stop and kick off grass and pieces of trash and paper that got stuck and dragged off their shoes."

These were probably the most words Ray had ever spoken to me at once, and he had me laughing. "Poor Martha. You and Daniel were brats."

Ray was still smiling. "That ole boy never did come around again."

"Was Martha heartbroken?"

"No," Ray scoffed. "Well, not so much as I know. Like I said, she grew up keeping pretty much to herself. Our mother was awful busy, and Martha liked her own company best of all." He turned to me. "But she sure does like you."

Martha, the matriarch of their family, had treated me as finely as I could have ever wished. Although she knew the real reason for my marrying Ray, she had welcomed me into the family, and Ruth, her oldest daughter, openly wanted to emulate me. I took my thoughts forward in time, to the day when the baby would come early. Ray had said no one would speak unkindly to me, but still, they would know. They would wonder what had happened to make a good girl fall so far.

Franklin came bounding out of the barn. When that old hound first hit snow, he stopped, sniffed, took another step, sniffed again, and then started to pounce into the powder with both front paws. You'd have thought he'd never seen snow before. Now he was diving into it and chopping it up with all four legs. Ray laughed aloud, and even I smiled. A minute later, Franklin saw me and started crossing the ground between the barn and the house, making a new path of churned snow along the way. Then he was galloping up the steps to the porch with chunks of snow spraying away behind him.

"There, boy," I said as he came up to me, tongue out and panting. I rubbed the top of his head and the soft folds of hide on the sides of his neck. I sank down to my knees so I could get closer to him.

"Careful," Ray said, and I was. Normal daily movements that

once I had taken for granted had become not nearly so easy. I felt heavier by the day and more uncomfortable with my own body and sense of balance. My arms and legs remained thin, but my breasts were larger, and my abdomen had turned into an upside-down bowl.

I continued to pet and scratch Franklin and made a mental note to let Ray see me thoroughly wash my hands before I made breakfast. "Isn't it possible, Ray, that he could freeze in the worst of the winter?"

"Not in the barn, he won't."

"But now he's getting older."

Ray slurped again. "He's been out there for years."

I continued scratching until my legs began to ache. I drew back to my feet, and Franklin took off for more romping in the snow. I followed him with my eyes. "You see, I always wanted a pet." What was coming over me? "My father never let us have a pet, not even a rabbit." I hadn't cried in front of anyone except Abby and Bea and wouldn't do it now. Crying made men cringe. "I'm sorry I let Franklin in the house. I didn't realize what an insult it would be to you."

"Livvy, it's okay."

I strained to see out into the sunshine.

"With all the other animals gathered in there, that dog'll be fine. Everything's going to be okay now. Trust me," he said.

We stood together watching Franklin paw at the snow in a search for life, for something to respond back to him. Now a goat was high-stepping its way out of the barn and into the snow, too.

Ray's voice changed. "Sometimes I wonder what would've happened if I'd been the one to go away. Daniel would be alive now." He looked out at the animals and took another sip of coffee.

"Ray, you can't ask yourself those questions. You'll only torment yourself." I stared away. "Why did Daniel enlist?"

"He didn't have to," Ray said. "The Draft Board put us 3-A, because we were the only ones left to run this farm, and farming is essential business nowadays."

"It is."

"But Daniel knew war was coming. Even before Pearl Harbor, he knew we were going to have to join the war in order to win it. Lots of local boys joined up on their own and left the farms to be run by their fathers. I was older. Maybe I should've talked him out of it." He paused. "But most of the time, I don't question it. Maybe I was just making a point."

I puzzled for a moment. "I didn't get it."

"Things happen for a reason. Even bad things." He seemed to be searching for words. "Or things that seem bad at first."

"Ray, what are you saying? Do you believe in fate?"

"Yeah," he said, taking another sip, this one silent. "I think I do. Otherwise, how could we take all the bad stuff?"

I looked back out. "I don't know. But discounting human choice and chance—I can't buy that, either."

"So you think everything comes about just by chance or by what we do?"

Maybe my heart had hardened more than I'd realized. "I didn't always."

His coffee mug now empty, he set it on the porch railing. "It seems to me," he said, "that you're the one tormenting yourself."

Back in the snow, Franklin had now churned his way around to the back of the barn, out of sight. Ray's voice was low, despite the silence of that morning. "You trusted someone who let you down. If only you could trust me."

It was the second time in one conversation that he'd asked me to do this.

"Is it so bad here? With me?"

"No."

"Is there anything I could do to make it better?"

I said, "You have made it better."

Nineteen

⁓⁓⁕⁓⁓

The next day was the first Tuesday in November, Election Day. While the war overseas continued to be fought with bullets, we in the U.S. prepared to make our choice for President at the ballot box. Roosevelt was running for his fourth term after already serving three. We'd had the same President for an unprecedented twelve years, so Roosevelt's opponent, the popular liberal governor from New York, Thomas Dewey, had campaigned on the platform of needed change. Dewey had also criticized our entry into the war and had even accused Roosevelt of lying to Americans in order to get us to join in.

Ray drove us to the post office in Wilson, where we placed our votes.

"We don't need to be switching our commanders in the middle of a war," Ray said as he drove us away after voting.

Ray and I finally had something upon which we could agree. I said, "Not only that, but don't forget that he brought this country out of the Depression."

"He's told us the truth from day one."

Dewey was still youthful at forty-two, in stark contrast to the incumbent, who seemed increasingly weak and fragile. And taken with the American penchant for change, my worry was that, although it was unlikely, a fluke might occur and Roosevelt might be defeated. I said, "Of course he has."

But the night before, I'd read an article in the paper and learned that in Washington, D.C., a movement to stop the exclusion of Japanese Americans was gaining momentum. Some evacuees had been slowly trickling back to their home cities over the past year. Even around me, many people had stopped referring to the interns as Japs. But Roosevelt was reluctant to do anything drastic before the election. He needed to carry California, where anti-Asian sentiment had always been strong. And I was experiencing negative feelings about Roosevelt for the first time because of it.

I opened my mouth to take a chance, to discuss it with Ray, when a group of three soldiers walking on the sidewalk made me stop still. One of those backs hit me like a fist in the neck. The way he set his shoulders, the width of the neck; it was so like Edward. I thought for just the briefest second it might be him. He would have had no business out here on the plains that I knew of, but then again, how much had I really known of Edward in the first place?

As Ray drove past the soldiers, I got a sideways glimpse of the man's profile. It was a younger man, actually just a big boy who couldn't have been much older than eighteen. But that brief moment of memory left me edgy. That time, that time of him, tried to come back to me.

In the evening, we had plans to go over to Martha's house, where we'd share supper and listen to the election reports on the radio. I wore maternity slacks and a barrel-shaped blouse sent to me from Abby. The outfit was comfortable, but the mountain in its middle made by heavy tucking along the bodice was so large the person filling it could still get lost. Maternity clothes. In the doctor's office waiting room, I'd noticed how frilly they tended to be—bows at the collar, smocking on the bodice, tiny prints on the fabric, almost as if intended for children and not for grown women. My body was so altered that it motivated me to fix my face and hair. I put on a bit of makeup for the first time in weeks, and I dampened my hair and put it up in pincurls until it was time to go. As I eventually emerged from the bathroom, Ray looked up at me for a moment, and in that brief second, I saw it again, that look of love he wanted so badly to hide.

At Martha's, we ate together and listened to the radio election news. The result was never in question, however. Roosevelt already had a big lead in both the popular vote and electoral votes, and after those one-sided results started to pour in, we could relax and simply bask in the victory. The surprising element of the election was that Roosevelt had replaced Vice President Henry Wallace with an unfamiliar senator from Missouri named Harry Truman, who would become the new Vice President. And to my satisfaction, an amendment to the state constitution that would've prevented Japanese aliens from owning land had been turned down.

Hank and Ray sat on the divan and talked farm business again. I was amazed as they went on and on. Farmers talked about their fields the same way women talked about their families. The seasons, the soil, and even the business side were discussed like the acts of moody and adored children. Hank and Ray started in on the price controls placed on farm crops during the war and their hopes that after the rationing period ended, they would be able to charge whatever they wanted. Martha could see that I was weary of that talk, so she brought out the old box of Singleton memorabilia for us to forage.

First, we found another faded photograph of their grandparents, who stood before a section of land planted in small trees. "Those are the first trees, the ones that didn't make it," she explained. "They tried apple orchards and other fruit and nut trees, but there were just too many late freezes, storms that came through in late spring and froze the buds. After these died off, they planted the elms that now grow back there beyond your house."

Next, we found another photograph, this one of children standing in front of a house. "That's the old shack," Martha said. "After the dugout, this house meant real progress."

It looked much like others I'd seen pictured in textbooks. Made of boards covered on the inside with tarpaper, sheets, or newspapers, crude shacks along with sod houses had dotted the treeless plains of the West throughout the homesteading days. The shacks often had packed dirt floors and roofs made with wide boards laid out flat and covered with a thick layer of dirt. The roofs leaked almost constantly, the prairie wind blew in dirt and dust through the cracks, and snakes regularly made their way inside. Upon first glimpse of the house in which they were to live, wives who had ventured west to join their husbands were known to break down and sob.

Nearby on the divan, Ray and Hank had finally stopped talking of farming. Out of his chest pocket, Ray pulled out a deck of cards. Chester and Hank Jr. plunked down on the floor at his feet, then to my surprise, Ray started doing a card trick. He fanned out the cards, face down, then asked the boys to each pick a card, secretly look at it, and place it back in the deck. Ray shuffled the deck over and over, smiling. He then sorted through the deck, found each boy's card, and gave it back. The boys sat looking at their cards and pondering for a moment. Then Chester checked the deck for markings, while Hank Jr. insisted Ray do it one more time. Ray did it more than once; in fact, he did that trick so many times I thought those boys would collapse from the concentration.

Wanda entered the room. She said to me, "I've seen his tricks before," but she ended up sitting at his side and watching, too. At one point, Chester made Ray do the trick with a different deck of cards, but still, he performed it perfectly.

While the card tricks continued nearby, Martha, Ruth, and I dug out more photographs and paperwork from the old box, including a receipt for a prairie-breaking plow bought in 1896 for $10.90, and some of the original papers that established the homestead.

"The filing fee cost fourteen dollars," Martha said. "They drove stakes into the corners of the land, then later they plowed furrows around the perimeter."

Martha went on to tell me about the dry fall seasons of 1874-77 when hordes of grasshoppers came through, eating all the crops and even the handles of farm implements along their way. All had been lost, yet her ancestors had stayed on and tried again. "After the grasshopper plague, they took over some of the abandoned claims and began to do some ranching. It was just too dry out here for much farming to be successful—that is, until all the irrigation canals were finished during the 1890s."

Ruth had been hanging over my shoulder and watching me all the while Martha and I dug through that box. After we made our way to the bottom, she asked me, "May I brush your hair?"

I touched a strand on my shoulder. Pregnancy was making my hair grow faster than usual, so now it hung long on the shoulders, where it spread about in loose curls. I leaned back in my chair and let Ruth brush it out, starting at the scalp and bringing it down to the ends. Long after it was neatly brushed, she kept on working, brushing it ever so gently from around my face and away from it. That brushing felt like caring. I found myself closing my eyes, and all the tension from long months of worry began to slip down, out of my body, like melted wax slides down the sides of a candle.

As she continued to brush, Ruth asked me, "Have you chosen names for the baby?"

Now the words dripped out of me as liquid wax. "I haven't thought." After a deep breath, I said, "We're open to suggestions."

"My favorite name is Patricia."

I could feel Ruth take one hand away and could imagine her pointing her finger at her mother as she fussed. "My parents had to go and name me Ruth." Then I heard Martha sigh.

"Ruth's an old biblical name," I said. "A very nice one, in my opinion."

Martha said, "Thank you. Maybe now she won't hate her name so much anymore."

Ruth brushed longer. "For a boy, I like Richard."

"But not Ricky, I hope," said Martha.

"No," said Ruth. "It could be shortened to Rich, but never Ricky."

I think Ruth would've brushed for hours. My hair became as silky as duck wings. Eventually Martha sent Ruth to cut the pie for dessert, leaving us alone. At last, I opened my eyes and found I had to take a moment to let them readjust to the glare of the light bulb. As my eyes focused again in the bright light, that worry I had sent melting into the floorboards started to climb back up and harden around me again.

I remembered the only girl I'd ever known before who got herself in trouble. But instead of an arranged marriage to save her, her family had fabricated a story of tuberculosis and told everyone at the high school she needed treatment far away in a sanitarium. Unfortunately for the family, a small panic ensued among students and parents, and the health officials had become involved, uncovering their false story. Their elaborate lie made the story even more compelling. It was whispered about for all of the next months. And after that, no one ever saw that girl again.

I straightened myself back in the chair. In a whisper, I asked Martha, "What will we do when the baby comes, full term, in March?"

She brushed a crumb off the table and looked at me dead in the center of my eyes. "Hold the biggest baby shower in the county."

And she was serious.

Twenty

On the ride back, I said to Ray, "I never imagined you as a magician."

He said, "Just a hobby."

"How do you do it? The card trick?"

He glanced over at me and smiled. "It's magic."

I smiled, too. "No, come on. It's a great trick. How did you learn it?"

"Really," he said. "It's magic."

I sighed. "I can see you're not going to tell me."

"You're a college girl, Livvy. You can figure it out."

I laughed. "Oh, I see. That was a low blow, there, Ray."

He laughed, then turned quiet again. "If you can't explain it, then it must be magic."

"Well, then." I put my hands into my lap as a selfish thought occurred to me. "Maybe you could conjure up some magic to get us a telephone line."

At first Ray didn't respond. "Do you mean it? You want a telephone?"

"It would be nice to call people from home instead of at the pay telephone."

"I didn't know you stopped there."

"I stop there often."

Ray seemed to be thinking. "If you want one, I'll look into it."

"If it's not too much trouble."

As we traveled over a wooden bridge, the rattle of rough boards underneath the tires shook the truck. On the other side, Ray said, "I always thought telephones were for matters of life and death. That's how I was raised, at least. But if you want one, if you'll just tell me these things," he said, "I'll be open to changing my mind."

I had gotten my way, but then I didn't feel as good as I had expected.

Ray went on. "I hear that vacuum man is in town. What's the name?"

"Electrolux."

"Maybe you could have him come out, too."

"No, Ray. Thank you, but the telephone would be plenty enough."

At home, Ray pulled out his manila folder and opened it on the table. I opened my latest find from the library—a history of Logan County, Colorado, with reminiscences by pioneers, published back in 1928. Between that and digging through that box at Martha's, my mind was churning backward in time. I wondered about the earliest women, those first ones out on the plains living in soddies, shacks, and dugouts. Some of the homesteaders had even been single women who came out without husbands. Others had worked claims on their own after husbands had died or left them.

While I was reading, I felt eyes resting heavily on me and realized that Ray hadn't even started on his paperwork. Instead he'd read briefly from his Bible, then after watching me read for a while longer, he arose from the table and stepped quietly around to stand behind me.

It had always annoyed me when someone read over my shoulder. Even teachers who had done it in class had brought up my ire. If he wanted to know more, he should read it for himself. I sat back in the chair and silently wished him to go away. But something was different about the way Ray stood behind me. He wasn't looking at the book. Instead his hands rested on the spindles at the corner backs of my chair, and his hands curved around them, caressing them.

Ray rubbed the spindles because he couldn't touch me.

I closed my eyes and tried to imagine it. Being touched by Ray.

Now I knew the farming life was plowing me under, just as Ray had plowed under the remains of that shack. Nothing could be further from what I wanted.

When I was eleven, I got a new world globe for my birthday. Of course, I received new dresses and a doll, too, but nothing fascinated me as much as that globe. I'd sit and turn it, letting my fingers travel lightly on its surface as it spun around. Often Mother would join me and we'd find all the countries, the ancient lands full of rich history, places that Mother would never see, but I would. She told me about the caste system in India and the Hindu religion. She drew an invisible line with her finger over the route followed by Marco Polo. And when we came to Egypt, I imagined the pyramids in all their symmetrical perfection. I pictured the mountain shrines raised out of the land of shifting sands, and knew I'd found the place where I most wanted to study. After that, I started delving into the hieroglyphs, the language of the pharaohs, all on my own.

What I missed most, however, were the conversations. Sometimes when I talked to myself, I was really talking to her, carrying on a seamless conversation that occurred only inside my head now. And during those mental talks, I would often feel something sweet drift in and alight on my skin, a sigh from the walls or the other world, I never knew which, but when I looked about, I was always surprised not to see her.

I opened my eyes. Ray was still standing behind me, his hands just as gentle on those spindles as they had been on that wounded fish. "Excuse me," I said to him and pushed back my chair. I walked into the bedroom without once looking his way.

The next morning, over breakfast, Ray wouldn't look near me, as if I had a layer of danger enclosing me, something that repelled his eyes each time they drew close. As he ate breakfast, Ray was instead studying every grain of food, every minute surface crack in the pottery of his plate.

I should've left him alone. But all I could see before me was a day without anything to do, in rooms without personality, in a house that held no memories. I said to him, "Last night, we went through Martha's box of family things." I set down my fork. "But I'm puzzled. She's keeping track of old records and photos, just as you told me. But primarily her things pertain to your grandparents and your parents when they were young, but not your family, Ray. Nothing of the three of you growing up."

Ray shrugged.

"You don't know what happened to all that?"

He looked up and passed a napkin across his mouth. Then he shrugged again and kept on eating.

Amazing. An entire chapter of family history was missing, and Ray didn't know about it or care. I washed and dried all of the breakfast dishes, except for Ray's, then wiped off all the countertops. I stood at the sink with my back to him until I built up the nerve to turn around and ask, "What are your plans for the up-coming holidays?"

Ray was still staring into his food, but now his hands were still. "We'd be welcome at Martha and Hank's."

"I'm sure we would." I took in a big breath. "But I'd like to go see my family, my sisters, in Denver."

It was out now, but I couldn't bear to look at him. Instead, now I was acting as shy as he was. I studied the nicks and dents on the countertop that couldn't be scrubbed away.

"If that's what you want," he said.

To the counter, I answered, "I haven't seen them since August, and it's the first holiday season without our mother, and with everything else that's happened . . ." I let my voice trail off.

Now I could feel his eyes upon me. "What else?"

I shook my head. "I'd just like to see them, that's all."

His voice was low. "I already told you. Do what you want."

I tried to think of a compromise. "I'll stay here for Thanks-giving and only go for Christmas and New Year's."

He stood, gathered his wool jacket, old felt hat, coffee thermos, and a canteen of water, and then he aimed for the door. "I'm taking the truck way over to the far side. You won't be needing to drive today?"

"I'll find something to do."

He went outside, and I stayed in the same spot. I looked about the empty house, and then, on sudden impulse, I went out through the screen door after him. "Could I please go along today?"

He gestured toward the truck bed filled with tools and rolls of barbed wire. "I'm going to repair fencing way out on the other side. It'll take all day."

"Fine. I've got all day."

He swept his arm toward the truck. "Then get in."

I went back inside, grabbed my overcoat and a sweater, then rushed back out to the truck. Ray drove us down narrow roadways that crossed the farm. When we reached the eastern property line, Ray gathered his tools and materials, and then he nodded over past the fence. "That there's Hank and Martha's. As the crow flies, it ain't far, but as you already know, it takes quite a spell by car."

The first snow had already melted away, but the ground remained damp. Decaying leaves and wet twigs were stamped into the soil like fossils. The sun drifted over us. I stood by and watched as Ray began to replace rusted and sagging lines of barbed-wire fencing. I found the work not interesting in the least, but in a strange way soothing. Ray had that ease of movement that one acquires after years of doing the same thing over and over again. He shifted his jaw just a bit forward as he worked, and his eyes never left sight of the things his hands were doing. He'd go back to the truck and pick out a tool, return with it, and begin working again in one smooth, fluid movement.

I think he could have done this work while dreaming. Ray was completely at home out here, giving his rapt attention to every last wire. He strung out the barbed wire, nailed it to the wood posts, cut it, and twisted it around until it was tight. Then he cut off the excess wire and tossed the remaining pieces into a pile.

As the day drew on longer, we were able to shed our overcoats. I'd noticed that farmers seemed to always wear long sleeves, even in summer heat. But although it was well into November, the midday warmth was intense enough to make Ray roll up his sleeves and wipe his brow occasionally with the back of his hand. Soon, however, I saw that Ray had been correct in not wanting me to join him. This was the most monotonous work I'd ever seen. How long would it take? I looked down the fence line and saw a rank of posts standing at attention and disappearing in both directions.

After a few hours, I'd had enough. I'd heard that factory work was inherently dull, but at least those workers had comrades with whom to talk. Every day Ray awakened and worked under this same broad stage of unmarked sky. What did he think about all day long as he worked by himself doing the same things repeatedly? What went on in that mind? I sat in the truck and rested my head on the back of the seat. It was oh-so-quiet again, now that the harvest had been completed and the workers had left us. I wondered what Lorelei and Rose were up to on this day.

I hadn't realized I'd drifted off until I heard the truck door close. Ray turned the key and started up the engine.

I rubbed my eyes awake. "What are you doing?"

"Taking you home."

He drove me back, and when we finally arrived at the house, I said, "I'm sorry."

At first he didn't respond, but then he said quietly, "It's no bother." He stretched his arm out on the seat back behind me. "I'll be back again around sunset."

"You had to make a special trip because of me."

But he just shook his head once and wouldn't let me see his eyes.

After trudging up the steps, I stretched out on the bed for a nap and dreamed of past holiday seasons. The candlelight services my father held on Christmas Eve, and the new dresses my mother chose especially for us girls to wear. The huge spreads of food in the fellowship hall, the presents individually chosen and wrapped up by my mother for each of us girls, and finding those gifts on Christmas morning underneath an evergreen tree in our living room.

That evening, the sunset lasted forever. In Denver, the mountains lifted the horizon and shortened the sunsets. But here, every tiny change of fading light could be appreciated. The sinking sun lit up the dust and each hovering cloud with gold and saffron and finally amber hues.

Before dinner, Ray took a longer time than usual praying. Well after I had finished with my blessing, his eyes were still closed and unmoving, his mouth soft. Even his nose looked relaxed, breathing invisibly. After dinner, we listened to Burns and Allen and found their comedy a nice break from the news of the war. Then I asked Ray for a game of rummy. I won the first few games easily, and afterward I started to let up on my strategy, deliberately discarding cards I would've normally kept. And still, I won the game. It took me a few more wins to realize what Ray was doing.

"Ray, you don't have to let me win." I started shuffling the deck for one more game. "I don't have to win every single time. Believe me, I've lost in many things before. It isn't necessary for me to—"

His hand was on mine.

The cards slid out of my hold and onto the table, fanning away. He took my hand off the table and held it in the warm flesh and blood of his palm. I didn't resist his touch, but I didn't return it, either.

My hands. With him, it had also begun with my hands.

It was early June, just weeks after Mother's death. Time mattered little to me. I spent my days on dirty sheets with half-read books stacked on the floor all around me. I was in the midst of a misery that nothing—not reading, talking, sleeping, or eating—

could relieve. By the time I felt able to get up and do something with myself, weeks had passed, and I had missed the deadline to enroll for summer classes.

My friend Dot had saved up her three gallons of gasoline so she could take me out for the first time since the funeral. We shopped, bought the khaki-colored dress for me, then Dot drove us over to the big USO on California Street to take in a show. A comedy troupe was performing for the soldiers, and we could watch the routine just by volunteering to help with refreshments at intermission and by cleaning up at the end of the program. When we arrived, the room that served as auditorium, the same room that sometimes doubled as dance floor, was packed with servicemen in uniform, and all of them, it seemed, smoking cigarettes and talking loudly, enjoying a cup of coffee or a glass of punch. Upon our arrival, many of the men looked our way, and some of them nodded or smiled. Dot was a real looker, not as classically beautiful as my sisters, but even more showy. She could always catch a man's eye.

As soon as the lights dimmed and the show began, Dot and I pulled out folding chairs and sat against the back wall. Everyone needed a laugh to combat the somber news of Allied preparations to invade France, a feat we knew would cost many American lives. So although the program wasn't all that funny, the crowd hollered out, laughed way too loudly, and clapped their approval. At intermission, as I was filling punch cups and serving coffee, I noticed a soldier slowly sidling his way up to Dot. It was always fun to watch Dot put her spell on a lonely guy. But to my surprise, the soldier didn't come up to Dot. Instead, he worked his way up to my side of the table, and as I served him coffee, he said, "You have lovely hands."

I smiled and thanked him, but I still assumed he was just

trying to get closer to Dot. But even after she edged her way into the conversation, he didn't show any interest in her. He kept talking to me.

He wore the silver bars of a first lieutenant, and he had suntanned skin, blond-streaked hair, a broad jaw, and deep-set eyes. The suntan, he told us, came from spending days in the high altitude, training out in the sun and snow up at Camp Hale near Leadville. Part of the Army's Tenth Mountain Division, he was preparing troops for the campaign in Italy, and his name was Edward. We talked all through the intermission, and when the show finally started up again, he invited me, not Dot, down front to sit with him.

Throughout the rest of the show, I couldn't concentrate on the entertainment going on just a few feet before me. Instead, I noticed the way he kept his arms loosely draped across his thighs, and how he laughed—long rolling flaps of laughter coming out of him like birds set free from a cage. After the show ended, he took me out on the sidewalk in the cool air, and we talked again. He had a manner of speaking that was a bit hesitant, as if he waited for just a second to think over his words before he spoke. But he held a gaze with calm confidence and smiled as if he knew it was dazzling.

Outside in the night and alone with him, I felt the intense draw of his looks. I had observed it for years—this power emitted by those with natural beauty. Abby and Bea had had it, even as young girls. But beauty had never before exerted a pull on me. I had always thought I could easily resist handsome looks if ever confronted by them in a man. But as I found out, I was no hardier than others were. I concentrated on keeping my voice steady and unbroken, but with each breath, I felt a crochet hook catching in my chest. Without even realizing it, I had taken another step closer to him. And I smiled, as I hadn't done, since when? Bea's wedding day, perhaps. With Edward, I smiled and laughed until my lips went dry.

When I told him I had been studying history before leaving school for family business, he asked, "And what part of history most interests you?"

"I'm fascinated by Egypt's history. But closer by, I love the history of our own country, especially the West."

"I grew up on a ranch outside of Durango. My brothers and I spent the whole summer exploring the canyons and ravines. We'd find pottery shards and obsidian flints and arrowheads."

"From the Anasazi?"

"Yes." His face broke into a smile. "You know about them?"

I said, "All it took for me was one trip to Mesa Verde. Ever since then, I've been hooked."

"Once my brother and I found an intact Anasazi cooking pot." He gave a short laugh. "We should have held on to it, but we sold it so my brother could buy a car, and now it's on display in a museum somewhere."

"That's not a bad thing." I smiled. "Now many people can enjoy it."

From the doorway, Dot appeared. "We need your help for the cleanup," she called out to me, and for the first time, I saw in her eyes an emotion that wasn't often directed at me. In her eyes, I could see envy.

"They're so small," Ray was saying.

"Yes." My voice cracked like pieces of ancient pottery. "Some people are small."

I looked into Ray's face.

"I was talking about your hands, Livvy. Your hands are so small."

Twenty-one

I pulled my hand away from Ray's, and then I couldn't look at the hurt I had caused him. After silence so heavy I could hear the walls groan, I shoved the cards together, stacked them, and put them away in the cupboard. Back at the table, I sat again. Ray simply sat, too, until the strain of it apparently grew too much for him, and he had to get up and leave the room.

That night, I tried to read in bed, but the words on the printed page kept swirling into leafy patterns before my eyes. This life, this life of isolation and more plants than people, was strangling me. The memories I couldn't bear to relive came to life as the substance of plants and crops living within me, their sharp stems and tangled roots growing and prodding me internally to let them come out.

By the next day, I couldn't stay in the house. I asked Ray to leave me the truck so I could drive over to Camp Amache to visit Rose and Lorelei and take one of those classes in *ikebana* from their mother. Before I left, however, I heard the newscasters on the radio announce the latest travel warnings. The government had decided to ban all holiday travel by civilians because troop movement would be particularly heavy during the coming season. All pleasure travel for Christmas was seriously discouraged. I clicked off the radio and headed on my way.

Forward movement had always set my mind into motion, sometimes against my will. As I drove, again the stems of past memories started spreading and poking their points within me, and I had to force them back into the ground pockets where they belonged. I had to concentrate on my driving. I tried to remember the lyrics to favorite songs, and I sang them aloud, or else I might end up choked by those emerging vines and pushy shoots.

At Camp Amache, the same guard remembered me, welcomed me in, and sent for Lorelei and Rose. When they came walking forward to meet me, Lorelei smiled and embraced me as was typical, but Rose held herself back. Eventually, she greeted me with a hug. But in her eyes I saw tension I'd never seen before, even worse than what I'd seen at the gas station in Swink. She forced a smile. "We've only a few minutes to visit."

I couldn't hide my disappointment. "I thought you two would come along and watch my lesson."

"We're helping in the shop."

Lorelei flicked her hair. "Making posters."

"Ah," I answered.

Camp Amache was home to a large silkscreen shop that produced hundreds of thousands of posters for the Navy. Since the beginning of the war, posters could be seen everywhere, most of them for recruitment and support of our troops, but others encouraging increased factory production and war jobs, even for women. Rosie the Riveter was mythical, but posters had made her famous nonetheless. I was reminded of a poster I'd seen at the train station in La Junta. It read, "Is Your Trip Necessary? Needless Travel Interferes with the War Effort."

Lorelei took my arm. "Pay no attention to Rose. We're so happy to see you." She steered me inside the camp. "At least we can walk you over and chat for a bit."

Rose fell into step with us, but haltingly. "We should return, Lorelei."

The skin on Lorelei's arm flinched. "Don't fret so much," she snapped at her sister. She continued to walk down the dusty row between barracks. "We can take a walk, after all."

Rose and Lorelei had always teased each other and disagreed, but this was different. These were bulleted words, the first truly angry words I'd ever heard from them, and Rose's face was twisted with worry.

I stopped walking. "What is it, Rose?"

Again, she tried to smile. "Nothing," she said. "We should return, that's all."

"You go back, then," said Lorelei. "I'm going to walk with Livvy."

Rose stopped, looked down at her shoes, then turned on a heel and left us.

Lorelei held tighter to my arm and kept us walking. "I warned you once about Rose. Always she must follow the rules."

We passed a group of older men working together. I stopped to look at their handiwork—vases, boxes, and toys made of tiny stones, the same ones that covered miles of open desert beyond the camp. Again they had created works of art out of this empty desert land. It reminded me of fireweed overtaking areas of forest burns, transforming charred wastelands into swaying red seas.

Lorelei urged me onward. "This is a hobby for the Issei." She glanced up at me with a sly smile and kept walking. "I have more important things to ponder."

I squeezed her arm. "Do you have something to tell me?"

Lorelei put a hand on her chest in a dramatic gesture. "I wish I could."

"Of course you can."

Lorelei then slowed her pace. Finally, she stopped walking altogether. She turned to me with a movie star smile and seemed to search for words. As I waited for her to tell me, I noticed a tiny gold chain that hung around her neck, one I'd never seen her wear before. "What's this?" I asked.

Lorelei pulled her collar in tighter around the neck. She lowered her voice. "Rose and I are involved with some men." After looking about, she fished the chain out from its hiding place inside her shirt. Hanging on the chain was a cameo pendant. "One of them gave it to me."

"It's quite lovely."

"It was his mother's."

She tucked the pendant back into her blouse. We locked arms again and strolled behind one of the large barrack buildings. How I missed conversations like this one, chatting on the telephone with my sisters, going to the diner with my girlfriends. This was a bond men couldn't understand, this sharing between women.

"He gave you something that belonged to his mother? You must be very special to him."

"I believe so." She beamed. "He tells me I am."

"Soldiers?" I asked her.

"Yes." She hesitated. "We met them on one of the farms we worked, just after we left your place. They were guarding the German POWs also working there."

I tried to picture their first meeting. Lorelei had probably flirted away shamelessly, while Rose had probably held herself back. Lorelei had most likely picked her man on the spot, whereas Rose had probably spent her time slowly getting to know hers. But even as I tried, I was having a hard time picturing it. The last time I'd passed through La Junta with Rose and Lorelei, they had acted as if the sight of soldiers was near to unbearable. The news of the kamikaze had even caused Lorelei to shy away. But perhaps something special had transpired between these two soldiers and the girls.

"How did you meet?"

Lorelei smiled. "I told you. On one of the farms."

I sounded like a drill sergeant but couldn't stop myself. "Did you get to go out with them?"

Lorelei stopped walking. "Not exactly. But now they're writing little notes to us."

"Love notes?"

"Sort of. But I really can't tell you anything else. It's a secret."

"Why must it be kept a secret?"

She took a deep breath. "It's complicated."

How foolish of me. Of course it would be.

"If I speak more about them, Rose will despise me. Please don't ask me another thing." She hugged my arm and picked up the pace again. "Just know that we are both very happy."

But Rose didn't seem happy.

"And don't worry for us."

"Why should I worry?"

Lorelei laughed. "No more questions, remember?"

I longed to know more, but I wouldn't press her. "Then take me for my lesson."

Before we moved on, Lorelei took me for a peek inside the silkscreen shop, but I didn't spot Rose among the workers. She dropped me off at their quarters before Lorelei said she, too, should return to the shop.

Itsu met me just inside the door. She led me in and began quietly talking as she pulled out two vases, some stems in a box, and an assortment of paper flowers for practicing.

"In *ikebana*, we do not use layer and layer of flowers as American florists do. Instead, we use only a few stems, leaves, and blooms, only as many as it takes to compose, along with the spaces in between, the perfect balance among them all."

She said we would begin with *rikka*, or standing flowers, appropriate for arrangement in bowl-shaped vases. She explained that it took years to perfect any of the styles, and that I would best learn by watching for the first of our lessons. I observed her select one of the vases, then begin to arrange the stems in exact positions using clippers to cut them and crosspieces to secure them. She used a *kenzan*, a holder with many sharp points about a half inch high, to firmly hold the flowers in their places.

As she continued to work, I heard the door open. Lorelei came back into the apartment. Itsu looked up briefly, then continued with our lesson. I looked at Lorelei and shot her a question with my eyes, *What are you doing?* Lorelei quickly got my meaning, but just shrugged, sat down beside me, and pretended to watch her mother. But out of the corner of my eye, I could see her gazing out the window and picking at her nails. Occasionally she would get up from the chair beside me, pace the floor back and forth once, then sit down again.

Now I was having a hard time concentrating, too. What trouble was coming between her and Rose? Why was Rose so tense? And why was Lorelei, who longed for a boyfriend so badly, being so secretive about the one she now had?

When I drove away, it was almost dusk. I looked back at the

camp in my rearview mirror until the dust cloud behind the truck obscured my sight. On the long drive back, once I thought I heard their laughter, in unison, coming from out of the seat cushion beside me. And although the season was long over, once I thought I saw a butterfly floating along the road. As I drew nearer, however, I could see it was only a bit of newspaper picked up by a breeze.

I stopped at the telephone booth in Wilson to call Abby. I wanted to hear her voice, and the question of restricted travel over the holidays was needling me. I wanted to visit my family for the holidays, but I was a patriot, after all. Perhaps Abby could help. As the telephone began to ring, I silently prayed for her to answer. Even before I had left Denver, she had been taking over Mother's charitable projects and could easily have been away, working somewhere in the city. When she picked up, I found myself almost speechless again, just as had happened before with Bea. Abby, my closest sister in age, was also the one whose mood often matched mine.

"Livvy. It's been so long. How are you?" she asked softly.

I put a hand on the spot where the baby had been kicking. I was five months along, over halfway there. "Huge."

She paused. "You couldn't be huge already. You must be exaggerating."

"Somewhat, I suppose."

I could hear Abby let out a low laugh. "I'm trying to picture you."

"Don't."

She laughed again. Then after a moment, she said, "Bea told you about Kent. He leaves next week. He'll be stationed at a military hospital somewhere in France."

"Abby, I'm so sorry."

"He'll be fine." I could feel her change faces right through the receiver. "I know he'll come back to me. Listen," she said. "This could work out well for us."

I had to laugh. "How can anything work out well from this?"

"What's happened? Is something wrong?"

"No, I'm fine."

"Has someone mistreated you?"

"No, Abby. I'm just having a tough time of it these days."

"Listen up, Livvy. When Kent leaves, I'll be living in our house all alone. You could come for the holidays, then simply remain for the rest of your term. It makes perfect sense that you would want to deliver in the city, near your own family."

We were so good at plausible explanations. "I don't know."

"Why?" she asked. "You can't stay out there forever."

I gazed out at the emptiness around me, and for a minute, I remembered the city. Memories of so many things—eating movie house popcorn in paper bags alongside Dot at the theater, being served by white-clad waiters in steak house restaurants, riding the streetcars full of people rushing about on business. I remembered running with my girlfriends, late for class, across parks of grass laid out like green wrapping paper rolled on the floor. And spending hours in the library studying up on all the places full of history that someday I would see in person. Then I looked down at my bulging abdomen. For me, it could never come back to that.

"Have you made many friends?" Abby was asking.

"Not many," I answered, thinking only of Rose and Lorelei. "But Ray and his family. They're so kind to me, Abby. I don't know if I can do it."

"Do what?" Abby sounded pained. "You don't mean you could stay out there, do you? Look . . ." She stopped. "You're having a spell of trouble, bad luck, really bad luck, but you don't have to ruin your entire life because of it. I have another idea. After the baby comes, if you want to go back to school, I'll baby-sit for you."

When I didn't respond, she went on. "You were so close to finishing your education. You must complete that master's degree. Then after that, you can do anything you want." She paused. "Well, maybe not the travel, but certainly you could teach. Listen to me. No one deserves to stay married to someone they don't love. Especially not you."

I gazed at Ray's truck sitting just a few feet beyond the telephone booth. How confusing it had all turned out to be. Now all our lives were linked and twisted together like that brush I had found caught in the bend of the creekbed. In one telephone conversation, I could never explain it to anyone, not even to Abby. That Ray was a simple and good man, that he had married out of loneliness, but now he loved. That he had married, as most people did, for life.

"How is Father?"

"He's fine. Pouring himself into church work so he doesn't miss Mother so much."

"And you?"

"I'm not so different from him, I suppose. I've been filling in for her. It makes me feel as if I'm doing something to carry on her legacy."

I summoned up some courage. "Does Father ever ask about me?"

She hesitated before answering. "Yes. He asks about you often."

But I could tell by something in her voice. She was lying.

Twenty-two

On the morning that Edward first called me, Father was already away from the house. Sleeping in late was a bad habit I had formed from idleness in the weeks since Mother's death. When I heard the telephone, I bounced out of bed, raced down the steps, nearly tripping over my nightgown in the process. When I reached the telephone, I grabbed the receiver and gasped "Hello" into it.

He wanted to meet me downtown, so I dressed in my favorite dress, spent a ridiculous amount of time styling my hair, then I took the streetcar down to the shopping district. He was waiting for me outside the five-and-dime, and when he saw me, he straightened up, stamped out his cigarette on the sidewalk, and took me inside for lunch at the snack counter.

We sat across from each other at the booth. For a few minutes, I couldn't think of anything to say, but strangely, the lack of conversation didn't seem to disturb him, and therefore it didn't disturb me, either. Instead, I studied his face, the smooth skin across his forehead, the barely discernible shadow line where beard would begin had he not shaved, a gleaming set of teeth. As he placed his order with the waitress, I noticed the way his smile rose just a tiny bit higher on the right side of his face.

Every time I found myself looking too closely at him or gazing for too long a period of time, I turned my eyes down into my plate and kept on eating, amazed that I could eat at all.

He fell into talking about himself. "When I was about twelve, my folks sold the ranch outside of Durango. They bought a hotel in Estes Park that they still operate to this day." He told me about the famous people who had visited their hotel, including governmental leaders, baseball players, and even a few actors and actresses out of Hollywood.

"Will you return to Estes Park after the war?" I asked.

"I think not." He crossed his arms into his lap after he finished eating. "I have other plans. I want to strike out on my own, make something new happen with my own ideas."

"That's exactly the way I feel, too." Then I told him about my particular interests in Egypt, about Akh-en-aten, his wife Nefertiti, and their six daughters.

Later, we rode the streetcar to the Museum of Natural History, where we walked through the exhibits. At each one, we paused to study the display and read the information. And at each one, we finished and turned to walk away at exactly the same moment. As we strolled about, he rested his hand on the small of my back and guided me through the doorways and up the stairs between floors. And something about that light touch on the back of my dress filled me with a body of pride I'd never felt before. We ended up riding the streetcar to Civic Center Park, where we spent the rest of the day talking and meandering about. Everywhere lilies were blooming. Lilies, the flower of weddings.

Even as the afternoon sun began to sink down low in the sky, we remained together. He told me that his infantry division, at

Camp Hale high in the mountains, was in survival training for the coldest of temperatures and the harshest of conditions. They were honing their mountaineering and skiing skills in preparation for secret campaigns against the Germans, for war in Southern Europe.

He stopped. "The land up there." He gestured west, toward the mountains. "It's the best terrain for skiing any of us has ever seen. When this war is over, some of us plan to come back."

In many regards, he was much like the other soldiers I'd met. Mostly they were lonely; they wanted a friend, a dance partner, someone to listen to their dreams and plans, someone to care if they came back dead or alive. Most of them were small-town boys away from home for the first time. They all had ideas and hopes for the future that they wanted to share with someone. But there the similarities ended; everything else about Edward was different. The confidence in his smile, the way he hung his hands easily and relaxed at his sides, the way he moved in closer as he spoke to me. That smile that pulled me in like ice cream melting down a cone.

I wanted to know everything about him, all the minute details of his past, his present-day thoughts and dreams, and everything that had come in between. Had he had many girlfriends?

As we walked onward, he continued to think out loud to me. "We'll come back here and buy up the property, develop the ski runs, and construct a base lodge, build places for equipment and restaurants. We'll turn it into a resort for skiing. Have you ever tried it?"

"Yes," I answered. "I can make my way down the mountain, although not with much finesse. I fall into the snow more often than I care to remember."

"But you get back up," he said.

"Yes, sometimes I have to force myself, but I do try again."

He took my hand then. He entwined each of his wide fingers between each of mine, and he looked at me with such intensity I had to turn away. And later, when we parted, when he raised my face up to his, I couldn't look at him then, either. I felt the soft warmth of lips upon mine, and that was all. I fell into a cave of stillness, and for that brief moment, nothing else on earth mattered. Not the war. For the moment, even my mother's death feathered away.

A woman shoved me aside. She knocked me away from Edward's lips and out of my daze. I said goodbye to Edward, turned away, and mounted the steps to the streetcar. But as it pulled away, clanging up the curving street, I watched him until he disappeared from my sight. He hadn't moved, and I touched my lips. It had been the best day, the perfect day, even better than dreaming, because it had been real.

That night, I tried listening to the radio but soon clicked it off. A book on Pueblo Indian religion that had earlier held my fascination could no longer hold me still. I couldn't read about others' lives when my own life had taken such an unexpected turn, when my own life held more promise than anything to be found on mere paper. I was experiencing the mixture of emotions others in love had felt for centuries. I had moments of fear, then reservation, and finally a sudden thrill knocked all the rest away until the cycle started over again. At night, I tossed and turned until I worked the sheets off the corners of my mattress. At home and by myself, I turned the radio volume high and danced with an imaginary Edward, and other times, I walked around with china plates balanced on the palms of my hands.

Twenty-three

*T*he night after I'd spent another full day at Camp Amache, Ray came up beside me as I was washing the dinner dishes. I was tired. At the camp, I'd stood on my feet watching Rose help out in one of the junior high school English classes. She was so proud to finally be able to teach English, as had always been her dream. For two hours, I had listened and watched as she taught a segment on grammar and then led her pupils through an exercise. I was hoping she'd have time to break away and talk to me, to tell me what she had been so worried about the last time I'd seen her. But she was so enjoying herself, proud of every rule of grammar she knew so well. I didn't want to ruin her day, and besides, she never left the classroom anyway. Later I'd found Itsu, who taught me another lesson in *ikebana*.

Ray searched out a cup towel and started drying off the dishes one by one. I knew he wanted to speak to me about something that was bothering him, so I waited until he built up the words to say it.

"You were gone a long time today."

"I'm learning how to arrange flowers, Japanese-style."

"What for?"

I smiled. "Just to learn something new."

He looked back at the plate he was drying. "I still don't know why."

"Ray, I like to do new things, to go to different places."

"So you were at the camp all day?"

"Yes."

He looked damaged.

I turned off the faucet. "Ray, there isn't enough for me to do around here." I sighed. "No, that's not exactly true. I'm sure other farm wives are very busy. I just don't know what else to do, how to help around here. At the camp, it seems there's so much going on, and I'm learning new things. It makes me feel useful again."

"You're useful here."

I turned back to the sink, wiped a circle of suds around on a plate, rinsed it, and passed it over to Ray. "Not very."

He dried the plate. "You could do more on the farm."

"Like what?"

He waited for a minute. "Let me think on it a bit."

By the next morning, he had come up with something. Ray found me on the porch, where I was standing around sipping on my coffee. "Come along with me today," he said.

"For what?"

"I got to get the dead branches that's come off the elm trees."

"Am I helping?"

He nodded, and a few minutes later we were heading out in the truck, driving toward the tall elm trees, now standing silently, bare branches making a spiderweb against the sky. At the grove, we piled out of the truck. Since the last snowfall, the ground and everything above it had dried out during sunny afternoons. The land was again spiked with crackling weeds, and the dead leaves beneath our feet were as stiff as hairbrush bristles, snapping as we walked over them. Ray retrieved a large handsaw from the truck bed, walked to the trees, then started lifting dead branches off the ground and sawing off smaller limbs so he could fit them into the bed of the truck.

Ray told me I could pick up the smaller branches and stems and carry them to the truck. And even though my abdomen now stuck out before me as a hard mound, I could still easily enough reach over and pick up small tree limbs off the ground. As I gathered and carried my collected stacks back to the truck, I felt my heart and breathing speed up a bit, felt the brisk air down deep inside my lungs. Ray and I piled the bed high, and when it was full, we took a load back toward the house, where we stored the wood in a stack Ray would later burn for mulch. We made several trips back and forth from the woodpile to the elm grove. The sun traveled overhead across cloudless blue sky without a hint of wind.

Moving about and working alongside Ray felt much as it had felt to work outside in the garden with my mother. After a few hours, the ground between trees was no longer tangled with branches, but instead was a dry carpet of curling leaves. These we raked up and pitched into the truck bed, too, as Ray said they posed a fire hazard. To my amazement, I found that close to the ground, having been sheltered by the layer of leaves, some patches of green grass still grew. After we finished, Ray parked the truck back out in the sunlight at the edge of the grove, facing it. I rolled down my window and breathed in the smells of fall, the crispness in the air, sweet as cider on your tongue.

"This was a great idea, Ray."

"Thought you might like it."

"But why is the grove so far from the house?"

"My grandfather started this orchard. I don't rightly know for sure why he put it so far away, but probably this was the worst soil he could find. Once you figure out the right trees, you can plant a grove like this one on the poorest soil of the farm, in land that isn't good for anything else."

"Now it's lovely."

"Thanks."

"And thank you for bringing me here and letting me help."

"You're sure welcome."

The next day, I wanted to catch up with Abby or Bea, but when I drove to the pay telephone in Wilson, I kept on driving past it. I went to Camp Amache instead, uninvited, yet Rose and Lorelei looked pleased to see me. They were working again in the silkscreen shop, however, and therefore I spent more time with Itsu learning to arrange flowers than I spent with either of them. They did manage to get away for lunch, which we ate together in the mess hall. It was typical mass-produced food, not even as good as the stuff that had been served in the hospital cafeteria the last time Mother was kept as an inpatient, and not nearly as good as the food served on campus.

I remembered the last time I'd seen them together, the tension between them, and Rose's worried face. Even though they seemed better now, I wanted to ask Lorelei about it, to reassure myself that whatever the trouble was, it was over. I wanted to know what was happening between her and Rose and the men with whom they'd been corresponding. If only I could get her off to herself, Lorelei would talk to me, I knew it. Instead, Itsu and Masaji joined us at the table, so we couldn't talk about anything personal for the rest of the meal.

I ate quickly and hoped Rose and Lorelei would, too. Then I followed them out. We walked full face into a wind blowing cold air straight through our clothes. Their short hair was whipping about their heads like ribbons caught in a fan. Rose wrapped herself in her sweater and hugged her arms around her body as she ducked into the door of their quarters. Rose's ability to read ideas off my face continued to amaze me. Lorelei and I followed her through the door.

We stood inside, rubbing our hands together and shivering.

Lorelei fluffed her hair with her fingers. "It's dreadful out there."

Rose checked her watch. "We've only a few minutes left."

I was still shaking despite the relative warmth inside their room. "I just want to know." I looked directly at Lorelei. "Is everything okay?"

"Yes." She beamed.

"Between you and the soldiers?"

Rose and Lorelei smiled at each other and then at me. "We're happy," said Lorelei.

But how serious were these relationships? I almost asked. But then I could see it, clearly. Just as long ago I'd seen Ray's love for me, even when he still didn't want me to, I could see theirs. People in love, especially a new love, have a certain look—of pain and joy all wrapped up in one inexplicable yearning few find in return. In both of their eyes I saw that restlessness, that vulnerable energy that could be nothing other than an early love. They smiled and laughed so easily. The world seemed so obvious; the future alive on their faces. But they also looked to me like delicate flowers that could so easily be crushed. Rose and Lorelei reminded me of the way I'd felt while I was seeing Edward, full of all those emotions that are fresh and exhilarating in one minute, intense and frightening the next.

Lorelei fingered something underneath her clothing. The cameo, of course.

Rose looked at the wall as if it weren't there, as if instead it were a face she loved, one that could be seen only by her mind's eye.

"Do you meet them?"

Rose answered, "We're writing to them, and occasionally they're able to call."

They looked at each other and smiled as though remembering.

"Do your parents know?"

Their faces fell at exactly the same moment, just after the words came out of my mouth.

"No," Lorelei said swiftly.

Of course not. Had I told Father about Edward?

Lorelei said, "They would never approve. Back in Long Beach, we weren't even allowed to date yet."

Rose said, "Our parents might not understand."

"Might not?" said Lorelei. "They never would."

Rose sighed. "But even if they did, our grandparents wouldn't. They would never approve of any men unlike us. Not only must our suitors be of Japanese descent, but from similar families, too."

Of course, I said to myself again. Then I realized something else, too. I couldn't save them from whatever was going to happen, good or bad. They were trying to find some joy despite their terrible circumstances in this camp. Just a bit of some happiness. They were taking a chance, and I could only hope they realized the risks. Yet how it worked out in the end, no one could know.

Twenty-four

≈≈≈≈≈≈

*I*n the mailbox down at the county road turnoff Ray and I picked up our contact with the outside world. The next day when I was making the retrieval, I found a card from the library in La Junta, notifying Ray that he had an overdue book and asking him to return it. I puzzled over that card. I had been the one checking out library books, not Ray. To my knowledge, he hadn't even gone inside any library doors since my arrival. I turned the card over again and verified that it was indeed addressed to him and not to me.

Turning books in on time had always been a priority to me. What could Ray have possibly checked out? Only rarely did he read the newspaper. And then he spread the pages all over the house and left them for days at a time. He caught up with current events by radio, but he usually spent the rest of his time at home working on farm paperwork and not reading at all.

I drove back to the house with the card and the rest of the mail sliding around on the seat beside me. When I arrived, Ray was nowhere to be seen. It always amazed me the distances he could get away from the house on foot or by tractor. I might not see him until dark, so I decided to check his room.

I found nothing beside his bed. I lifted the pillow and checked the crack between bed and wall. Then I ducked into the bunk and sat, thinking. Next, I looked under the bed and from there, I pulled it out. The cover was unmarked; no title on the spine, either. I opened the book and saw diagrams of pregnant women and stages of fetal development.

Now I slammed it shut. I could feel heat creeping up into my neck.

Why was he reading this? I didn't expect anything of him. I stood and faced his chest of drawers. Not since the first morning after my arrival had I considered looking in it. Every few days I brought in Ray's fresh laundry, but I always left the folded clothes on the chest top for him to put away.

Now I strode right up to the chest of drawers and opened the top one. Underwear and socks. In the next drawer, undershirts and handkerchiefs. Continuing to search downward, I found nothing but personal articles of clothing, and in the bottom drawer, letters from his brother Daniel, but I wouldn't stoop so low as to read them. On top of the letters lay a man's gold pocket watch, one I guessed had probably belonged to his father. So this was what I had heard ticking on my first morning in this house.

Now the watch lay silent. I picked it up and wound it until the ticking resumed. But why had I heard it ticking on that first morning? I'd never even seen Ray wear this watch, not even for church. After I put it back and closed the drawer, I picked up the pregnancy book, marched back into the kitchen, all the while chastising my own behavior. What had I expected to find in Ray's drawers? Evidence of secrets? I had been foolish. Mother had once told me that every person had a secret compartment within himself or herself, a locked door. But Ray was exactly the way he appeared to be, nothing more and nothing less.

I let the book drop on the table with a thump. When Ray finally came in that night, he glanced at it, went to the bunkroom to change clothes, then came back to the kitchen without acknowledging that the thing existed. I found his eyes. In them, I saw those same held-back tears he would never cry, and I found I'd lost hold of my anger. As he stood at the sink, shoving up his sleeves and washing his hands, I had the strangest of thoughts. I wondered how large was the circle of his arms, if ever I found myself in it.

"I have to tell you something, Ray," I said. "I looked in your drawers today. I can't even explain to you why I did it. I invaded your privacy, and I'm sorry."

He turned away from the sink and dried his hands. That familiar line sank down into the center of his forehead. "You could've looked in there anytime you wanted. I got nothing to hide from you."

I swallowed hard. "It's a beautiful watch. Did it belong to your father?"

He nodded.

"I heard it ticking once. On my first morning here."

Ray sat down and rubbed the red thorns in his eyes. "Sometimes I wind it up. When I want to remember him."

I peered into his face. "And on that morning?"

He cleared his throat. "I remembered how good he was to my mother. The kind of husband I want to be." He sat back and smiled through suffering eyes. He looked off then, as if remembering. "He took care of himself. When he spilled his coffee, he never waited for her to clean it up. And he'd pick her whole bunches of wildflowers, and she'd keep them in water until they got to dropping their dead petals on the table." He turned to me. "That first morning you were here, I wound up that watch." He shrugged. "For no good reason. Just for luck."

Ray got up again, put his coat back on, and headed toward the door.

"You haven't eaten," I callēd out to him before he could leave.

He stopped and turned in my direction. Then he moved one step closer and took my arm. He was so close I could see the threads in his shirt collar and every line in his lips. He took my face in one hand and moved closer still. Then he pressed soft, closed lips into mine in a way so awkward, but so sweet, it glued my shoes to the floor.

"Is there anything you like about me, Livvy?"

Now my lungs caved in. I could smell my attempt at Italian lasagna burning in the oven, and Ray had just kissed me. The book about pregnancy was sitting on the table, and Ray was standing over me demanding an answer.

I had enjoyed the day of fishing. I had taken some pleasure in watching him work. I remembered the gentle way he held that fish in the water, the way he lost himself in prayer. His faith in God's will made him more of a true believer than even those deacons in my father's church. I even appreciated that he had checked out a book, any book. But I couldn't give him false hopes that I'd grow to love him as a husband. I thought we had entered this arrangement for the convenience of us both, not expecting love.

"I never meant to hurt you," I began.

But he turned and walked out the door before I could finish what I had to say.

Twenty-five

⁙

he third time I saw Edward, it was only days after D-Day during the ongoing Allied invasion of Normandy. He had managed to get leave from his base, and at first chance, had called me to meet him. We met again outside the five-and-dime, then we went for lunch at an old saloon-turned-steak-house, where the owner walked around and talked to customers weighted down with a holster belt and a six-shooter. On the walls were hundreds of animal heads, spoils from the chase. After eating, we walked along the path that followed the Platte River. Some of the Canada geese were already returning to build their nests there, and the river ran full to its brim with early summer runoff.

Edward most enjoyed talking of his plans. "I learned more from watching my parents operate a business than from anything else," he said. He smiled in that way I now imagined whenever I closed my eyes. "But the degree I earned will help to open opportunity." He gazed up and down the river. "My resort will be the finest and most efficiently run."

"Would your parents help you get started?" I asked him.

"They would." He glanced my way. "But I won't ask them." He reached down to pull a blade of grass. "I want to take on the risk, no one else."

"You'll start small, then?"

He nodded. "We'll start with a T-bar." He looked to see if I understood. When I nodded, he continued, "They're far superior to a rope tow. Then we'll need to buy rental skis and some equipment to groom the snow, but after that, we could go ahead and open."

He held that blade of grass in his fingers like it was a stem of crystal. "As the years go by and we start to pull in a profit, we'll invest in further improvements, such as a base lodge, a hotel, a restaurant."

I pictured a modern resort for skiing high in the mountains and being there with Edward. I saw myself gliding down the slopes alongside him during the day, cuddling together in warm sweaters before a fire at night. "It sounds wonderful, Edward."

He stopped walking and turned to me. "If I make it back."

But I couldn't allow myself to think about that.

Along the riverbank, purple lupine and white candytuft grew up through the soil. "I heard something on the radio this morning," I said. "Our troops in France have started moving inland, and they've found fields spread far and wide with red poppies waiting for them."

He moved closer and touched my face. "That proves it, then. Even in these tough times, it's possible to find something good."

I closed my eyes.

"Look at us," he whispered, "I'm shipping out soon, but I've found someone to love."

I could look at him now. "Maybe the war will end before you have to go."

"No," he said softly. "I'll go. I'll do my part."

"Europe is lost to the Nazis."

"Shhh," he said, putting a finger to my lips. "Don't even talk about that. Let's just make the most of this time we have left together."

He took me for dining and dancing at the Brown Palace, and I do believe he spent all the money he carried in his wallet. When he first took me out to the dance floor, I was so nervous with anticipation of his arms around me that I tripped over his shoes and half stumbled into the center of the dance area. Surely I would die from embarrassment. And surely he'd never been with someone as clumsy as me before. But to my surprise, I found Edward grinning at me, not in a mocking way, but in a way that was nice.

And when he slipped his arms about my waist, I found myself no longer nervous. Instead, waters of calm and confidence came coursing through me. My feet were fluid on the dance floor. Not much later, that newfound sense of pride visited me again, and I danced high in Edward's arms, a sailing ship rising high out of the waves. If only my sisters could see me now. And wouldn't Mother, too, have been proud? Not to speak of Aunt Eloise and Aunt Pearl. There I was, floating over the dance floor in the arms of a handsome man. Me, Livvy.

After we grew tired of dancing, he took me to a bar. We sat leaning close to each other on our barstools in a place that played jazz, where hazy cigarette smoke drifted in the air, and where laughter became contagious. Nearby, the bartender splashed honey-hued liquor over ice cubes in small glasses, pouring with both hands at once to keep up with orders.

I cupped a hand to my face and said over the sound of the music and the other voices, "I've never been to one of these places before."

He cocked his head my way. "Why is that?"

I shrugged. "My father is a minister. He doesn't believe in alcohol."

A look of reservation came over Edward's face.

"It's okay. I've always made my own decisions, and I want to try it."

He thought for a minute, then seemed to relax again. "Better start off easy, then. Try orange juice and gin. It's a fairly mild one."

Edward drank heartily and with confidence, downing two small tumblers of whiskey while I sipped on my drink. I found it not bad at all—orange juice with an aftertaste of white fire. He hummed along with the music and occasionally glanced over at me with a smile. The bartender served me just as he did everyone else, without a falter. I must have looked as if I belonged, and when I finished the first drink, Edward ordered me another.

I thought the alcohol was having no effect on me until I rose to leave. Then I found myself woozy on my feet as Edward steered me outside into the cool night air. I walked onward, but I could have sworn my legs had been sliced away at the thigh. I put one foot before the other, but it seemed to be happening by some other's will, not my own.

I would have followed him anywhere he wished to take me.

Even now, however, I don't use the alcohol as an excuse for what I later did. I went to his room willingly. My body was reacting quickly, instinctively, subliminally, before rational thought had a chance to compete in the race. I fell so deeply in love that night, and since I had so little to give, I gave it all.

He didn't seem to mind my inexperience. In a hotel room lit by a yellow light, he undressed me tenderly. The act itself began painfully, and at first I found his weight on me a bit frightening, but I loved it anyway. I took in every thrust of the way he desired me so. How hungry and desperate he seemed to be for my body, and how new and unexpected it all was—the feeling of our chests pressed together, sounds that came involuntarily from the back of his throat, the happy exhaustion that came after. Never had I felt wanted in this way, never had I felt the power a woman possesses to give a man pleasure.

Afterward, we lay together on top of the covers. Murmuring words of love, he kissed my neck and face and nose and ears, and of course my lips, too many times to recall. His touch on my skin was eloquent; he wrote words on my body never uttered before. And when he entered me again, this time his love was given slowly. After long moments with my eyes sealed shut, I opened them to look at the molding on the ceiling, breathe in the damp air of his neck, and remind myself that this was actually happening to me.

In the early hours of morning, I slipped back into my father's house, praying that he would not be up waiting for me. But instead I found that I probably could have remained out the entire night, could have spent even more time in Edward's arms. Father was sleeping soundly in his room, his snores so loud that I could hear them in the hallway as I tiptoed by.

In only a few hours, Edward would be arriving alone at the bus station to return to Camp Hale. I had wanted badly to see him off, but he had insisted that our last memories come from our night together, in the yellow-lit hotel room, that he would take that memory away with him instead of one of us having to say goodbye.

"Don't be sad. And don't worry for me," he had said as he kissed my face for the last time outside of the hotel.

"When will I see you again?"

He kissed me again. "A soldier never knows."

"But you can let me know. Keep in touch with letters."

He smiled and smoothed back my hair on either side of my face. "I'm not much of a writer, but for you, I'll make an exception."

"Oh, please do," I said and clung to his shoulders. "Write to me every day."

He kissed me for the last time, then took a step away. "For the next few weeks, we'll be in the last of our backcountry training. But as soon as I get back to base, before I ship out, I'll write. Okay?"

At the breakfast table the following morning, Father ripped off his glasses and stared me down over the top of his newspaper. "Olivia. What has gotten into you?" he demanded.

I shook myself. In front of me, I held a large spoonful of oatmeal. I had no idea how long the spoon had been hanging up there in the air, dripping globs of oatmeal onto a lace tablecloth that had been Mother's favorite.

I laughed at myself and set the spoon down in my bowl. "Just daydreaming, I guess."

Father grumbled as he turned back to his newspaper. "Daydreaming? Folly for Abigail and Beatrice. But never before for you."

I laughed again. Yes, how dull my days had been before this joyous creature had come to sit beside me, to ride with me. "True enough, Father. Never before for me."

Twenty-six

꩜

he night after Ray kissed me found me rolling and turning in bed like potatoes boiling in water, and I slept little. I tried flicking on the light and reading but couldn't
keep my eyes focused on the page. I kept thinking about leaving
the farm, going back and finishing my graduate work, as Abby
had suggested.

As a divorced woman with a baby, I wouldn't be allowed on an
expedition to Egypt, but probably I could teach at any of several
colleges. And maybe I could work at an excavation site nearby.
I'd once visited the center of the world of the Anasazi, Chaco
Canyon, and found it magnificent. Much work still needed to be
done there. Or I could take the baby and work at Mesa Verde.
Those Indians who lived on and around Mesa Verde had been
Colorado's first farmers. And perhaps I'd feel closer to Edward
there. I remembered the first time he and I had talked out on the
sidewalk in front of the USO, and how he had smiled when he
realized we shared an interest in the Anasazi. Edward had smiled,
that crooked smile.

But now I lay still. Which side rose up higher? Already I was forgetting his face. The father of my unborn child. I'd never had a chance to take a snapshot of him, so it would be up to me to remember. I closed my eyes and tried to picture sitting across from him at the snack counter in the bright artificial light. I took myself back to those precious hours when his face lingered just above mine, kissing me. But still, hard as I tried to recall, I couldn't remember the details. The memory of his face was starting to fade away from me. Instead, I kept seeing Ray's face, demanding an answer.

Is there anything you like about me, Livvy?

I made mental lists of Ray's faults, so I wouldn't forget. He had few interests beyond this farm and no good friends beyond his family. He was inexperienced, but his lack of exposure to women didn't bother me as much as his lack of interest in the larger world. He was prejudiced or ignorant; either way, he didn't see people like Rose and Lorelei as true Americans.

The next evening, I drove over to the camp again. Rose and Lorelei had invited me to help chaperone a high school dance in the mess hall, a themed "barn dance," and to bring some bales of hay out with me to be used for decoration. I arrived in time to help move tables and chairs out of the way after dinner, then we decorated the room with the bales of hay I'd brought out, some pumpkins and gourds and Indian corn, and finally with orange, red, and yellow crepe paper and balloons.

I was surprised to find that the tension between Rose and Lorelei had returned. They had dressed for the dance—Lorelei in denims cut off just below her knees and Rose in men's overalls over a plaid shirt. But they seemed uncomfortable every time they moved near each other, and therefore we worked together in silence until the dance began. When the music started, we sat in chairs pushed up against the wall and tapped our toes to the beat of the four-boy band, named the Jive Bombers. The mess hall soon filled with high school boys and girls all dressed in their cotton shirts and rolled-up jeans, some of them wearing straw hats and freckles painted on their cheeks. The musicians were quite good. After we had listened and watched for an hour or so, Rose and Lorelei looked more relaxed. Lorelei looked over at Rose and me. "Come on," she said. "We can't just sit here listening all night. Let's try some steps."

At first Rose and I didn't move. Then Lorelei looked at me again, pleadingly. When I told her I knew how to do the jitterbug, Lorelei sprang off the chair. "Oh, please show us," she pleaded.

Rose jumped to her feet, too.

"This should be interesting." I half laughed. "I feel much too heavy for dancing."

Even Rose was begging me now. "Oh, come on. Please try."

I pushed to my feet and we danced together, the three of us. We practiced the fast steps and swings, bops and twists, taking turns in the lead. I stood back as Rose swung Lorelei behind her back, and Lorelei slid Rose in between her legs. Dust came puffing out of the wood floor beneath our feet. I found myself laughing and saw them smile and laugh, too. I hoped things would be better between the girls after this. When we finished trying some Lindy Hop steps, they were panting and brushing the hair off their foreheads. And when they smiled at each other again, I laughed like no war ever existed.

It made me remember past New Year's Eve parties. Our family had listened to the countdown in Times Square on the radio, passing the time by dancing to all the previous year's best tunes. Mother would let us girls sip apple juice out of wineglasses and pretend to be grown-ups. It was the only time we were allowed to stay up until midnight. And how my mother could sing. She never played the piano or organ, musical skills almost expected of a minister's wife, but she could sing along with the music so well, it would be hard to distinguish her voice from that of the professional. Father was usually in one of his better moods for this occasion, and always he took turns with each of us girls, letting us dance on the toes of his polished shoes, moving us about in the dance steps that Mother said once he had practiced with her for hours. I remembered how Abby, Bea, and I would fight for our turns, and how sophisticated I felt swaying about in his arms.

After the dance ended, I couldn't face driving back alone to the farm, not yet. The girls and I found the Umahara quarters empty, and there we sprawled out together across one of the lower beds. I flipped through the butterfly notebook, the same one they'd carried with them when we had taken our drives during the harvest. Rose stretched out beside me and glanced over at the butterfly drawings before me. She pushed the curls away from her forehead. "If you could be a butterfly, what kind would you be?"

I turned another page. "Oh, probably one with very large, false eyes."

Rose looked me over and shifted forward on the bed so her face was close. In a whisper, she asked, "Livvy, why would you say that?"

I still don't know why I told them. It was unplanned, escaped from me before I knew it. "The baby isn't Ray's."

Lorelei was right beside me now, too. She and Rose looked helpless, confused.

"I got in trouble. My father arranged this marriage."

Now they looked wounded.

Rose waited for a moment, then said, "You don't love him. Your husband."

I shook my head.

Lorelei barely nodded, then breathed out her words. "You married him for the honor of your family."

I took in a deep breath, trying to get the weight to lift off my chest. "Yes. I guess so."

I looked back at the butterfly drawings Rose had long ago sketched in the book.

"It shouldn't have happened to you," said Lorelei, a bit louder now.

"I caused it."

When I looked at her, I saw tears in the hollows of Lorelei's beautiful, almond-shaped eyes. I couldn't believe it. Lorelei, tough Lorelei. Now I was consoling her. "It's okay," I whispered.

"No, it isn't," Lorelei said and wiped her tears away. "It isn't fair." Then she met my gaze. "But no one ever said that life was fair."

Of course it wasn't. My penance could have been avoided, but what had happened to them, having to live away in this camp, had nothing to do with them personally. My mistake was about as personal as one could get. They had done nothing wrong, yet they were receiving the worst punishment.

Rose spoke up softly beside me. "It's how you handle the unfairness of life—that's what matters most, I think."

I pictured the rock gardens, the vases made of tiny desert stones, the majorette uniforms. In this city of imprisonment, I had seen faith and optimism, strength and fortitude in the face of adversity. Resilience. I could only hope to grow in that direction.

Lorelei added, "And the bolder you handle it, the better."

"No, Lorelei," Rose said quietly.

They were silent. I had to ask them then, "What's happening between you two? Please tell me."

Rose began, "It's the men we've met."

"Rose, don't," Lorelei said between clenched teeth. They continued to stare at each other.

"Have you seen them again? Is there a problem?"

The sisters glared at each other. "We haven't seen them since the harvest ended, but they call us now. Almost every day."

"Isn't that good? I mean, if you care for them, it's good, isn't it?"

Rose finally had to look away from her sister. Lorelei answered me while still looking at Rose. "We do care for them. We just haven't had the chance to get to know them well enough."

"What do you know of them?"

Lorelei shrugged. "We're learning more and more as we continue to talk." She tried to smile and turned to me. "We discuss important things, just as we do with you, Livvy. They're still working, guarding the POWs who remain at the Rocky Ford fairgrounds. They have no means to come and see us, and before long, they'll be returning to Camp Trinidad, where they'll be even farther away. I'm afraid we won't get to see them again."

"I could drive you over if you like."

Lorelei said, "We couldn't impose."

"It's no imposition, really. I'm always ready and willing to leave the farm. Just let me know when you'd like to go."

"Really?" asked Lorelei.

"Of course."

At that moment, Itsu and Masaji came in, ending our conversation.

"I should leave," I told them and rose from the bed, gathered my purse, and said goodbye to them all. Itsu held on to Lorelei as I headed for the door, so it was Rose who walked me out on that night. We walked down the dark passageways between barracks, in and out of elongated rectangles of light streaming out of the windows, arms made of nothing substantial, arms stretched out of shadows. Rose walked me past the gate and all the way to the truck.

Before I opened the truck door, she touched my sleeve again. "Lorelei seems so strong, so sure of herself."

"She is strong."

Rose shook her head. "That's what everyone thinks. But she's the one who cries at night."

"Oh, Rose."

She hugged me then.

I said, "I'm sorry." Again those useless words.

She released me and stood before me, holding my arms. "Do you remember earlier when I asked you what butterfly you would be?"

I nodded.

"When you said one with large false eyes, something else came to my mind. About Lorelei. Now I see her as a very old butterfly, one who is trying so hard to keep flying and still losing her colors anyway."

In my mind's eye, the vision came easily. I also could see Lorelei's wings flapping in a desperate attempt for acceptance and love, and all the while losing the substance of her own being in the process. Without my studies, without my plans for travel and learning in other parts of the world, I, too, had lost pieces of myself.

"I'm worried about her, Livvy. The things she wants to do . . ."

"What things?"

Rose's eyebrows came together. "It's the soldiers' ideas."

"What ideas?"

"They're pressuring us."

"To do what?"

Rose looked down at her feet and shook her head slowly.

"You can tell me." But as I waited for her to answer, my back began to ache. I placed my palms against the lower half of my spine and began rubbing.

Rose looked at me, then back inside the camp. "I don't know."

And still she didn't tell me.

I should have probed harder, waited longer. Instead I said, "Don't worry. Lorelei is stronger than you think, and so are you. You'll both get through this. I know it." After all, they were both making the best of a situation that was much worse than mine.

Now Rose took a step backward.

"Send for me. Anytime you want to go anywhere or do anything. Promise?"

Rose nodded. "We will."

Then I drove off, leaving her standing there, surrounded by the dust stirred up by the truck's old tires.

Twenty-seven

~~~

inter came in its completeness. Even in the middle of the days bright with sunlight, the temperature barely hovered above freezing. Crumbling, ridged snow sleeves, built up by the plows, closed in the road leading to the farm.

On Thanksgiving Day, I had to force myself up after only a few hours of sleep. In the kitchen, I listened to mixed news on the radio. Despite American victories, the costs continued to be so high it was difficult to listen. Battles in the South Pacific continued to rage, with huge numbers of casualties. Kamikaze pilots continued to dive-bomb our ships, but by all accounts, the Allies were winning; victory would come.

Ray and I had planned a full day of events. First we would drive out to Camp Amache to visit Rose and Lorelei, and later we'd head back to Martha's for a family meal. For several days before, I had been experimenting with baking and preparing side dishes. I tried the simplest of pies—custard and pumpkin—and left the fruit and meringue concoctions up to Martha, who was also in charge of the turkey and dressing. Early in the morning,

Ray and I stacked the casserole dishes and pie plates on the seat of the truck between us and set out on our way.

We met Rose and Lorelei outside the camp's dining hall. Bundled up in their coats, they took us inside, where we sat across from them at a long table. I handed over two pies as gifts, and they gave me the maternity suit made of gray wool they had just recently finished. Both Rose and Lorelei seemed relaxed, smiling easily and sitting close to each other, and I hoped this meant that whatever had been troubling them before had now been resolved.

"This suit," I said and looked it over. "It's the finest one I've ever owned."

I passed it over so Ray could have a look.

"It's our first maternity suit. Look," Rose said as she reached across the table to where the suit now lay in front of Ray. She moved the jacket aside and showed me the cutout area in the skirt that would allow my abdomen to keep on growing. "We gave you lots of room for the baby."

I gazed at that gaping hole in the skirt and wondered if I could ever fill it. Rose showed me some tie strings on either side of the hole. "You can adjust the waistline as you get larger."

Lorelei stifled a laugh. All at once, Rose seemed to realize she had spoken of a taboo subject in front of Ray. Her face flushed, and she quickly plopped back in her chair.

I said, "You've made me a lovely dress, and now a suit, too. My sister sent me a slacks set, so I have all the clothes I need. Don't spend any more time on me. Promise?"

They exchanged smiles.

"What is it?" I asked. "What are you scheming?"

Lorelei smoothed back her hair. "Nothing special." She was lying. "Just something for Christmas."

"I love your work, but please spend no more time on me. You

should concentrate on yourselves." I meant the clothing just then, but I meant other things, too.

"The piece we're now working on will last you forever," said Rose.

"For all your future babies," Lorelei said, then looked down. Now she, too, had embarrassed herself.

As the conversation lapsed, I tried to get a glimpse of Lorelei's neck. Was she still wearing the cameo pendant hidden beneath her blouse? What was happening between them and the MPs over in Rocky Ford? Unfortunately for me, the neckline of Lorelei's sweater was high, and I could see nothing. I wanted badly to ask them about it but couldn't mention it in front of Ray. They were way too shy to talk about boyfriends with him around.

The conversation came to a halt. Everything had changed because Ray was with us.

It would be much too uncomfortable for us to speak of the war. I jabbered on about my efforts to make pies in the kitchen, but after a while, my talk felt as empty as that hole in my skirt. Ray was sitting next to me with his hands in his lap and hadn't said a word. A draft of cold air coming into the dining hall from under the door made Rose slip her arms back into her coat.

"What will you do today? For Thanksgiving?" I finally asked.

Rose answered, "Eat here in the mess hall."

Lorelei appeared untouched by the lack of real conversation. She hugged herself. "In California, we could eat Thanksgiving dinner outside in our garden."

"The yard was forever green," said Rose. "We had vines of red bougainvillea that overflowed the fence between our yard and the neighbor's and attracted butterflies."

"And we had an orange tree and huge Birds of Paradise," Lorelei added.

I tried to imagine a place that was always green, where something was always blooming. The cold season on the plains had only just started, but those green days I'd enjoyed after my arrival now palled under a layer of ice and snow.

"The begonias and pansies bloomed most of the year," said Rose.

"We also had a pond nearly covered with floating lilies and full of koi fish that grew to over a foot in length," Lorelei added. "The water never froze."

Still Ray hadn't said anything. I glanced once in his direction to see if he was even listening. He must have taken my glance as a dictate because finally he said something. "Fishing from a pond year-round. That'd be nice."

Rose's face fell.

Lorelei put a hand over her mouth, but I could still hear her gasp. She said, "Oh, my gosh. I never thought of this before. Those fish were like pets to us. I certainly hope the new owners of our house knew that koi were not for eating."

Rose paled. "Don't even say such a thing."

I said, "They knew." When I looked over at Ray again, his cheek buckled in and he turned down his eyes. We chatted on about the weather and food; then, as the conversation was so strained with Ray around, I said we should be on our way.

"Long drive ahead of us," Ray finally spoke again as we rose to leave. Then we wished them a happy holiday and left.

In the truck, Ray drove away in silence. Miles away, his body at last conformed to the seat. He glanced my way. "Sorry I said that about the fish."

I bit my lip so I wouldn't smile. "It's okay." Now I could see the humor in the situation, but I doubted Ray could.

He focused ahead on the road. "What are koi fish anyway?"

"They look like big orange and white goldfish," I told him. "They're ornamental. People put them in garden ponds, just for show."

Again, he glanced my way. "I didn't know."

Of course he didn't. And how would he? "Don't give it another thought."

But for the rest of the drive out to Martha's, I think Ray gave it plenty of thought. Almost at their house, he said to me in a whisper, "I'm not any good with new people."

"Ray." I turned to look at him across the pile of pies and casserole dishes. "In school, science was always my worst subject. One day in biology class, I was distracted, when all of a sudden my professor asked me to name the four chambers of the heart. I guess I thought I was back in English Romantic poetry, because I thought he had asked me to name the four 'dangers' of the heart. I pondered for a minute, then I said the first danger of the heart was probably falling in love." I stopped and remembered my embarrassment. "Everyone in my class nearly died from laughter, except the professor, who asked me if I thought science was a joke." I shook my head. "I had to force myself to return to class again after that."

Now I had him smiling. "Sure enough?" he said. "You did that?"

As we drove on, I remembered how foolish I'd felt. I was mad at myself for weeks afterward. Dangers of the heart indeed. And how odd the way things had turned out. That love had come dangerously for me, just as then I'd predicted it would.

I stared out at the slick, icy road and remembered the days after Edward left. In only four days, I had mailed him four letters. I couldn't sit still. I had to talk about it, so I met up with Abby and Bea. I remembered how we sat together in Father's car at the drive-in, eating cheeseburgers. I told them every detail about Edward—our dancing together, his crooked smile and suntanned skin, his hesitant manner of speaking. How close I felt to my sisters on that day. All three of us, after all, were women in love.

In the first few weeks, it never occurred to me that Edward wouldn't keep his word. When no letters had come in four weeks, I excused it as lack of time, his backcountry training, of course. Perhaps weather had hindered the mail delivery. But each empty-handed walk away from the mailbox put more weight into my shoes. Each day, I was beaten down lower, just as the flowers in Mother's garden had been drummed into the dirt by strange summer hailstorms. At first I accepted that perhaps his feelings hadn't been as deep as mine, but I still never imagined I wouldn't see him again.

Edward had said he wasn't much of a writer, so perhaps he'd telephone me instead. I started staying home all the time, just in case. As each day passed and as I realized that the unspeakable had happened, claws of despair tore me off my very bones. Not only had I suffered the worst loss of faith, I had created a problem unthinkable for me to have. I told Abby, not so much out of pain as out of panic.

Ray ground the truck to a stop in front of the house, and then he started lifting out the dishes and pies we'd brought to share. Finally, I moved, too. I found Martha busy in the kitchen making final preparations for the feast we'd all later share. Ray joined Hank somewhere outside, and Ruth helped me to don an apron. As she tied the strings behind my back, she asked, "May I touch the baby?"

I took her hand and placed it on the ball of my abdomen. "If you wait for a few minutes, you might be able to feel a kick."

Ruth looked up at me in the way I used to look up to my professors. We stood like that until the baby, as if on command, shifted inside me and gave Ruth what she had been waiting for. Her face spread open in a smile. "I can't believe it," she said. "She feels so strong."

"She?" Martha quipped as she steamed around the kitchen. "So you've decided this child will be a girl?"

Ruth blushed. "I can always hope, can't I?"

A thought occurred to me. If this child turned out to be a boy, he would carry on the Singleton name for both Ray and Daniel. The Singleton name without an ounce of Singleton blood flowing inside him. "I wish for a girl, too."

Before dinner, Ray tormented Chester and Hank Jr. with still another card trick while Ruth sat beside me and finally said, "You didn't notice."

I took a good look at her. She had a new hairstyle, a bob. "Oh, yes, I did," I lied. "I noticed right away, but I decided to tease you and say nothing." Now she smiled. "By the way, it looks lovely." She turned her eyes down. "You look more grown up than ever."

At the dinner table, we said a prayer of Thanksgiving. We circled a feast of ham and a stuffed turkey, nutty and fruity salads, peeled mashed potatoes with gravy, and sweet potatoes baked with marshmallows. Before she started passing around the dishes, Martha explained to me that in their family, they held a round of personal thanks before Thanksgiving dinner. "We each say what we're most grateful for."

Martha smiled, looked around the table, and began. "I'm grateful for all of you, of course. But I'd also like to say that I'm thankful this war is nearing its end. And I'd like to pray that never again should we have to go through another world war."

She looked to her side, at Hank. He cleared his throat, then spoke, one elongated word at a time. "I'd have to say I'm thankful for the harvest this year."

Chester said he was thankful for Christmas vacation and the time he'd have off from school, and Hank Jr. seconded his brother's sentiments.

Wanda was going to be a woman taken seriously someday. She said, "I'm grateful that none of us has polio." That holiday season, over twenty thousand cases had been reported in the U.S. alone.

Ruth, who went next, fixed her eyes on me. "The baby coming. I'm going to have a cousin!"

Then Ray, who seemed to have prepared his response, spoke. He looked over at me and said, "Daniel's seat beside me isn't empty."

Ray had unruly eyebrows that, at that moment, I wanted to smooth out with the tips of my fingers. On the table before me sat Martha's food, mixed of a kind of clan language I didn't yet know. Something was gnawing at the fisted, beating muscle inside my chest.

I looked up. To my surprise, I saw that everyone was waiting for me. I hadn't realized I'd be expected to take a turn. What could I possibly say?

I began searching my mind. It had to be something not too sentimental but meaningful, and certainly nothing that would come across as trite. In my classes during discussion time, often I wouldn't hear other students' comments because I was so deep in the throes of practicing my own lines. But here, I'd had no rehearsal time.

"Flowers," I blurted out. "For the poppies in the field at Normandy. For the tulip bulbs that saved so many Dutch people from starving."

I looked around at each of them. But they didn't reply, nor did they move. I had gone last, but still, no one was beginning to eat.

"After a fire, did you know that red fireweed grows in and covers all the burnt ruins of the forest?"

Now I looked around at their faces filled with silent compassion and waiting for something else from me. "And for my mother. She loved all flowers, you know."

Ray reached over and took my hand in his. And this time, I had no urge to pull it away.

Twenty-eight

*T*hat night, as we drove back from Martha's, exhaustion came over me. A rod of iron rode across my shoulders, and my legs felt as heavy as telephone poles. Perhaps the fatigue had resulted from my restless night before, or from the full day of travel, or perhaps because we had begun the day with that strained visit at Camp Amache. Or maybe the pregnancy was finally beginning to push its weight down on top of me.

When Ray and I came into the house, I set the empty Thanksgiving dishes on the table and didn't bother putting them in the cupboards. Instead I washed my face and brushed my teeth, then bade Ray a good night. But as I stretched out into bed, although my body ached for rest, I found my eyes open.

Outside there was no wind. Instead I listened to pinging sounds coming from the pipes in the bathroom, and later, I could hear Ray's rhythmic breathing coming from the bunkroom. I tried turning from side to side and clearing my mind of all the day's events, but despite my attempts to relax, something was needling me. I closed my eyes and the world was green again. The plants of the summer past tried again to grow up, not out of the ground, but instead out of the center soil of me. The small of my back grew roots that twisted into the flesh.

I got up out of bed and tiptoed to the bathroom. After closing the door, I turned on the light. The brightness of the bulb blinded me for an instant, then as my eyes began to adjust, I looked in the mirror. My former sunflower eyes now looked glazed over with a layer of dust. My face was full, and along the sides of my neck I could see bulging veins. I looked so bad it was almost exciting. I opened the medicine cabinet. Perhaps a couple of aspirin tablets would ease the pain and help me to sleep. I downed the aspirin and opened the door.

I met Ray, wearing an open robe, standing just beyond the doorway. "What's wrong?" he asked me.

I wore only my nylon nightgown. Over these months since my arrival, often Ray had seen me wrapped in a robe over night-clothes, but never had he seen my body so flimsily covered as now I found it. I was aware of my engorged breasts pushing through the thin fabric of my gown and the curved melon that had re-placed my waist. "My back," I answered him. "I have a backache. I took some aspirin."

"Maybe you did too much today. Hurt yourself."

I started to move past him. "I'm sure it's just fatigue."

I brushed by his arm as I headed toward the bedroom.

"I could give you a back rub," he was saying.

I turned around and opened my mouth to say it wasn't neces-sary. But he was explaining, "Back when my folks were still alive, my father had the arthritis. At night, I'd watch Mom give him a rubdown." He held up his hands. "I think I could help."

The pain was now coming out of the small of my back and stemming down my legs in wild creepers and roots. Maybe he could help.

Ray followed me into the bedroom, where I stretched out on top of the covers and turned to my side. He sat on the edge of the bed at my back and put his hands on my shoulder blades. His hands were gentle, just as they'd been on that hooked fish.

"I hope they're not too cold."

"No," I said and let myself sink farther into the mattress. "They're not cold at all."

He started by lightly rubbing the skin all over my back, warming it. "Where is it worst?" he asked.

"Low," I answered. "Where I used to have a waist."

I felt his breath on my bare arms. Now he took that skin over my lower back and rolled it under his palms. He kneaded and plied it until I could feel the root coils begin to unravel. I'd never have believed those callused hands could feel so good. Through the nylon of my gown, they had the same effect that the wonder drug morphine had once had on my mother. All unnecessary things went away, pain first. I hadn't felt this good since Ruth brushed out my hair. I took a long deep breath and let myself start to drift away.

I don't know how much time passed. I became aware of heaviness on the mattress, and when my eyes popped open, I realized that Ray had stretched out on the bed behind me. Now his body was big and warm just at my back. I felt him now, up against my buttocks, and he was hard. He was hard, but his hands, which curved around my arms, touched me lightly, gently.

"Ray," I said.

His head moved up, and his mouth found my ear. "Don't worry. I wouldn't. I just wanted to hold you, is all."

I closed my eyes again and let myself enjoy the weight of him behind me, the support of his body against my back. After all the nights I'd been sleeping alone, his body beside me made me think of animals curled together on hay in the barn. I began to drift back to sleep.

"After the baby comes . . ." he started.

Now my eyes flew open. Once before, at the Harvey House in La Junta, he'd tried to have this conversation with me.

"We can start over, you and me. Just like newlyweds."

My body remained motionless, but my mind started unfurling.

"Could you feel that way about me?" He buried his face into the hair at the back of my neck. "Could you feel like you did about him?"

Now I was back in the weeks of waiting by the telephone and rushing to an empty mailbox. The questions that plagued me then were the same ones that haunted me now. What had happened after Edward left me for the last time? Had he met someone else, had he changed his mind, or was the worst true? That he never meant any of it. That he had seen me as nothing but an object of conquest, a nonperson whose feelings mattered not at all.

And what of me? Why had I trusted so completely? Why had I been susceptible to the seduction of a handsome man who flattered me, just like so many other girls I'd once thought myself over and above? Had it happened because of the grief after my mother's death, or was I just fooling myself? Would it have happened anyway?

Now Ray's hand was softly stroking the length of my arm. "I'll wait," he was saying. "For as long as it takes."

I closed my eyes and wished for a gentler way to say it. "You deserve better, Ray." Then I stated the obvious. "The child isn't yours."

Now his hand stopped moving. "Whose is it, then? On this farm, I've watched animals abandon their own blood kin for years. Blood ain't the most important thing, you know."

I closed my eyes even tighter. This was the reason I'd acted distantly to Ray ever since my arrival: to prevent this. I had no right to tempt someone so innocent and unexposed. Of course, Ray would easily fall in love. I had kept him at a safe distance until tonight. How could I have let this happen?

Now my mouth went dry. How could I explain that this life, his life, was far from what I'd wanted? That I'd once had dreams of an extraordinary life, and that maybe someday I'd find my way back to those dreams? "You're a good man, Ray."

I could hear his breath catch and stop. "You're a good woman."

"But I'm not the right woman," I whispered. "For you."

Now he lay still for a long time. Against my back, his chest rose and fell. His hands, which had before felt so light on my skin, now felt like bricks. Finally he turned over and lifted himself off the bed, leaving me alone again.

In the morning when I awakened, I found all the dishes I'd left out on the table sitting untouched. No signs of breakfast, not even his coffee. The truck was gone, and I could see no sign of Ray anywhere.

Twenty-nine

*Overnight, new snow had fallen, every inch of earth iced with dropped scales of angel wings. Even the grooves left by Ray's tires were pure white impressions of tread. I found that his tracks headed toward town. Back inside and in the bunkroom, I found the lower bunk unmade. A rumpled pillow hung off one side of the mattress, and the sheets and blankets were wadded up into a punching bag. I opened his closet, half expecting to find it empty, but his few articles of clothing still sagged off the hangers just as before.

I let myself take a deep breath and, telling myself to relax, I also told myself not to be ridiculous. This was Ray's family home, after all. He wouldn't be the one leaving it.

Now I sat at the table and folded the same napkin over and over. If I had a car, I would go after him. But where would he go when he suffered? Would he go to Martha or to visit Daniel's grave? Would he perhaps talk to Reverend Case? I tried to picture him sharing his pain with someone, but I couldn't shake visions of the most likely scenario: that he would suffer alone.

By afternoon, I couldn't stand my own company any longer.

The sun blazed in a cloudless sky, making it warm enough for a walk outside. I threw on my overcoat and headed down the road toward the bridge, my feet making squeaking noises with each step on the snow. Just past the bridge, I saw the truck coming in my direction. Ray was at the wheel driving slowly, and I was so relieved to see him that I waved to him like a schoolgirl. He slowed down so the tires wouldn't spray me with snow, but then he kept on creeping by without acknowledging me at all.

I found him inside, sitting at the table with his back to the door. The sight of his rounded-over shoulders made me remember exactly this lovesickness. At that moment, I wished with everything in my body that things could be different. I wished I could pluck out the threads of him that I didn't care for and keep the ones I liked. But then again, I knew that people couldn't be pulled apart in that way. Those severed threads would just cause the whole of him to unravel. I came up behind him and put my hand at the back of his neck. "You haven't eaten anything all day, have you?"

I felt him take a deep breath, but he didn't answer me.

"Let me make something for you."

He shook his head. "No need."

I made him a plate of food anyway, and finally, he started eating. As Ray chewed the pot roast, I could hear his jaw working. When he ate the carrots, he stabbed the slices with his fork as if he were spearfishing, and he slurped up his coffee with such force it sounded like a storm wind. When he chewed, he looked as if he had dice in his mouth. How powerfully Ray's pain had turned into anger.

I watched him eating and sat still. "Ray, I made a mistake."

For a moment, he didn't move. His cheek quivered, and at one edge of his parched lips, I saw raw pink skin. "Which one?" he asked in a voice so roughly trembling it surprised me. "Which mistake are you speaking of? Being with him or marrying me?"

He surprised me. "I was speaking of a mistake I made last night. Getting so near to each other wasn't a good idea."

"For me, it was no mistake. Sorry you don't feel the same way." He stabbed a chunk of potato on his plate. "If you think you can run me away, you're wrong. I said I'll wait and I mean it."

He would wait; I had no doubt he did mean it. And that meant it would be up to me to end this thing, this awful, hurtful thing my father had sent me to bear.

Now he stared at me. "Aren't you used to people meaning what they say?"

Did he expect an answer? I wanted to shout, *No! People don't mean what they say*. But as I continued to look at him, I no longer felt like shouting. Instead I had the strange urge to help smooth out his hair, to comb it down over the bald spots, to touch the veins that were standing out on his temples.

I answered, "Some people mean what they say. Others don't."

Now his voice was gentle, and his shoulders sagged into his chest. "When you figure out which kind I am, please let me know."

When I said these words, I could hear the bones in my skull snapping. "Would it be easier if I left?"

His head jerked up. He put down the fork and then covered his eyes with both palms. "No!" he cried out with such force it could've split the sky, and all my lists of his faults, all my anger at what he wasn't and could probably never be, disappeared like chalk powder blown by a breeze. He put down his hands. It was the closest he'd come to tears, but the restraint of men never ceased to amaze me. Although the barrels of his eyes filled to their brim, he wouldn't allow one drop to fall.

I said, "Then I won't go back to Denver for the holidays."

He shrugged and looked away, still fighting for his composure. "I'll stay here."

He started jabbing at the food on his plate again.

"I'm staying because I want to."

Again he shrugged and kept on eating.

The next day, when I heard Ray up early in the morning making his own breakfast, I decided to stay in bed. I couldn't stand to sit and share another angry meal. Instead, as soon as I heard him close the door behind him, I arose and readied myself for a day of driving and shopping.

I had held off on Christmas buying in hopes that I might be able to shop in Denver with Abby and Bea or with Dot. The best I could do here was to head out for JC Penney and Montgomery Ward in La Junta. For my sisters, nothing ordinary would do. After I walked the aisles of the stores several times over, I picked up a bottle of cologne for Bea and a flowered china dish filled with scented soaps for Abby. I was heading for the checkout counter when I passed by some leather goods. A wallet caught my eye. Made of unusually soft leather, it had a scene of mountains hand-engraved on the front. It was the most unusual item I'd ever seen in one of these stores. Father would like this, I said to myself. But would he want to receive it from me?

I held that wallet in my hand for so long I caught the smart of others' stares on my skin. Finally I took it with the other items to the cash register, paid, and left. Before I faced going back home, I stopped at the pay telephone to call Abby. Once she picked up, I let her relate to me the details of Kent's leaving, then I asked about their holiday. "It was terrible to celebrate Thanksgiving without Mother and without you and Kent, too, but we made the best of it. How was your day?"

"Fine," I told her. Then I had to get it out. "Look, Abby, I can't come for Christmas after all." I could hear her sigh. "With all these travel restrictions, I don't see how I could justify the trip."

Abby said, "You need your family."

I leaned my forehead against the wall of the booth. "I can't."

I could hear Abby breathing into the receiver. At last, she said, "If you feel so strongly about it, then I'm sure you're doing the right thing."

"It's not that I don't miss you and Bea."

"I know."

"And Father."

Again, I could hear her sigh. "It's still hard to believe everything that's happened over the past year. I used to think we were one of the lucky families, that nothing really bad would ever happen to us."

"Me, too," I told her. I could feel the baby buckling a knee under my rib cage, and I stood up straight. "The baby moves all the time now."

"Oh, my gosh. Sometimes I forget. Have you seen a doctor? Is all well?"

"As well as can be expected."

"Do you think often about what you'll do?"

"Only when I'm not still pretending it didn't happen."

I thought I heard her sniffle.

"At least Mother didn't have to see this."

Abby reined herself in. "Mother would never have bound you to marriage."

But that's exactly what she had done to herself. "Let's not talk about Mother anymore."

"I agree," said Abby. "Tell me about him."

I stood still and thought, how could I explain Ray? "He's a good man. Honest. Loyal." I didn't say angry.

"Livvy," Abby said. "That's all well and good. But do you love him?"

Again, I leaned my head against the wall. "Truthfully, Abby, I can't say. I'm not sure what it feels like to really love."

"You loved Edward."

"I thought so, but the truth is—I never knew Edward."

Abby waited. "You doubt yourself now, and that's understandable. I think you should come back to your family as soon as possible. We can help you figure this all out."

Funny how I'd planned to always figure things out on my own. But perhaps I'd been strong because I did have them. "I'll call again soon," I told her.

"Just hold on and don't make any decisions until we can talk in person. Come as soon as the restrictions are lifted. You're welcome anytime."

The next morning, Ray disappeared in the truck for all of the daylight hours. When he strode in that evening, he handed me a letter. I had recently received letters from both Abby and Bea, so I was immediately curious. The return address was a box at Camp Amache. I tore open the envelope and read a note penned by Lorelei on the palest of pink stationery. She was asking me to meet them and go for a drive the following week. I held that letter in my hands the way the organist at my father's church once held her new sheet music. Finally we would have time alone. Finally we could catch up. And I could find out what was really happening in their lives. I continued to read. But the other lines contained only a meeting place, well-wishes, and a goodbye.

That night, Ray started speaking to me again, but only in

the most perfunctory tones, nothing beyond necessities. And the next day, he left me alone again. I stared out the kitchen window while I listened to more gloomy radio news reports of war in the Pacific. On the island of Leyte, the land battle was progressing, but not without huge casualties. The high numbers were especially tragic because one of the main objectives of the operation wouldn't be met. The Americans had planned to build airfields to launch future missions, but found that the monsoons and the topography of the island, mainly the swampy ground, would make it impossible.

Ray and I went on for two more days in a similar manner. I found myself living in silence again, exactly as I'd done in the weeks following Mother's death. One afternoon, as I was putting away Ray's clean undershirts, I noticed his calendar lying open on the dresser top. The month of December lay out before me in small squares, and one day stood out at me and screamed. December seventh, Pearl Harbor Day, and the date of Daniel's death. I picked up the calendar, then sat on the edge of the bed with it opened in my lap. Today was December 2. In just five days, our country would acknowledge the third anniversary of the day that would live in infamy. For the rest of us in this country, it marked U.S. entrance into the war and numbers of casualties too high to fathom, but for Ray, the pain would be more personal.

Ray used his calendar to keep track of bills and orders, deliveries and other such needs for running the farm. I looked at the days before me and studied his rough scrawl, which tried to fit into the small squares of one day on paper. I turned back one page, to the month of November. On the thirtieth, just two days ago, Ray had written inside the square, "Livvy, 3 months together."

Ray's handwriting in those few words differed from his scrawl on the rest of the page. The lead markings were paler, more faint, as if he had written with a soft touch as he formed the letters of my name. I put my fingers on the pencil markings made by his hand and looked about the room.

Three months and I wondered, how much longer? Every time I asked myself if I could rein back my dreams and live my life as a farmer's wife, if I could just give up on what I'd once wanted so badly, if I could settle for something simpler like teaching history instead of rewriting it, something inside me screamed, No! But I couldn't picture myself walking out on Ray, either. I looked back at the calendar. At the end of 1944, I could never have imagined I'd end up here.

Already, I knew much about him: that he awakened early before dawn, and nearly every morning he made up his bed. He read the Bible more than any other book, he could do card tricks, of all things, and this family farm was his life, his life's commitment. I put the calendar back where I had found it, and then continued to put away Ray's clean clothes. Now I knew the plaid shirt he favored for work on warmer days, the heavier flannel shirt for chilly ones. I knew the herringbone pattern woven into the wool of his one suit, and the two dress shirts he alternated wearing on Sundays. I could fold socks in the way he liked them, wrapped one inside the other and flattened out. He had accepted me into his home without asking questions, had loved me despite the way I'd come to him. Once I'd thought such a simple love could only come from simple people, or from those who didn't know better.

That evening after dinner, I sprawled out on the floor and began wrapping Christmas presents. When I came to that wallet for Father, my offering, I rubbed my fingers along the grooves in the leather. I placed the wallet in a box and began wrapping. Father and I weren't so different from each other. He had lost himself before her death, but I had crumbled afterward. Neither of us had been as strong as we'd wanted to be. Perhaps the scene on the front would remind him of those days in the mountains after the first snow, those good times.

Ray was finishing up the last of a cobbler I'd made for dessert. He stood up from the table and put his plate in the sink. Then he stood around in different spots on the kitchen floor. Finally he came forward, stood over me, and pointed to the wrapped packages. His scent of earth and soap came with him. "You've done your shopping?"

"Well, I'm not finished yet." I had purchased presents for my family in Denver, but had bought nothing for Martha, Hank, and the kids. I would've loved to buy a bicycle for the boys, but with rubber and metal so scarce, new ones weren't available. And what would I get for Ray? I sat back and rested on the heels of my hands. "But I've made a good dent."

Ray pulled up a chair and sat before me. The tips of his old work boots looked up at me like a pair of wise old eyes. I tied a ribbon around the last package. Now finished, I shoved the box aside and looked down at my hands. "I'm sorry for all I've done to hurt you, Ray. Maybe I should never have come here."

His boots hadn't moved, and his voice was the softest I'd ever heard it. "You were supposed to come here. I knew it the second I saw you."

Now I sat still. "Ray, I wasn't supposed to come here. I had dreams far different from this. I thought I did have a destiny, but it wasn't this one." I wanted him to understand. "There are so many things I planned on doing, places I dreamed of going. What you know of me is simply the outside shell. You don't know what creature lives inside me yet."

His hands, which I'd watched for over three months now, hung down before me, the curled fingers motionless. Underneath his nails, I could still see faint lines of dirt from this land he so loved. "I know enough," he said. "And I want to know more."

I shook my head. "I never imagined a marriage like this."

"I didn't, either."

I wanted to understand his love, to see it clearly before me, to put it into a form I could roll around in my palm and examine like modeling clay. Or I wanted to write it with words of reason and illustrate it with romance. I wanted to study it as once I'd studied my books. I still remember the way the kitchen light filled the room behind him when I said, "I don't understand, Ray. Many girls get in trouble. I could've been any one of them. Do you love me just because I came here?"

"Of course not," he said in a whisper.

I cocked my head to one side. "Then why?"

Ray continued to defy all logic. "I love you because you came here to me."

Thirty

erhaps because Ray and I were speaking again, I rested well throughout that night. The tension that had run through the house like wire on fire seemed to be burning itself out.

The next day was Sunday. I wore the new suit Lorelei and Rose had made for me to church. In the kitchen after the service, Ruth came rushing up to me to get a closer look at it, her eyes as big and wide open as ever. "Where did you get this?" she asked me and touched a finger to the shoulder seam.

Ruth was such an observant girl. She could tell just by the sight of this suit that I hadn't bought it anywhere close by or even ordered it from a mail-order catalog. "My friends from Amache custom-made it just for me. In their family, everyone is an expert tailor."

Ruth ran her hand down the collar, then took a step back to get the overall effect. "It's wonderful."

"We could hire them," I said. "To make a suit for you."

Ruth put her hand over her mouth to hide a grin. "A suit for me?"

"Sure. You're a young woman now. With a bright future, too. You never know when you might need a good suit."

Ruth looked amazed, and I could swear she blushed. She was still lost in wonder over my suggestion when Martha came up and handed me something on a covered plate. "It's angel food cake," she said with a sad little smile. "Angel food for the baby."

I took it from her, but wondered why she would be baking for Ray and me. We still received pies and cakes from Mrs. Pratt all the time, and I'd been trying some recipes for new holiday desserts I'd found in the newspaper. "Thank you," I told her. "But you shouldn't have bothered."

Martha had dullness in her eyes I'd not seen before, and she looked tired, too, but she kept the smile on her face anyway. "We've been baking a lot lately." She glanced over at Ruth, who had now been taken away from her thoughts of new suits, I could tell, and was looking at the floor. "To get our minds off of other things, you know."

Ruth glanced up and gave me a knowing look.

Pearl Harbor Day coming up on Thursday, of course. The loss of Daniel. The next few days were going to be tough ones for this family. But Martha would never say it aloud.

"Maybe we could go shopping together," I suggested. "I don't really know what I should be buying for the baby."

Ruth now beamed at me from beside her mother, and Martha looked pleased, too.

"I haven't bought anything yet, and I'm sure I should be stocking up."

Martha said, "We'd sure enjoy helping you."

"Love to," echoed Ruth.

The next morning, I stretched out in bed and waited for the now familiar baby kicks to begin. After the first nudge or two, I got up, threw on my robe, and headed for the kitchen. On the table, instead of Ray's breakfast dishes, I found a dusty old box. I moved in closer. Ray apparently had ripped off the tape, so I opened the flaps.

Inside, I found stacks of old framed photographs. On top was one of Ray's family. In it, Martha looked to be a preteenager, Ray was a boy of about five, and then, in their mother's arms, I saw the tiny plumped face of a baby who could only be Daniel. I didn't touch anything, didn't lift anything out, but I did peer closer into the dark corners of the box. I could see bronzed baby shoes in one corner, and in another, a stack of silver baby cups. Beneath the framed photos, it looked like albums, perhaps yearbooks and scrapbooks, too.

Back in my room, I threw on clothes and thrust my arms into my overcoat. I found Ray outside the barn, moving haystacks from the truck bed inside.

"Morning," he said as he lifted a bale of hay and tossed it inside the barn.

I gave a half smile. "I saw the box." I put my hands in my pockets. "I looked inside, but I won't touch anything without your permission."

He kept working. "I got it down for you."

"From the attic?"

He nodded and slowed for a moment. "I told you once Martha had pretty much everything. But I didn't tell you that Daniel had put a bunch of stuff in our attic after our folks died." He stopped to catch his breath. "It did make it easier." He gestured around, outside the barn. "They're everywhere around here, anyway." Then he looked at me. "But those photos and other things, why, they were like flags waving sadness in our faces. After Daniel died, I did the same thing with his stuff, too."

Just outside his ear, I saw a thin line of shaving cream he had apparently missed that morning. I wanted to brush it away, to touch his cheek, to see how soft it would feel after a shave. "After I look through the box, what shall I do with it?"

He leaned on the pitchfork. "I couldn't face it before, but now . . ." His voice trailed off, then he said, "You can do anything you want."

The sun was beginning to burn off the chill of the morning. Icicles that hung from the barn eaves began dropping tears on the ground. But Ray looked relieved, as if he'd finally shed his sadness. Three years since Daniel's death, and even longer since his parents'. Three years it had taken him to get to this spot.

"I'd like to put them out. The house is so bare anyway. And I think it's those personal things, those remembrances, that make a house into a home."

He nodded. "Go on ahead, then."

But as I walked back up the steps into the kitchen, and then found myself standing before the box again, I hesitated to do it. It wouldn't be fair to pry into these lives, especially those ones dead and gone that meant so much to Ray, if I wasn't at least willing to try it. I looked back outside and watched the easy, comfortable shape of him stepping outside the barn as he hooked another bale of hay.

The house did seem warmer when he came home. The awful news of the war had been easier to take when he was here to share and validate the horror of it with me. He continually surprised me by doing things, such as magic tricks, I'd never have imagined him likely to do, such as checking out that book from the library, marking on his calendar with my name, thanking me for the strangest things. We didn't share a single interest, but he had found things in me to love. And over the past months, the pain of losing Mother had become less dreadful in his company.

I opened the box and touched the top photo frame. What would happen if I just gave in and allowed him to love me? Could I continue to be the seeker I'd always been, only planted here on this growing ground instead of far away? Outside, Ray had paused from his work to throw a stick to Franklin. When that dog came loping back up to him with the stick in his mouth, panting and so proud of himself, Ray crouched down and scratched both sides of Franklin's neck at once.

I lifted the first photo out of the box, brushed it off, and started back in time. I didn't know it then, but as I went down into that box of Ray's gentle love, I was traveling back in time, too, peeling off layers of past pain and grief, and beginning to heal my own damaged heart.

On Wednesday, I went shopping with Martha and Ruth. We bought diapers and diaper pins, some yellow receiving blankets, and a few long white baby gowns. We looked at cradles and bassinets, but I didn't find one I liked enough to buy.

The next day, December 7, Ray emerged from his room as if the day were like any other. He sat down, prayed as usual, and then began eating the eggs over easy and sausage I'd made for breakfast.

I waited until he had finished up, had downed each bite and emptied his coffee mug, too. Then I whispered, "Ray, I want to help you." I put my napkin on the table and moved in closer. "To get through this day. Maybe we could go somewhere, do something special."

He looked up at me, and to my surprise, his eyes were dry.

I asked, "Where would you like to go?"

He rubbed his chin. "The truth is"—he sat back in the chair—"I'd like to stay around the farm. I could show you more parts you never seen before."

I smiled. "That sounds fine. Whatever you want."

The sun was coming up warm, but still we loaded up coats and a thermos full of hot coffee. Ray drove away in the direction opposite where he'd taken me before. We passed by clumpy dirt in empty fields spiked with every shade of brown dry plants, then, unexpectedly, a broad green rectangle of winter wheat lit up the landscape, looking to me exactly like a park of summer grass.

As we drove out, I asked Ray, "How does it feel to have all the photos and things around?" The night before, after I'd sifted through the box, I'd dusted and found a spot for each item around the house. The photos of Ray's parents; childhood pictures of Martha, Ray, and Daniel; scrapbooks; yearbooks; Ray's and Daniel's bronzed baby shoes—silver baby cups engraved with their names; and the greatest find of them all—the Singleton family Bible filled with information and words of inspiration on every birth and death over generations. These treasures now adorned every room.

"It's not bad," Ray said and looked over. "There's more, you know. In the attic. Her china, her knickknacks, and whatnot. She collected buttons."

"Your mother? Buttons? I knew she collected stones for the garden, but I didn't know she could sew."

"She did sew." Ray nodded. "But most of those buttons never got put on clothes. There's all kinds. Old ones, brass ones, ones with tiny birds and other things painted on the fronts. They're in the attic, a whole box of them in jars."

I tried to imagine what else might be up there. Even in my exalted, blown-up physical state, I could climb up there and find it, examine it all.

Ray seemed to know what I was thinking. "Oh, no, you don't. You're not going up there after it." He put his hand on the seat between us. "It's yours," he said. "If you want it. But please let me get it down for you. Promise?"

I nodded.

He pulled to a stop where the fence met the railroad tracks. "End of the line," he said.

Outside, the sun was rising high in clear skies marked only with an occasional pearl of cloud. Crisscrossed with the tracks of coyotes, the snow beneath our feet hadn't yet been touched with human shoes.

"I didn't know the property went all the way to the tracks," I said over my shoulder to Ray as I crunched through the snow in that direction.

He was right behind me. At the escarpment, we stopped.

"Daniel and I used to come out here as kids," he said as he squinted into the sunshine. "Back then, we had a mule both of us could ride." Ray gazed at the railroad tracks rising up in front of us. "Daniel liked it out here." He looked my way and smiled. "You and he would've got along swell. He wanted to see the world, too. He'd come down to these tracks and tell me that one day, he was going to go riding off somewhere."

I hadn't thought often of Daniel before. But since I'd seen his face in the photos, a younger and leaner version of Ray with a bigger smile, I could also picture the farm boy out here along the railroad tracks, dreaming.

"He joined the Navy since he'd never seen the sea. He wanted to come back here, of course," Ray said. "Just wanted to sow some wild oats, as they say." Ray lifted his hat, then put it back on. "Less than six months before Pearl Harbor. Our part of the war hadn't even started yet." He kicked at clumps of hard snow underneath his boot. "We figured one of us could run the farm, and one should join up. Daniel said this was his chance to see the world. And me, I was happy to stay back here and feed people instead of fighting them." He looked relieved when he turned to me. "He got to see Hawaii, that's something."

I waited for a plane to pass overhead, long enough, too, to fight off tears for the young man who had died on that beautiful island. "It is."

We started walking the line where the snow-covered prairie ended and the rock bank leading up to the tracks began.

"Dangerous place for kids to play." My own words jolted me for a second. Now I was leaving off the first word or two of my sentences, just as Ray so often did.

"Not really," he said. "We kept off the track, except for setting pennies." He explained, "We'd save up a penny or two, bring them down here, and set them on the tracks. When a train comes, it flattens out that penny, leaving it thin as paper and shaped long, like an egg. But it happens so fast, you can't see where the train sends that penny flying. Daniel and I used to spend hours searching out our mashed pennies. We'd look all around, in the sagebrush and the prickly pear cactus, until we found them. And you know what?"

He stopped walking and turned to gaze at me now. "We always found them closer than we thought."

He looked at me openly then, let me see it then, that sweet vulnerability in his eyes that he'd worked so long to hide from me. The curtain that shielded them gone, his eyes were now an empty stage ready for whatever act I was willing to play out with him.

"After we'd looked all over Creation, we'd find them somewhere near to the tracks, after all."

Looking into those eyes, the pain and worry that had been clinging to me for too long began to fall away, replaced by a feeling of fullness that swelled to the point of near pain, then landed as a deep, sweet ache.

He said, "Sometimes you do find what you're looking for, closer than you think."

Thirty-one

❦

The next day, I was to meet Rose and Lorelei early in the morning, but I got a late start. When I finally awakened, Ray had gone out somewhere on the farm, but left me with the truck, as was planned. I dressed quickly and drove to the meeting place in Wilson, all the while stealing nervous glances at my watch. I had never been late before.

When I ground the truck to a halt at the pay telephone, I saw that Rose and Lorelei weren't alone. With them stood two good-looking soldiers I immediately knew had to be the boyfriends they'd been telling me about. As I stepped down from the truck to meet them, I noticed they wore their stripes on brand-new MP uniforms. Their shirts looked as if they'd just been laundered and starched, and a pressed crease ran down the front of their trouser legs. How well they were groomed. Even their shoes looked new.

Lorelei introduced them by first name, Walter and Steven. After the introductions, both men surprised me by barely saying a word. Instead, they merely nodded as we shook hands. They weren't boys; they were at least in their mid-twenties. And I hadn't met men this shy since the day I met Ray.

At their sides, they held duffel bags. I turned to Rose with a question on my face.

"We'll explain in the car."

The soldiers tossed their duffel bags into the truck bed, then jumped over the side to ride back there themselves. Rose and Lorelei slid in on the seat beside me, and I started the engine again.

"Can you go south?" asked Lorelei as she ran her fingers through her hair. "We want to go to that canyon where we found the Hairstreak. Do you remember it?"

"Of course I do." But that canyon was all the way down in New Mexico. "It's a long drive."

Rose looked around Lorelei. "They're on leave. They want to spend a day or two camping out. But don't worry, we're coming back with you."

Now they had me smiling. "By necessity or by choice?"

Lorelei laughed. "Choice, for the most part."

I glanced in my rearview mirror. Both soldiers sat backed up against the truck cab, braced against December winds. "They must be freezing back there. If they took turns, we could fit one of them inside." And that way I'd have a chance to talk with these boyfriends, to form an impression. I could already read Rose's and Lorelei's feelings all over their shining faces. If it was possible, I'd swear they'd fallen even more in love. But what of these men?

"They're fine. They want to ride in the back," said Lorelei.

"Okay, then." I pushed down on the accelerator. We had a long way to go, and I didn't want to return so late I'd worry Ray. I glanced at Lorelei. "Now, which one is yours?"

She laughed again. "Walter is mine. Rose has Stephan—I mean Steven."

I nearly laughed. Lorelei and Rose hardly ever mispronounced anything. Their English was as good as mine was, so if cool Lorelei was stumbling over a word, she had to be pretty wound up about spending a day in the company of these men. "You wouldn't be nervous, would you?"

Lorelei laughed again, then answered, "We haven't seen them in so long. In fact, we barely get to meet at all."

Rose said, "This day is what we've been waiting for."

But with the men riding in the back and such a long drive ahead of us, it made no sense. "You won't be spending much time with them at all."

Lorelei only shrugged.

"I'm so happy for you," I said. "The cameo pendant?" I asked Lorelei.

As an answer, she pulled it out from her blouse and let it lay outside of her open collar.

"Tell me more about them," I urged.

"They'll both be shipping out soon." This was familiar territory. "They want to do a little sightseeing before they go."

"Why so far away?" I asked. "Bent's Fort would have been closer."

"They've already been there," answered Rose.

Up ahead, I watched a whirlwind spin along the side of the road. The Navajo believed whirlwinds to be the worst of bad luck. They would do just about anything, even turning around and deliberately going miles out of their way, just to avoid one. There was nothing to it, of course. Just superstition. Whirlwinds, also called dust devils, were just a natural phenomenon.

Dust devils. Devils. There it was again, something evil in

the name. That whirlwind did seem sinister to me at that moment, so full of its own power. I let up on the accelerator to avoid it, but I was too late. It spun over the road and whipped right over the truck, jerking the wheel away from me for a fraction of a second despite my firm grip. Then I remembered Rose's comment to me that night after the dance. They're pressuring us, she had said.

I glanced over at Rose and Lorelei. "Just be careful," I told them.

When we arrived at the canyon, Walter and Steven were red-faced and bone-stiff from the cold. They creaked out of the truck bed and sank down onto the ground. Lorelei hooked an arm through Walter's, and Rose walked along close beside Steven. I took up the rear as we made our way down the path and into the depths of the canyon.

All the branches of the cottonwoods were as bare as steel bars, and any fall-colored leaves had long since been blown away. The ground was hard but dry, and not frozen. A light breeze kept the branches of bushes rattling against each other like keys jangling on a chain.

On the canyon floor, Lorelei turned around and said to me, "We're going to keep on walking. You can wait for us here, if you like."

Funny how most people treated pregnant women like invalids. I was six months along, but had barely slowed down. Just as before, I worked in the house and took walks whenever the weather allowed. "I don't mind walking," I told her.

Rose spun around. "You should wait here for us." Then she looked at me as if pleading. Obviously, they wanted to be alone.

"Okay," I replied.

I found myself a flat rock and sat for close to an hour. I didn't mind the solitude, and the scenery inside the canyon was a nice change from the flat map of the farm. But I couldn't imagine what Rose and Lorelei were doing with the men. Rose and Lorelei were not the kind of girls to go off and have affairs in broad daylight, even in this remote canyon. I could barely imagine them kissing.

Up and down my back, a prickle began to run. I stood up, walked for a few minutes, and then sat back on the rock again. I knew what Rose and Lorelei were going through, falling in love with handsome soldiers. I knew what they were dreaming of—love letters, kisses in the shadows—and I knew what they were planning—futures together. I knew how much they trusted, just as I had.

I checked my watch repeatedly and told myself to stop fretting. They were probably just off kissing those boyfriends, doing nothing more. And they were bright girls. At the camp, they were handling the worst of circumstances. Certainly they could handle male company. And just as many male soldiers had suffered broken hearts at the hands of their girlfriends as vice versa. "Dear John" letters sent to men overseas and "Allotment Annie" stories of women marrying for a soldier's paycheck had become just as common as stories of the girl who got left behind. It was so like me to analyze everything into bits and shreds. For once, I would just stop it.

Instead, I thought about the last few days with Ray and found myself smiling at the memories. I'd been trying to impress him with cooking, while he had complimented my every movement and feature, even my feet. In the evenings, we had left the table for the divan and had worked closer and closer to each other until we sat shoulder to shoulder. Only the night before I'd discovered that I could turn around and face him on the divan, tuck my legs to one side, and curl against his chest. So close I could hear the slow thumping of his heart and his breathing coming in and out, equally, without a pause. And when he whispered to me, I could feel the words start in his chest, rumble through his throat, then leave his body to fill the room with wishes.

I heard a rustling in the thicket along the trail, and then Rose and Lorelei appeared by themselves. "We're ready," announced Rose.

I stood up from the rock and brushed off the back of my slack-clad legs. "The temperature will dip down below freezing tonight. Are you sure they should camp out this time of year?"

Lorelei answered, "They found a good place. Now we should let you get back."

As we drove away, it occurred to me that I hadn't even so much as shared one sentence with Walter and Steven. I knew no more about them than I had before—only that they were handsome, well groomed, and foolish enough to freeze themselves camping out in the December elements. What I had hoped to glean from conversation was a sense of their feelings. As it ended, I could only hope they really cared for Rose and Lorelei.

On the way back, Lorelei launched a long conversation about upcoming plans for Christmas at the camp—the parties to be held, special entertainment arranged, and traditional American dinners to be served. Rose told me that her English students were making her a present, but she didn't yet know what it would be. One of the girls had spilled the beans about the gift, but would only say it had something to do with butterflies.

By the time we returned to the telephone booth, dusk was upon us. Still we had a long way to go before we would reach the camp. My back throbbed from hours spent in the driver's seat, but I had to ignore it. After all, I had extended this offer. I turned toward Granada and sped up the road. Rose fell asleep against the window, while Lorelei kept me company for the remainder of the drive.

"Is Rose okay now?" I asked her.

Lorelei rubbed the cameo pendant, then slipped it inside her shirt as we pulled up to the camp. "Everything is great. Thank you."

I wanted badly for them to confide in me, to tell me specifics about the soldiers, to tell me about their feelings. I had told them my deepest secret, yet they had shared little of how they felt about the men. I whispered it out. "He was a soldier, too, you know."

Lorelei waited, then lowered her voice. "The father?"

"Yes."

Rose was awake now. She asked me softly, so that I could just barely hear her voice over the sound of the truck's engine, "Livvy, where is the father?"

I shrugged. "Somewhere in Europe, I suppose."

Lorelei touched my arm and looked at me with eyes full of pain.

I tried smiling at her. "I made a mistake. A big one. And I just don't want anything like it to happen to either of you."

Lorelei said, "Everything is wonderful."

"But what about the men? Do you really know them?"

"Well enough." Lorelei stared out the windshield into a hazy three-quarter moon. "We've been worried over you."

Worried over me? With so much going on in their own lives, why were they worried over me? Then I remembered again that feeling of being in love. Even though danger exists, love blinds you to any bad possibilities. It makes you believe the end result will be good, makes you discount all other outcomes because you can't bear to believe in them. Instead of protecting their own hearts, Rose and Lorelei were worrying over mine.

Rose turned away from the window and blinked hard. "Will you be happy, Livvy?"

"We want you to be happy," said Lorelei, almost like a command.

"Before I wasn't trying, not really. But I've already learned a few things. A lot of them from you."

"You've learned from us?" Lorelei asked, her face surprised.

"Of course." I bit my lip and had to look down. "You've helped me."

Rose and Lorelei glanced at each other. "You've helped us, too," said Rose.

"More than you know," added Lorelei.

I wanted to believe them. Maybe that's why I saw nothing at all.

At day's end, I had driven more county roads in one day than ever before. When I finally made my way down Red Church Road, I parked the truck in front of the house and found Ray standing on the porch waiting for me.

"I thought you must've run away."

I trudged up the steps. "I'm so happy to be back."

"Long day," he said. "Run you a bath?"

"That sounds wonderful." Inside, I dropped my handbag on the table beside the dishes Ray had left out for dinner. As the bathtub filled, I made myself a plate of food and wolfed it down.

I sank into the tub up to my neck. In front of me, the island of my abdomen rose out of an ocean of water. I soaked until the tub water started to cool, then I took the bar of soap and lathered my entire body. As I was handling the soap, letting it slip back and forth from one hand to the other, it hit me. Something was wrong. Just beyond my grip, like the slippery soap in my hand, I couldn't hold on to it or even put a name to it, but I knew it anyway.

Thirty-two

⟡

The next morning brought bad news of the war in Europe. Just when most of us in America could smell Hitler's defeat, he launched a great offensive in the same region where once he had crushed the Allies and captured most of Western Europe four years before. The operation, code-named Autumn Mist but later known as the Battle of the Bulge, caught the Allies ill-prepared and split the American and British forces in two.

Ray and I listened to the news report as we tried to swallow down breakfast. Only eighty thousand war-weary or new Allied forces were battling two hunderd fifty thousand experienced Axis troops. The Germans had encircled the inexperienced 106th Division near St. Vith and captured two-thirds of our men.

I pushed my plate away. Perhaps the sense of doom I'd felt the night before was a preparation for this news. Abby's Kent was stationed near the fighting. People all over Europe were starved, sick, and living in ruin. In addition to unimaginable human loss, once-grand cities lay in rubble, and museums, priceless works of art, artifacts, and rare books had gone up in flames.

Ray rose from the table. "Storm's coming," he said. "I'll be working in the barn. Need to shore it up, replace some boards, and bring in some hay." He waited before leaving. "You'll be okay?"

I nodded, but he was still waiting. I tried to smile. "It's just this news."

Now he swung into his heavy jacket. "Come after me if you need anything."

After he left, the cold air that had crept in through the open door closed in around my arms. I went searching for a sweater and pondered what I would do with myself on such a day. Beyond the bedroom window, I saw low gray clouds moving in from the northwest. Not a good day for driving or walking, as the weather would be dreary. Instead, I decided to try some holiday baking.

After I stirred up cookie batter and had the first batch baking in the oven, I pulled out extra quilts I found on the top shelf of the coat closet and spread these on Ray's bed and on mine. At the bottom of the stack I found an old blanket full of holes and decided maybe I could lay it out on some hay in the barn for Franklin. But when I mentioned my idea to Ray, he said, "The goat will just eat that blanket." And I had to believe him that Franklin would be warm enough without it.

Throughout the day, Ray returned periodically to fill his thermos with hot coffee and to catch up as more news reports continued to stream in. Details of increasing casualties and unexpected defeats caused some of the radio announcers to halt their speeches and gather themselves. On the few occasions when the radio station played music, I turned up the volume and let my mind dance to the tune of anything besides bad news. But when the news reports resumed, I couldn't just click the radio off. A need to know, to try to understand, still drove me. We turned it off, however, when Ray started bringing down the remaining boxes from the attic.

The first one he plunked down on the table contained his mother's buttons. In one jar, I found plain buttons of all different sizes and colors that looked like an assortment of hard candy or jelly beans. In the other jars, I found her more unusual buttons— brass and silver ones that had come from uniforms, painted porcelains, black glass and rhinestone-covered ones, even some made with mother-of-pearl. I found celluloid-covered buttons covered with pictures of MGM movie stars—Loretta Young, Robert Taylor, Errol Flynn, and Myrna Loy. One button held the image of the Eiffel Tower, and one very old and rare-looking perfumery button still contained a swatch of wool inside that once had been moistened with scent.

In another jar, I found long strings of buttons. Girls in the latter part of the nineteenth century had collected buttons in this way as some kind of good luck charm. I'd have to ask Martha if she remembered the details.

Ray also carried down a box of his mother's china and a box of Daniel's things. A catcher's glove and baseball cards held together with rubber bands topped that box. Inside were a deflated basketball, a few trophies, and some fishing books. "He must have liked sports," I said to Ray.

Ray nodded. "There wasn't much Daniel couldn't do. He came out on top more often than not. I guess he figured with that kind of luck, he'd make it back." Ray sat down for a moment. "I always thought he'd end up married and I'd be the third wheel living around here. I thought he'd be the one with a wife and children, and I'd be a fine uncle, you know, helping out and watching over the kids while Daniel and his wife went to the picture show."

Ray brought down the last thing, an old wooden bassinet covered with yellowed and stained cotton. After Ray set it down, he caught his breath. "That's it." He pointed at the old bassinet. "I only brought that down to clear everything out up there. I'm sure we can order a new one from the Sears and Roebuck catalog."

I carefully tore away the old fabric from around the bassinet and found the bent wood beneath. "Oh, no," I said to Ray and ran my hands around its curved middle. "I'd rather have this one. I can refinish it and make it beautiful again."

Ray looked surprised, but said only, "Whatever you want."

That evening, after Ray came in for the last time, we turned the radio back on to listen to updated news while we ate dinner. Ray always ate voraciously after a day out in the cold, and this night was no exception. I studied the raw red streaks painted by bitter winds on his cheeks and found myself wanting to smooth out the cracks I saw dried into his lips. When I looked at him across the table, it didn't seem possible that he was the same man who once held me in bed. But then again, it seemed to be him, exactly.

Finally, I dove into my stew.

A few minutes later, a local announcer broke into the news report already in progress. I listened as the man's excited voice announced that two German POWs had escaped from Camp Trinidad and were still at large. Local police officers were on the men's trail, but the officials were warning all citizens to be on the lookout and to lock their doors.

As those words sank into me, my throat narrowed, and pressure built inside my cheeks. Ray was standing over me now, and I had to make myself swallow the tasteless mass of food in my mouth.

"Go down the wrong way?" he was asking.

I shook my head. I caught my breath and asked myself what had come over me.

"What is it? What's wrong?" Ray was saying. He put a hand on my shoulder. "They'll catch those prisoners. They always do. Most of them speak such broken English, they never get far."

Speak such broken English? Never get far?

Now I was breathing regularly again, but I couldn't eat another bite. I kept remembering that whirlwind I'd driven through the day before, and then chastising myself for giving any credence to that kind of superstition. But then I remembered the strong sense of impending doom that had come over me later the same evening, in the bathtub, its sweep of me as deadly as a breath of the gases made at the Rocky Mountain Arsenal. What had caused that? In twenty-four years, I'd never known such a strong sense of foreboding to come to me without some reason.

Today, two German POWs escaped from Camp Trinidad and are still at large.

Now I had to stand up and go to the sink. I ran water and started scrubbing dishes, my thoughts racing around in circles as I rubbed the sponge outside and inside each glass, over and over, getting off every single spot, just as my father had once cleaned those glasses of his. As I worked, Ray sat and watched me with worried eyes. "Please tell me what it is."

"It's nothing."

I cleaned and dried every dish, then took a broom and swept away new cobwebs that had recently formed in the kitchen corners. The news continued with a report from the Pacific theater, which wasn't good, either. In the Philippines, two more ships were sunk by kamikazes on the way to the island of Mindoro, and a storm hit the island with ninety-mile-per-hour winds, sinking three destroyers and drowning 279 men. Reports of brutality by the Japanese toward prisoners also came streaming in, with such horrific revelations as Americans ignited with gasoline-lit torches and buried alive.

Ray shook his head. "At least at Pearl Harbor, they died quick."

I came to him then, sat in his lap, wrapped my arms around him, and held him to me as closely as I could. I wanted to kiss his eyes, his cheeks, his mouth, but something stopped me. On the radio, the local news announcer came back on, preempting the nationals and updating an earlier story of interest. The two escaped German POWs, Afrika Korps corporals, had been captured in northern New Mexico after having camped out in a remote canyon.

I stood up and went to the radio. The announcer went on. A trucker who picked up the POWs hitchhiking on the highway had immediately recognized strong German accents. Instead of driving them farther south as they had requested, he drove them to the local county sheriff's office. The prisoners surrendered without a fight, and according to the deputy on duty, even expressed relief that their ordeal, however short, was over. They hadn't known a winter storm was coming, hadn't worn adequate clothing or brought with them appropriate supplies. They sat before the stove at the sheriff's office, warming up, until guards from Camp Trinidad could travel down and pick them up.

Now I knew. They hadn't spoken a word to me because they couldn't do it without giving away who they were. But because of me, they did get far.

Now I was covered by a hoard of hungry bees and they were besting me. The radio on the counter blurred before me, and pressure built in my cheekbones. I blasted out the first sneeze, then a second.

Lorelei had said Stephan, not because she was nervous, but because that was how she knew him. And the uniforms, the perfectly neat and new-appearing uniforms. With Rose and Lorelei's skills in tailoring, an American Army uniform would have been a snap to duplicate. Once they had told me of meeting German POWs while working the same farms. Now it all made sense to me, the tension between the two of them, the secrecy about these boyfriends.

Ray came to stand behind me while continued reports of the escape screamed at me from the radio. "Tell me," he pleaded.

But I only sneezed once more before I calmed myself. The POWs had been recaptured, I kept saying to myself. No harm had been done. And perhaps I was jumping to conclusions. Perhaps Walter and Steven were American soldiers, just as I'd believed them to be only a few minutes before. Perhaps the similarities were simply coincidences. I had no evidence to the contrary. But hard as I tried to convince myself, in some center place of me, I already knew. Much as I kept trying to push it out of my mind's knowing eye, it sat there nonetheless, for no one else except me to see.

Later, I must have looked quite content standing at my kitchen sink and gazing past the ice-encrusted windowpanes into the night. Funny that sometimes people undergoing the worst kind of discord in their lives can look so calm. But Ray could see. He pushed aside the paperwork he usually worked on in the evenings and watched me. Occasionally he'd ask me to sit down and please tell him what was bothering me, but I hadn't as yet fully admitted it to myself, so how could I tell another?

Bedtime couldn't come. All I could see before me was a night of tangling with the sheets, and when I did slip into the bed where once Ray's parents had slept together, I curled my legs high into my rounded body and dreamed of those green summer days that now seemed years ago. It was the first subzero night of the winter, and from the walls, I could feel the frigid air oozing into my room through invisible seams. Although I bunched the quilts in all around me, and although we had the propane stove burning full out, the chill inside me refused to budge. Every time I started to drift away into slumber, the words of the radio announcer came pouring back in over me as if I were a rock at the base of a waterfall.

Rose and Lorelei had lied to me and used me for transportation. How long ago had the plan been hatched? So many things began to make sense. I'd never seen them working in the silkscreen shop because they were probably sewing clothes for the men off in a place where no one could find them. But it wasn't their betrayal that bothered me. I understood going against everything taught and drilled since childhood. I had done it, too, and all for the promise of love.

My right calf drew up into a cramp. I threw back the covers, jumped out of bed, and stepped down on my foot, effectively stopping the cramping. But then I couldn't make myself get back in bed. Instead, I found myself in Ray's open doorway. He slept on his side under smooth quilts, facing me. I listened to the long deep breaths he took while soundly sleeping. I studied the gentle curve of his fingers laid out on the pillow in front of his face. And when I sank down on the bed beside him, he awakened, but moved only enough to give me more space on the narrow mattress of the bunk bed. Then he held me from behind, as once he'd done before, and kissed the back of my neck and the tops of my shoulders. In his arms, even the anguished cries of coyotes coming out of the black night sounded like songs. Ray's body and mine rested together like a pair of stacked bowls, and finally, I slept.

I slept until the earliest gray of daybreak sent my eyes flying open.

In the warm circle of Ray's arms, thoughts began to bat around inside me. I had knowledge of the escape, information that, as a good citizen, I should share with the authorities. But if I talked, I would doom Rose and Lorelei to pay for the parts they had played. And now I found that I disagreed with my father. Rose and Lorelei had made the worst of mistakes, and I couldn't imagine the anguish that had led them to do it. Despite Lorelei's justifiable anger for their imprisonment, for everything they'd been through, she had never seemed vengeful to me. I'd never imagined them concocting so elaborate a deception and crime. The German POWs had convinced them; I was sure of it. Rose and Lorelei had fallen in love and wanted to rescue soldiers, just like so many other women before them had done. And even though it didn't excuse their parts, I understood it.

But must all persons bear the consequences of their actions, at all costs, as my father believed? The POWs had been recaptured without incident, without any harm having been done. I kept telling myself this. And wasn't guilt of the deed itself sometimes punishment enough?

I remembered the man at the gas station who'd refused to talk to me, just because I was in their company. I remembered the pain on their faces even when they were working so hard to conceal it. I remembered new love on their faces, too. And I saw Lorelei's wings flapping, her colors falling to the ground.

Later, I found myself standing at the kitchen window again and staring down the dawn of a new day. And still I didn't know what I was going to do.

Thirty-three

J knew the day ahead would be one of the toughest of my life, yet Ray was the happiest I'd ever seen him. I had come to him in the night, and he couldn't stop smiling. In the bathroom, I heard him humming over the sound of the shower. He came out dressed in his newest flannel shirt tucked in with a belt and his hair combed carefully over the thinning area on top. As usual, he had missed the bald spot in back, but I wouldn't tell him.

He pointed out the kitchen window. "Not too much snow last night, but more's coming."

"Could we drive to the telephone?"

He looked out the window again and up at the sky. "Not a good idea. We could get stuck on the road."

I couldn't make my bottom lip stop dipping and jerking. And I couldn't stop thinking about Rose and Lorelei, the only ones who could tell me the truth. Although the POWs were back in captivity, I had to know if I'd played a part in their escape. My plan was to call Camp Amache, tell the guards it was a matter of grave importance that they bring one of the girls to the telephone, then simply ask Rose or Lorelei if they had done it. I wouldn't chastise; I wouldn't complain. I simply had to know the truth.

"Ray, I need to make a phone call."

"Come here," Ray whispered before I found myself back in his arms.

After we ate a hot breakfast, Ray got the truck running while I bundled into my coat and muffler and closed up the house. Once we were heading down Red Church Road into town, the truck's heater finally started to send warmth up from the floorboards, but little blasts of freezing wind squeaked in from poor seals around the windows.

Ray kept glancing over at me, but he didn't ask me why I needed so badly to place this call. And even if he had, I wouldn't have known what to tell him. If I told him the truth about Rose and Lorelei, then he would have information he, too, was withholding. Or would he report it? It didn't take me long to decide to stay silent. Perhaps I'd never find it necessary to tell anyone. The POWs were back in custody, the weather had made any trip to the sheriff's office impossible anyway, and hadn't Rose and Lorelei suffered enough already?

Big snow started pouring out of a sky capped by low-lying storm clouds. The flakes blew in sideways, building up on the windshield and nearly blocking our view of the road. Stiff gusts made Ray grip the steering wheel with both hands just to keep control of the truck. He kept creeping onward for a mile or so longer, then he gradually put on the brake and turned to me. "Whatever it is, it'll have to wait. It's just too dangerous. I got to turn back."

Slowly he inched the truck around in a circle and started urging it back in the direction of the house. He had the wipers going, but they couldn't keep up with the ragged chips of snow now clattering down on the windshield. The weather worsened by the minute, but Ray worked the truck back toward the house, taking extra precaution when we passed over a bridge. I heard him let out a big sigh as we finally saw the triangular shadow of the barn's roof rising out of a world suddenly gone devoid of color and depth.

Snow was already building up, covering everything slippery white. After he helped me up the porch steps, Ray said, "I need to go close up the milk cows and the horses in the barn. I'll be back soon."

I entered the house by myself and clicked on the radio.

After a song ended, the announcer began to relay more details of the POW escape incident. The most bizarre twist in the story had only recently been revealed, he said. The recaptured Germans named two Japanese interns as accomplices in their escape. The interns, Rose and Lorelei Umahara, living in Camp Amache, had immediately been arrested and charged with treason.

Now I knew the source of the doomed sensation that had plagued me for nearly two days. As full realization clamped down on me, the room became a dark and cold dungeon. I became small and shaking and full of anguish more profound than the pain I'd felt even when I first realized Edward had left me and that I was pregnant. It couldn't be true. Their betrayal was worse, worse even than mine had been. A more cruel breach of faith I could never have imagined. The POWs would receive some token punishment within camp, such as a few days of solitary confinement or loss of rations, but nothing more. After all, the Geneva Convention maintained that it was a POW's duty to try to escape. But the Umahara sisters, the announcer said, would be prosecuted to the full extent of the law, ironically, because they were citizens.

I wasn't prepared for the gravity of this tragedy. The pain of it turned my lungs into sponge, made it impossible for me to go on breathing. I flew out the front door without turning off the radio. I stumbled down the porch steps and ran out into the storm as fast as my burdened legs could carry me.

A monstrous ghost of snow and storm bore down on me from above, but I didn't care. I ran full-face right into it. Now I was pounding the ground, trying to send it all away with every heavy thump of my feet and each new boot track laid out in the snow. I didn't wish for summer, didn't think of the city. As I ran, I longed only for a return to the recent past, for one last opportunity to change that grievous mistake of faith committed by girls who couldn't have realized the dreadful consequences of their actions.

Before long, my feet and fingers began to sting and burn, as if thrust into a fire rather than freezing. Cutting winds made my clothes and coat into transparent gauze. But I kept stumbling and trudging myself through the snow, drawn to the spot on the road between the fields where first I'd met them, back on a day of sunshine and Indian summer. I stopped running and stood in the place where once, so long ago, we had introduced ourselves and talked of butterflies. Their wonderful lives had come down to this, this one mistake, caused by belief in men who professed to love them.

If only they had told me the truth, I could have cautioned them not to do it. I could have warned them. But in that instant, my own truth came over me. At the same time the snowflakes were encasing my body into a frozen shroud, the realization of my own part oozed its way out of me and into the gray daylight.

Rose had tried to tell me. That night of the barn dance, when she walked me out to the truck, she had tried. But I had been so consumed with my own problems that I hadn't given her the time and attention she needed in order to be able to get it out. I had underestimated what they were going through by daring to compare their pain and suffering to mine. I had underestimated their endurance because I assumed them too strong to be easily manipulated by others. I had underestimated everything about them. I had failed them by taking them for granted, too, along with everyone else.

I thought of the water nymph Clytie, who, too, had given it all away. As friends, Rose, Lorelei, and I had started swimming together on the surface of the water. We had at times dipped below the surface as we went along. But we hadn't taken a deep dive, hadn't delved into those dark waters, the ones where we kept hidden the unseen frailties that lie in wait. In the end, the friendship had failed because we failed to dive deep.

I stood adrift in the snowstorm until my shivering stopped, until my body settled into an artificial calm. Now my feet and hands no longer existed, and sky tears froze into silence on my face.

I don't know how long I languished in the middle of the storm. I remember making my way back through a soup of snow, seeing the lights coming from the house windows, and feeling the heat envelop my body as I walked through the door.

Ray stood before me. His voice was full of frustration, but gentle on me nonetheless. "What are you doing? Trying to kill yourself out there?"

But my lips were too cold to form words.

Ray gestured toward the radio, then stared at me. "I heard the news." Now he shook his head. "I couldn't find you anywhere. Why were you out in this storm? You could have froze to death."

As we stood in silence, finally warmth began to work its way back into my bloodstream. I looked out the window at heavier snow than I'd seen in years. I caught my reflection in the glass and saw a polar cap encrusting my hair. Now the snow was beginning to melt and drop big clumps of slush onto the floor.

I turned back to Ray and said, "I promise I'm not this crazy."

He took my arms. "Do you have something to tell me?"

With the storm screeching and swirling outside, Ray and I swam together in a calm sea. It's a difficult thing to do, once you've been deceived. But my time was now.

"His name was Edward," I said aloud. "He was a lieutenant from the Mountain Division. I let him sweep me away. He said he loved me, and after one night together, he disappeared."

Ray was looking over every inch of my face. In his eyes, I didn't see pity. Instead, in the colored strands of his eyes, I saw the soft seeds of something like hope. Finally, he asked, "Do you still love him?"

I stood still. "Is that what it was? Love?"

He blinked. "You got to answer that question."

Now I could feel blood making its way back into the skin of my face. "It wasn't love, even though at the time I thought so. And maybe it no longer matters."

I looked over his windburned face, those cracks in his lips that now I realized I wanted to smooth away with my own. Melting globs of snow continued to fall out of my hair, but I no longer cared how ridiculous or pitiful I looked.

"What does matter to you?" he asked.

In the past, I would've listed things such as common interests, mutual attraction, worldliness, and higher education. My freedom above all else. If I had found love, it would have had to be the kind that overwhelmed and overpowered all else.

I passed a hand between Ray and me. "Once you told me that

this," I said, "is a beginning." I searched his face. "But how do you know, Ray? How do you know it's the beginning of something good?"

"I know." His breath was warm on my face as he moved in closer. "Because someday, you're bound to forgive yourself."

Thirty-four

*I*n the safety of our house and the warmth of our bed, I got to know the fullness of Ray's lips on my face and the taste of his skin, the soft bend of his ear and the touch of his breath on my shoulder. I discovered the silky strands of hair at the base of his head and the feel of his shoulder blades beneath my outstretched hands. I discovered just how far around my arms could encircle his back. He touched me as if I were the curved and delicate handle of a china cup, but he held me tightly just as I was, flesh and blood and full of human flaws and fears. In his arms, I wasn't a girl dreaming of sailing the high seas, and I wasn't a farm kid jumping the train, either, but a fully grown woman riding the soft side of a crescent moon.

As we lay together under the covers, I told him, "I drove them into New Mexico, but I didn't know those men were German prisoners."

He smoothed away wisps of hair on my forehead. "I know you didn't."

And then, in his arms, I cried for Rose and Lorelei.

Under clearing skies the next morning, I listened to the news report. In Washington, the Cabinet had just announced an end to the exclusion and detention of Japanese citizens. The concentration camps had been deemed by legal resources to be against the law. Public Proclamation 21 outlawed the holding of loyal U.S. citizens of any ancestry; therefore the Japanese American evacuees would be allowed to leave the camps with their personal belongings, twenty-five dollars, and train fare.

After I listened to the report, I took that old hound dog Franklin galloping out into the fields covered in deep, flat snow. Before me, V-shaped animal tracks nicked across acres of topcrust, but I took the first human steps, each one sinking me lower into the soles of remembrance. Snow now covered all the dust lost from all the other butterfly wings, all the shining human details from the previous green seasons, those from the past season and those from many other seasons before mine, too.

As the sun faithfully opened its bright bald eye, visions of the place where Rose and Lorelei might be at that moment, somewhere behind bars, sent me pain I couldn't bear. I had to refuse thoughts of them in that level of confinement. The camp they had been forced to endure had been bad enough. Instead, I would remember them as I chose to, walking the green fields, searching the canyon for butterflies, and laughing in unison.

When Franklin and I returned to the house, I saw that the Otero County sheriff had made his way down the roads behind a snowplow to our farm. Ray and I sat with him at the table while he questioned me about the part I had played in aiding the POWs' escape. I told every ounce the truth, although I didn't altogether admire the way it rang in my ears. After the sheriff satisfied himself that I had known nothing of the men's identities, he sat longer than I would have liked, slurping on coffee and chatting on with Ray about the aftereffects of the storm.

I couldn't listen to them casually converse about the weather, or anything else, for that matter, when the future of two valuable lives had so recently been forfeited. I knew what would happen next. Rose and Lorelei would be painted in the newspapers and on the radio as traitors by people who'd never met them, by people who could never understand what torments and desires had driven them to their sad, ill-fated decision.

Instead, I found my eyes drawn to the window outside, to that square of blue sky, where I could see white shafts of sunlight reaching down to earth, the fingers of God telling me that we could survive it. In only a few hours after the sheriff drove off, the news came out. I was portrayed as the innocent victim, the newcomer who'd befriended the wrong people, and who'd been duped into providing transportation after the escape.

By dinnertime, solace arrived in the form of Reverend Case and Martha on our doorstep. I hadn't spoken privately with the reverend since my arrival here, and the sight of that kind face gave me a sense of hope that someday these wrongs would be analyzed and prevented in the future. In church, he spoke so eloquently of forgiveness, so perhaps someday this country would give apologies for wrongs committed under extraordinary circumstances. And would the world ever count Rose and Lorelei among the casualties of the war? Perhaps someday they could be forgiven for their mistake, too.

"Olivia, dear," he said as he took my hand. "I came to see if you and Ray are in need of prayer."

Martha brought in fried chicken and roasted potatoes, and of course dessert. We sat together and shared a plate of consolation at the table. In this farmland I have come to call home, food is seen as a sure cure for just about anything that ails you. People shovel in piled-high plates of heavy meats and casseroles, salads and desserts, even during the most trying of times.

After we finished eating, I stacked the plates in the sink, and Reverend Case readied himself to begin our prayers. We sat around the table, Ray, Martha, Reverend Case, and I, with hands clasped together. Speaking softly, Reverend Case began praying to God, asking Him to help me to weather this storm.

I stopped him in midsentence. "Please."

I don't think anyone had ever interrupted Reverend Case in prayer before. The dear man's eyes couldn't hide his surprise and concern.

I told him, "I don't desire prayer for me, personally." Because I hadn't paid such a high price after all. When I'd headed out here on my wedding day, I hadn't realized I'd bought a ticket to my own history, a different one from studying Akh-en-aten and Horizon-of-the-Aten, maybe, but a living, ongoing one. I pictured Daniel, all the other dead soldiers and civilians, and prisoners all over the world. "Couldn't we pray for those who have paid with their lives?"

Reverend Case prayed as I had requested, then he and Martha stayed for coffee before heading out. "We have congregation members and others out there without adequate heat," he explained. I hadn't realized that others around me were going cold. Before he and Martha left us, I gathered up our extra quilts and carried them out to the car.

"Careful," he said to me as I peered over the load and made my way down the porch steps.

"You sound just like Ray," I told him.

Reverend Case looked pleased with himself. "You two seem to be getting along mighty well."

I placed the quilts in his trunk, then turned back into the sunlight. I was open, exposed, without intending to be. "I love him," I said to Reverend Case. Then I turned to Martha. "I love your brother."

On the plains, people rarely speak openly of their feelings, especially of one so personal as love between husband and wife. Reverend Case raised his eyebrows for a second, then he smiled and said, "I'm so happy for the both of you."

But Martha didn't respond with words. Instead she walked up, kissed me on the cheek, and turned toward the car door in a waltzlike move. In all the years I've come to know Martha, I've never heard her talk of such personal feelings as I'd just done. It seems that certain lines of privacy aren't often crossed in a land where physical distance keeps people independent by necessity and by choice.

This land of distances, this land of buffalo grass, locoweed, crops, and churches, became my home. Change comes to these farmlands slowly. Harvest time is still the best season, everyone still talks endlessly about the weather, and contrary to what Ray once told me, he has always been kind.

One afternoon the following August, I took the baby, whom we named Daniel, outside on the porch and left him to nap in his bassinet while I worked in the flower garden. Hiroshima and Nagasaki had just exploded onto the pages of history, V-J Day had passed, and negotiations over the terms of Japan's surrender were under way. Earlier in the year, before the war's end, Camp Amache had been closed. Finally, the shadows had begun to fall on the most deadly war in human history, and on the Singleton farm, the tall Shasta daisies and black-eyed Susans in my garden nodded their heads and scraped against each other's arms as a warm prairie wind blew in ever so gently. The whirligigs that once belonged to Ray's mother, which I had repainted in red, white, and blue, stood above the flowers, and her collection of stones scattered out among waxy geranium stems.

Earlier that morning, I'd pulled weeds that had taken root and wrapped themselves around the flower stems. As Daniel slept nearby on the porch, I stood out in the sunlight, looking for any remaining weeds and examining this flower garden that would most certainly have pleased my mother.

One small yellow butterfly floated in and landed on a daisy petal. I didn't know the name of that species, but as I watched it open and close its wings, I thought how it reminded me of a single petal of a yellow rose.

Rose.

Then I watched as more came, until perhaps a dozen of the same kind of butterfly did a sunny swing over the flower heads and landed on their centers.

Lorelei.

I thanked the butterflies, as if they were responsible. Memories are fragile things to hold, but many times, it's what we have. The flowers grew for my mother, the whirligigs twirled for Ray's, and the butterflies came for the sisters—Rose and Lorelei, Abby and Bea, Aunt Eloise and Aunt Pearl—perhaps for all sisters everywhere.

I had never seen them again after the day we took that drive. Once I'd tried to visit them while they were being held in Denver awaiting trial, but they had refused me, probably out of shame. After their arrest, reporters and others had tried to ascribe all kinds of political and ideological reasons for what Rose and Lorelei had done. It was conjectured about and editorialized and discussed by the so-called experts, and many times during those days, I felt that I alone understood their reasons. Maybe the girls had at times questioned how much they owed to this country that had imprisoned them, yet it hadn't been nearly as complex as most people believed. They were simply two lonely, isolated women who fell in love and gave their trust away.

In their well-publicized trial, the German corporals testified against them, and the jury returned a guilty verdict to the reduced charge of obstructing justice. Rose and Lorelei each received a three-year prison sentence and a ten-thousand-dollar fine. After their release, I could only assume they returned to their home state of California.

The baby let out a cry. By the time I reached the bassinet, he was yelling, as if he'd awakened from a bad dream and found me missing.

"I'm here," I said, then lifted him and held his face to my cheek. My love for him had come as a surprise to me. Once he had arrived in howling perfection, it had come swiftly, intensely.

As a child, when I first heard the story of Creation, I'd closed my eyes and pictured the earth as a ball rolling off the palm of God and into dark space, then drifting around until it found its home in sunny orbit. Never perfect, but ever spinning, and holding on to her course, despite it all.

A PENGUIN READERS GUIDE TO

THE MAGIC OF
ORDINARY DAYS

Ann Howard Creel

An Introduction to
The Magic of Ordinary Days

History has a way of bringing the past to life, conjuring up people and places that have long since disappeared. Living in the past is also a way to flee the present, to experience and perhaps live in a world that is not complicated by emotion and regret. Livvy could never have imagined that her life would take a course that was so distant from the dream she had for herself—her hopes to become an archaeologist, to lead a cloistered yet fulfilling life. But she becomes pregnant and unexpectedly finds herself far from home and her family, married to a man she does not know, as the country is on the brink of war. As she explains it, "in one fleeting moment I stripped away the petals of my future, let them catch wind, and fly away."

At first, Livvy feels almost as though she is in exile as she struggles to come to terms with her feelings of loneliness. "Ever since I had been quite young," she admits, "I could resist those who went against me, had been able to deny their opinions. . . . My inner strength came from an ability to handle, then separate myself from adversity." But the strength and intellect that allowed her to break through the barriers faced by most American women in the 1940s are frustrated by life on a prairie farm where there is no one to talk to, few books to read, and nowhere to go.

Slowly she takes to exploring her new environment and immersing herself in the history of the Plains. She begins a friendship with Rose and Lorelei, two Japanese American women confined at a nearby internment camp, and begins to find stimulation and comfort in the companionship.

Meanwhile, through radio and newspaper reports and her friendship with Rose and Lorelei, Livvy becomes aware of the history being made in her own lifetime. Stories of Nazi concentration camps, reports of enormous American losses in the Pacific, and the realities of Rose's and Lorelei's lives remind her daily that her own troubles seem small in comparison. But when Livvy plays an unwitting role in the escape of two German POWs, she finally realizes that she, too, has a role in the history being made around her.

A history buff, Livvy yearns to know more about the circumstances behind this mysterious event. Though she has forged a strong friendship, she suddenly realizes that she knows very little about Rose and Lorelei and their dangerous plot—a scandal to which she had suddenly become an accomplice. She observes, "Rose, Lorelei and I had started swimming together on the surface of the water. We had at times dipped below the surface as we went along. But we hadn't taken a deep dive, hadn't delved into those dark waters, the ones where we kept hidden the unseen frailties that lie in wait."

Through her relationship with Rose and Lorelei, Livvy slowly begins to accept her present life, finding a new appreciation for the kind of freedom she had always taken for granted, and a growing love for her simple yet kind husband who is devoted to her happiness. She realizes that the most valuable lesson in life is how each person creates her own history day by day.

A Conversation with
Ann Howard Creel

1. Until this book you have been known as a writer of young-adult fiction. Is writing for an older audience different?

Whether it's a book for children or for adults, when I sit down at the keyboard, the writing process is essentially the same. The same story elements—character, plot, setting, style, voice, etc.—must all be present. The difference comes from finding the voice of a child versus that of an adult. Subject matter may differ, too; however, children's books involve serious topics now more than ever before.

2. What could a young reader learn from Livvy's story?

A young reader might learn that mistakes don't always hinder, that growth may follow mistakes, and that happiness may be found in unexpected places and in the company of unexpected people. Livvy's outlook on her mistake began to change as the book progressed, as Ray's love began to touch her, and as she started to see the special qualities that shimmered beneath his surface.

3. Some readers might disagree with Livvy's decision to stay with Ray instead of returning to Denver. What would you say to them?

Livvy ended up staying because in Ray's presence she learned to love and trust again. I wanted the choice to be a difficult one without a clear or easy answer, and certainly for some women, leaving might have been a better choice. I enjoy the disagreement on this point because in my experience, each person views it differently based on his or her past and inclinations. It makes for heated discussions, too.

4. You have said that the novel was inspired, in part, by an actual event that occurred in a Nazi POW camp. Can you tell us more about this incident, and why you found it so compelling? Is Livvy herself based on a real-life person?

Livvy is fictitious; however, I based Rose and Lorelei on three Japanese American sisters who were interned at Camp Amache and who aided in a POW escape. They were later prosecuted for treason. I latched onto this story because the aid rendered by the women seemed to be motivated by love, the results were tragic, and the story, although widely sensationalized in the past, has largely been forgotten, even in the area of Colorado where it took place.

5. You have also said that you wanted to write a novel about an arranged marriage. Why?

I'm fascinated with relationships and marriage to begin with, and arranged marriages, which have been a common occurrence throughout history, are particularly compelling. I've always wondered how two strangers, thrown together most often by their parents, would manage to open up the doors to each other. Given the daunting task of maintaining a good marriage in any circumstances, I've wondered how often love ripens between people who didn't know each other to begin with.

6. Although Livvy calls herself a "practice rug," she is determined to find her own way in the world and wants to put off marriage until after

5

she has settled into a career. What kinds of role models were available to independent-minded women like Livvy?

During World War II, women entered college and the work force in numbers never seen before. Women did everything from assembling fighter planes to organizing Red Cross disaster relief to serving in the military in several newly established women's corps. Role models ranged from First Lady Eleanor Roosevelt to Rosie the Riveter.

7. Can you recommend any other books for readers who are interested in learning more about rural Colorado and its history, or about American life during World War II?

Although there are a host of excellent books available about America during the war, the following painted a vivid picture of life during that time period:

- *V is for Victory: America's Homefront During World War II*, by Stan Cohen
- *The Homefront: America During World War II*, by Mark Jonathan Harris, Franklin Mitchell, and Steven Schechter
- *Prisoners without Trial: Japanese Americans During World War II*, by Roger Daniels
- *Nazi Prisoners of War in America*, by Arnold Krammer

8. What are you working on now?

I continue to be fascinated by our country's history and enjoy weaving together fact and fiction. Unlike other authors who tell me they often begin with a character or a plot, my inspiration usually comes from history and from a particular place and time. My current endeavor takes place in the West and is an exploration of family ties, love, and loyalty, and how they relate to human connectedness to the land.

QUESTIONS FOR DISCUSSION

1. Was Livvy's father right to insist on her finding a husband before she gave birth? What other options were available to her? What would have been the repercussions of these options?

2. It takes Livvy a while to warm up to Ray, let alone love him. Do you think she was too hard on him? Were you surprised that she *could* come to love him at all?

3. What are some of the qualities that make Livvy and Ray such well-developed characters? How does Creel make them human? How does each surprise you?

4. Creel reveals the story behind Livvy's pregnancy gradually; we don't find out what really happened until more than halfway through the novel. How does knowing she is pregnant change the opinions you had begun to form about her?

5. Why is it so easy for Livvy to make friends with Rose and Lorelei? How are their situations similar?

6. How did you feel about Rose and Lorelei after they used Livvy to help the POWs escape? Did they betray Livvy's friendship? Did you, like Livvy, feel any sympathy toward them because of their feelings for these soldiers?

7. Do you think the girls befriended Livvy because they knew she could help them with their plan? Why or why not?

8. What is the significance of Rose and Lorelei's fascination with butterflies?

9. What did you learn from this book about World War II and its effects on the home front?

10. Did Livvy make the right choice in remaining with Ray? What was she giving up by not returning to Denver? What do you think you would have done in her situation?

11. Would you attribute her whirlwind romance and pregnancy to grief over her mother's death? Why would a sensible, self-assured, independent woman "strip away the petals of her future to let them catch wind, and fly away?" Why is this metaphor so suitable to the book?

For more information about or to order other Penguin Readers Guides, please call the Penguin Marketing Department at (800) 778-6425, e-mail us at reading@penguinputnam.com, or write to us at:

> Penguin Books Marketing Dept. CC
> Readers Guides
> 375 Hudson Street
> New York, NY 10014-3657

Please allow 4–6 weeks for delivery
To access Penguin Readers Guides online, visit the PPI Web site at www.penguinputnam.com